Praise for Dharma Kelleher

THE SHEA STEVENS THRILLER SERIES

"Kelleher keeps the reader guessing until the very end."
—Book Reviews to Ponder

"Gritty, dangerous, and hard to put down"
—Pure Textuality

"The pacing is excellent and fast-moving and the prose is tight and a pleasure to read. The protagonist is just as cool!"
—Son of Spade

"Her first book in the series, Iron Goddess, *set a high bar but* Snitch *jumps it with ease. This is money well spent. Fire up that bike and get ready for a hot trip down a highway with no speed limit."*
—Steve Shadow, author of *Savage Little Flea*

"Shea Stevens is just about the most interesting and sympathetic criminal you'll meet."
—Paula Berinstein, author of the Amanda Lester detective series

EXTREME PREJUDICE

EXTREME PREJUDICE

A Jinx Ballou Novel

Dharma Kelleher

Dark Pariah Press

Dark Pariah Press, Phoenix, Arizona, USA

Copyright © 2018 by Dharma Kelleher.

Cover design by Damonza.com

Paperback ISBN: 978-0-9791730-5-9

For my wife, Eileen, as always.

1

I don't typically show up at a fugitive's door dressed as Wonder Woman. I'm a professional bounty hunter licensed by the State of Arizona, for fuck's sake. And yet there I was knocking on a bail jumper's hotel suite, dressed in a homemade foam-and-leather Wonder Woman costume. Maybe it's true what they say—dress for the job you want, not the one you have.

I was armed with a rubber sword and a Lasso of Truth made from electroluminescent wire. All of my real weapons and my handcuffs were at home. If things went sideways, I'd be in deep shit.

Earlier that morning, I'd been enjoying the Winter Con comic book convention, meeting my favorite celebrities, hanging with fellow cosplayers, taking selfies with fans. Sure as hell beat fighting the crowds at the mall less than three weeks before Christmas.

A teenage Wonder Woman fan was about to take a selfie with me when my phone rang. "Hold on a moment," I told her.

The *Game of Thrones* ringtone indicated the caller was Becca Alvarez. We'd been best friends since junior high, having met soon after I began my gender transition. These days she worked as an IT security consultant while doing electronic skip tracing for me on the side.

I pulled my phone out of my gold-lamé fanny pack. "What's up, Becks?"

"Sorry to interrupt your fangirl weekend, Jinxie, but I believe I've located Danny Warren."

Daniel Warren was the sixty-year-old star of *Danny & Friends*, a local sci-fi children's TV show that ran in the 1980s and '90s. Recently, the aging role model's squeaky-clean façade was shattered when several former child stars came forward making tearful accusations against him. Scottsdale police had charged him with multiple accounts of sexual assault on minors.

When he failed to appear for trial, his bail bond agent, Sadie Levinson, assigned me to go after him. He'd dodged me for weeks, and time was running out. If I didn't apprehend him soon, Sadie would have to pay the court Warren's full bail amount. I had conflicting feelings about arresting a childhood hero. But after Warren had harmed so many people, I wasn't letting the creepy fucker escape justice.

"Where's the old perv hiding out?"

"You're still at Winter Con, right?"

"Yup."

"He's there at the Calderwood Hotel."

"He's here? Why?"

"Winter Con invited him as a guest speaker. Apparently, he's got lots of adult fans who grew up watching the show. Or did before he was indicted."

"The con didn't ban him?"

"The convention organizers did, but the hotel didn't. I accessed the Calderwood Hotel database and confirmed his sister checked into suite 623 a couple weeks ago. And yet the same credit card was just used at a Walgreens near her house in Fountain Hills. I think he's there at the con."

"That sneaky little shit. I knew his sister was lying to me." I scanned the crowd, wondering whether he'd snuck into the convention. "Thanks for the 411, Becks. I'll be in touch."

I hung up and turned to my young fan, who was looking rather impatient. "Sorry, girl. One more quick photo, and then I have to go catch a bad guy."

The girl's eyes widened. "You're a real superhero?"

I grinned. "No superpowers, but I do bring bad guys to justice."

After the girl took a final selfie with me, she hugged me and moved on to someone cosplaying Rey from *Star Wars: The Force Awakens.*

I considered running to my vehicle to retrieve my weapons, handcuffs, and body armor. I didn't like apprehending fugitives when I was unarmed. But with the convention going on, there was no way security would let me in carrying a Taser, much less a revolver. Then again, Warren was a skinny old guy. How much trouble could he be?

But first I had to find him. I figured there was a fair chance he would be on the convention floor, even if he'd been banned. Celebrities thrived on attention, even if it was negative. Why else would he be here?

Security guards stood at all of the entrances, but they were looking for people with dangerous weapons or without the proper badges. Not sixty-year-old pedophiles.

For fifteen minutes, I wandered the crowded convention floor past comic book dealers, prop vendors, and T-shirt booths. But unless Warren was disguised in a costume, I didn't see him.

I approached one of the security guards at the convention floor entrance and pulled up Warren's photo on my phone. "Excuse me, have you seen this man?" I asked. "I've been assigned to return him to custody."

The guard glanced at my costume and gave me a bemused look. "This is a joke, right?"

I flipped out my state-issued bail enforcement license and badge. "No joke. I'm a bail enforcement agent. Have you seen him?"

He studied the photo. "That's the guy who molested kids from his TV show."

"Yeah, Daniel Warren. You seen him around the con?"

"No, they banned his sorry ass."

"My sources tell me he checked in to the hotel after missing his court date."

The security guard shrugged. "Sorry, haven't seen him."

"If he shows up, call me." I handed him my business card and walked into the lobby.

I considered going directly up to the sixth floor and forcing my way into his room, but that could lead to problems of its own. Better to have an employee with a key let me in. So I approached the registration desk.

"Welcome to Calderwood Hotel and Convention Center. How may I help you?" asked a pleasant fortyish woman with chestnut hair and a name badge that read Nancy.

I held up my ID. "Jinx Ballou, bail enforcement agent working for Assurity Bail Bonds. One of my fugitives, Daniel Warren, is checked in to suite 623. I need someone here to let me into his room."

Nancy looked at my ID, then began typing at her computer. "I'm sorry, we don't have a Daniel Warren checked in to any room."

"He's registered under his sister's name."

"What name would that be?"

Shit, I forgot to ask Becca. "I don't know. But he's the one in suite 623. I need to get in there to arrest him."

She glanced down at my costume and gave me a snooty look. "I'm sorry, but I can't help you. Our high-profile guests value their privacy. Fans go to great lengths to sneak into their rooms. I can't let you in unless you have a warrant or something."

"Look, lady, you have a serial child molester staying in your hotel. As a licensed bounty hunter, I'm allowed to enter any location where I believe my fugitive is hiding. I don't need a warrant. Supreme Court said so."

"I'm sorry, ma'am, but you don't exactly look like a bounty hunter to me."

"I'm here for Winter Con. Not my fault you let fugitive sexual predators stay in your hotel."

"Do you have any paperwork showing he's your fugitive?"

I sighed. "Not on me. I wasn't expecting Warren to be here."

"Then I'm sorry. Come back when you have a warrant."

I rolled my eyes and turned away. "Bitch," I said under my breath as I strode to the elevators.

If I couldn't go through official channels, I'd have to do things the fun way. I rode the elevator to the sixth floor and followed the signs to suite 623. I was about to knock when a stern voice caught my attention.

"Can I help you, miss?" The voice belonged to a hulking security guard who outweighed me by a hundred pounds.

"Nope, I'm good. Thanks!"

"I'm gonna have to ask you to come with me." This guy was getting on my nerves.

I approached him. "Look, I'm here to arrest a child molester who's jumped bail. Now let me do my job, and you can go back to harassing people at the convention."

He grabbed my arm. Bad move. No one touches me without my permission.

In the span of a heartbeat, I twisted back his wrist and drove him to his knees. Keeping his wrist pinned, I pivoted and locked my arm around his thick neck in a chokehold. Guys this big are tough to choke out, but I've had a lot of practice. He struggled for ten seconds, frantically reaching for the Taser on his belt before going limp.

He wouldn't be unconscious long, so I rushed back to Warren's door and knocked, keeping an eye on the guard.

A familiar but tired voice asked, "Who is it?"

"Mr. Warren, I was hoping to get an autograph." It was a stupid cover story, but then I was dressed as Wonder Woman. The doors to the hotel rooms were solid and would be hard to kick in.

The door inched open with the security latch engaged. "I'm sorry, but I'm not up for signing autographs at this time."

"Please, I've been a fan since I was three." My voice was urgent. "I've been waiting my whole life for this chance."

"How'd you know I was here?"

I fake blushed. "Girlfriend of mine works the front desk. She knows I'm a die-hard fan."

Warren sighed. "Okay, but please make it quick."

He closed the door and released the security latch. Down the hall, the guard was starting to stir.

The door opened, revealing Warren in a white undershirt and a pair of blue gym shorts. I flashed my bail enforcement ID and badge. "Daniel Warren, you're under arrest for failure to appear at your court date."

For an old guy, he was fast. The dude turned on his heel and hauled ass through the suite's spacious living room. He tried to shut the bedroom door, but I put my weight against it before he could latch it. He stumbled back and picked up a nickel-plated Colt 1911 from the nightstand. It trembled in his hand as he pointed it at me.

"I…I'm not going back to jail. Y-You know what they do to people who've molested kids?"

In situations like this, I asked myself WWWWD—What would Wonder Woman do? I held up my hand in a de-escalating gesture, trying to ignore the .45-caliber barrel pointed at my chest. "Whoa, take it easy, Danny."

"I'm not going back."

"Calm down. No one believes the charges." I was lying out my ass because I couldn't deflect bullets as Gal Gadot did on screen. "We can work this out, but you gotta put down the gun. You don't see me with a gun, do ya?"

"I didn't mean to hurt nobody." His face colored and tightened like a fist. "I loved those kids."

"I know you did. And you don't want to hurt me either, do you? I really am a lifelong fan." I started humming the show's theme song.

The gun lowered a bit. "I just…I can't go back to jail."

"Look, we can get your bail reset and your court date

rescheduled. No big deal. You can beat this rap but not if you shoot me."

He looked up at me. Sorrow and a disturbing resolve haunted his eyes. "I'm sorry." He raised the pistol again.

I rushed him, reaching for the gun as his finger squeezed the trigger.

2

The hammer clicked without firing. I snatched the Colt out of his hand and tackled him to the floor.

"Try chambering a round next time you try shooting someone, dumb ass." I reached for my handcuffs only to find the loops of my homemade Lasso of Truth. *Oh well. When necessary, improvise.*

I unsnapped the lasso and lashed Warren's wrists together behind his back.

"Please don't do this," he whimpered. "I never meant to hurt nobody."

"Like you didn't mean to shoot me just now?" I applied more pressure on his arm until he yelped in pain.

"I'm...I'm sorry. I just...I panicked."

"Shut the fuck up, perv." I yanked him to his feet. "To think you were once my hero. Makes me wanna puke. Or kick the shit out of you."

"Just kill me and get it over with," Warren whined.

"Kill you? Ha! Like I'd throw away my future over filth like you. Au contraire, I want you to spend the rest of your miserable life in some hellhole bent over as someone's prison bitch." I'm not a fan of prison rape, but in his case, I'd make an exception.

I stashed his pistol in my fanny pack and pushed him toward the living room. "Okay, perv. Let's move."

"I'm not even dressed."

"I'm sure the corrections officers in Scottsdale will be happy to hook you up with a fancy orange jumpsuit."

"It's cold outside. I'll freeze to death."

"Ask me if I care?"

Warren hung his head like a scolded child.

I sighed as my conscience got the best of me. "Fine. You got a coat?"

"In the closet. There's a pair of loafers in there too."

I helped him on with the loafers and draped the heavy winter coat over his shoulders. "There. Now let's go."

A loud pounding shook the front door. "Security!" said a familiar baritone voice.

"Shit," I grumbled.

The lock clicked, and in rushed the hulking security guard I'd choked out. Next to him was a smaller, squatter guard with a buzz cut. Both stood with Tasers trained on me.

"Hands up!" they shouted in unison.

I kept my grip on Warren in case he tried to bolt. "Easy, boys. I'm a licensed bail enforcement agent hired to apprehend this scumbag, who failed to appear in court. Now get out of my way, or I'll charge you both with interference in the apprehension of a fugitive." It was a made-up charge, but they didn't know that.

"Get those hands up, or I will light you up, lady," said Hulk.

"Hey, big guy. I already kicked your ass once this morning. You want a rematch?"

Buzz Cut peered up at his taller cohort. "She kicked your ass?"

Hulk's face screwed up in anger. Hulk's Taser shot two metal darts into my thick leather costume, but they didn't penetrate enough to affect me. I smacked them away with the braces covering my forearms.

Hulk tossed his Taser and swung at me. I grabbed his arm and twisted him around into an elbow lock. His buddy got a panicked look in his eye and drew down on me. I used Hulk as a shield. Buzz Cut's Taser darts hit Hulk in the back. He bellowed as his muscles constricted at once, dropping him to the floor like a felled tree.

I drew Warren's pistol and aimed it at Buzz Cut. "Drop the Taser!"

"Crap." Buzz Cut tossed his weapon and held up his hands in surrender.

Hulk groaned but stayed down.

"Now listen up, boys! All I want is to return my prisoner to custody. So if you two are quite done playing Keystone Kops, I'll be on my way."

Buzz Cut eyed me warily. Hulk managed to utter a muffled "Cunt." My work here was done.

"Come on, perv. Let's take you back to lockup."

I kept a firm grip on Warren's arm as we rode the elevator to the lobby. From his drooping posture, I gathered he'd resolved himself to his fate.

I caught my reflection in the polished steel doors. My hair was mussed, making me look less like a demigod superhero and more like a wild woman raised by wolves. I did what I could to finger comb it back into place, but it didn't help much.

"Could you loosen the rope? I've lost feeling in my hands," Warren muttered quietly between the third and second floors.

"Shut up, perv, or I'll make it tighter." Never let it be said that I'm one of those TV bounty hunters who gets all touchy-feely once a perp was apprehended.

"I could lose my hands if I don't get the blood flowing."

"Oh, wouldn't that be a shame," I said with dripping sarcasm. "How would you ever fondle little kids without your hands?"

The elevator doors opened to a lobby filled with the costumed masses of my fellow comic book geeks. Several of them noticed me perp walking Warren toward the hotel entrance and started applauding. Others held up their phones to capture the Kodak moment. I had to admit, getting cheered on by my fellow cosplayers kinda rocked.

Outside, the early December air was cool but not cold.

Phoenix doesn't have the same four seasons most places do. Autumn doesn't begin until mid-October and lasts until New Year's. Winter is a myth. Spring starts in January. By mid-April, summer arrives with temps climbing into the triple digits. In July, the dry heat of summer cranks up into the muggy hell of monsoon season, with spectacular thunderstorms, widespread flooding, and nightmarish dust storms called haboobs.

For now, I savored the all-too-brief cool weather as I guided Warren down the street, while the sapphire sky played peekaboo between the glass-and-steel buildings. A few blocks away, we reached the parking garage.

Warren froze as I tried to lead him up the outside staircase. "I can't climb stairs with my hands behind my back."

"Move, asshole! I'm only parked on the third floor. You can make it."

"Untie my hands first so I can hold the rail."

"Fat chance."

He leaned away from the concrete steps as if they were made of lava. "I'll fall and break my hip." His voice trembled.

"Fine, we'll take the elevator." I punched the call button with my fist. "Big baby."

On the third floor, I pressed the key fob to unlock my SUV. Nicknamed the Gray Ghost, the seven-year-old Nissan Pathfinder was pockmarked with scrapes, dents, and broken trim, rendering it virtually invisible in most Phoenix neighborhoods.

I shoved Warren into the back seat and secured him with the seat belt. "Comfy?" I asked with a sneer.

"You know what they'll do to me in prison."

"Maybe you should've thought of that before you molested those kids."

"I'll pay you double whatever the bounty is just to let me

go." His face looked deathly pale under the dim glow of the Gray Ghost's dome light.

"So you can hurt more kids? I don't fucking think so."

His gaze fell. "It's not my fault. I have a problem."

"Oh, is that what you call it?" I chuckled darkly. "Alcoholism is a problem. Missing your court date is a problem. Molesting children is an abomination."

"I get urges I can't control."

"Maybe your fellow inmates can help you with those urges." I slammed the side door shut and climbed into the driver's seat.

"Can't we make some sort of deal?" he whined as I started the engine.

"The only deal I'm interested in involves returning your sorry ass to jail. Now pipe down, or I'll strap you to the bumper. You got me, perv?"

He stayed silent for the remainder of the trip.

I drove north to I-10, then transitioned onto the Loop 202 before taking the McDowell exit. As I waited for the light to change, my phone rang. Becca again.

"Jinxie, did you seriously just arrest Daniel Warren while dressed as Wonder Woman?" She sounded excited and tired at the same time.

"Yeah, why?" I asked nervously.

"It's trending all over social media with the hashtag #WonderWomanPerpWalk. Hold on. I'm clicking on a video."

"There's video?" I felt a lump in my throat.

"Wow! That's seriously badass. No wonder the local news stations are all over it."

"The news stations? Seriously? Shit." I've had an aversion to the press ever since the *Phoenix Living* weekly newspaper outed me as transgender. Bail bond agents around town blackballed me when they read it.

"Don't worry. Your name's not mentioned. But folks are wondering who this mystery Wonder Woman is. Most think you're a cop."

"Let them keep thinking that. You at the Hub today?" The Hub was a coworking space near Fifteenth Avenue and Grand, where we both worked.

"Yeah, but about to call it a day. Chronic fatigue's kicking in. I'm done out of spoons."

"That's why I keep telling you to switch to knives. They're much more fun."

"Ha ha."

"You need me to pick up anything for you?" I often helped her out whenever her chronic fatigue flared up.

"A friend of mine already did some shopping for me."

I scoffed. "Hey! That's *my* job."

"You were at Winter Con. I didn't want to bother you. But you're still my bestie."

"Damn straight! I'm headed to Scottsdale lockup to drop off Warren. You need anything else, you call me. Got that?"

"Will do."

I'd dealt with the correction officers at the Scottsdale Jail for years. All in all, they were good folks. But they weren't above catcalling, whistling, and otherwise giving me shit when I walked in.

CO Bennett, a woman with a coppery ponytail and freckles, smirked while she pulled up Warren's records. "Damn, Ballou, you can arrest me in that costume anytime," she teased.

My face warmed as I untied Warren. "Thanks, Bennett, but I prefer guys."

"Oh well, a girl can dream." She gave me a coy wink.

I had to admit I felt a little physical attraction when she handed me Warren's body receipt.

"See you around, superhero," she said.

I waved and walked out the door, hoping she didn't see my face turning red. Things were getting way too hot in there.

3

With paperwork in hand, I pointed the Gray Ghost toward Phoenix. I debated whether to return to Winter Con or turn in Daniel Warren's paperwork and get paid. The last few days, Sadie Levinson had been having a cow over Warren's defaulted bail bond. I decided to drop off the body receipt and put her fears to rest.

The con would continue into the weekend, so I could go back tomorrow and with more money to spend on rare comics and maybe some Funko Pop figures. I'd had my eye on a Funko version of Negasonic Teenage Warhead from *Deadpool*.

But first, a change in attire was called for. I was not showing up at Assurity Bail Bonds in costume. Sadie already had a stick up her butt. I didn't need her giving me shit about being dressed as Wonder Woman when I captured Warren. So I pulled off the highway at Seventh Avenue and headed home.

I lived in a cozy house in Phoenix's trendy Willo District, north of downtown along the Central Corridor. The neighborhood dated back to the 1930s. The homes were small but solid and tended to be on the pricey side.

My brother, Jake, who remodeled and flipped houses for a living, had acquired the two-bedroom, two-bath on the cheap after the housing bubble burst. He'd restored the hardwood floors, brought the wiring up to code, and installed Saltillo tile in the kitchen and dining area. I converted the spare room into workout space with an exercise station for strength training and a human-shaped punching bag for combat practice.

My decor could best be described as millennial Bohemian meets sci-fi/fantasy fangirl. Lots of bright colors and different textures throughout the house. Roy Lichtenstein prints and movie posters covered the walls, including one autographed by Gal Gadot. A bamboo bookshelf in the living room was filled with comics in plastic sleeves. A breakfront in the dining room displayed a carefully curated collection of action figures. It wasn't the tidiest place, but it was clean. Mostly.

The best thing was that my boyfriend, Conor Doyle, lived only a few streets south of me. We alternated spending the night at each other's houses, so the proximity was a real time-saver.

Once in my bedroom, I shimmied out of the Wonder Woman outfit and pulled on a Pink Trinkets concert T-shirt, cargo pants, and a well-worn pair of black Doc Martens—my preferred business attire.

For safety, I strapped on a ballistic vest emblazoned with the words "Bail Enforcement." A tactical belt around my waist held my Taser in a holster on my right side, and a snub-nosed Rossi .357 revolver for backup nestled in an ankle holster. I hooked a walkie-talkie on the belt and slipped two sets of handcuffs in a thigh pocket.

A pair of my wraparound shades, fingerless leather gloves, and a black ball cap embroidered with the words Ballou Fugitive Recovery completed the ensemble. Time to rock and roll.

I opened the fridge to grab a bottle of water for the road, only to find there weren't any left. I would've sworn there'd been at least a few last time I checked. I made a note to pick up another case on the way home.

As I walked out the door, my phone began playing a Flogging Molly's "Drunken Lullabies"—Conor's ringtone.

"Heard ya nicked that pedo Danny Warren," he said in his Irish brogue. "Nice catch, love."

"Thanks," I said, feeling a flush of embarrassment. Maybe Conor hadn't heard how I was dressed.

"By the way, ya looked mighty deadly in your Super Girl getup."

I chuckled. He was intentionally tweaking me with the misreference. "It's Wonder Woman, ya dodgy bloke," I replied in a poor imitation of his accent.

"So ya say, love. Wear it tonight, or I'll remain unconvinced."

I felt myself getting aroused thinking about getting him in bed, with or without the costume. Mostly without. "You're on, mister," I replied.

"We at your place or mine tonight?"

"Mine, if that's all right. I've got paperwork and stuff to catch up on."

"Ya know, this would be a lot easier if ya just moved in with me already. All this back and forth between houses is driving me mad."

And with that, the passion escaped like air from a balloon. "We talked about this, Conor." It came out more sternly than I intended.

"We've been dating for two and a half years. Don't ya think it's time we stop this sleepover madness and live together like normal people?"

"Normal?" I scoffed, trying to lighten the mood. "When've you *ever* known me to be normal?"

"You're dodging the issue, love." His voice stiffened. "Been wondering if ya really fancy me or if ya just want me for the occasional shag."

Ouch! That one hurt. "I love you, Conor. Really, I do. It's just...I like having my own space."

"Ya want to hold on to your bungalow, fine. But for Christ's sake, can't we live under a single roof? After what that fucker Milo Volkov did last year—"

"Volkov's dead. I killed him. Remember?"

"Aye, but not before he left that reporter's body wrapped up in plastic on your doorstep."

"I can take care of myself."

"That ya can." The silence between us stretched. "Maybe you're just scared."

"Scared? What've I got to be scared of?" I made sure my voice didn't shake, even though he was hitting a little close to the mark.

"Scared of commitment, maybe. Not sure exactly."

"I have to go. Sadie's been shitting kittens over Daniel Warren. I have to bring her the body receipt."

"Fine. I'll see ya tonight." He sounded hurt, which piled onto the guilt I was already feeling.

"See you then." I felt like a heel. He was a sweet guy who treated me with respect and was great in the sack. So why did I resist moving in with him? Hell if I knew. But my gut was telling me not to, and I'd learned to trust it.

I hopped in the Gray Ghost and floored down Central Avenue with the windows open and Le Tigre playing full blast on the stereo.

Assurity Bail Bonds was wedged between an accounting firm and a temp staffing office on the second floor of the Arizona Center. Sadie Levinson had opened it a few years back when the touristy outdoor shopping mall was rebranding itself as a corporate business center downtown. Lately, management had been opening stores that catered more to year-round residents.

I parked in the adjacent garage and hustled along the sidewalk, past a smorgasbord of restaurants, clothing shops, and kiosks. Mothers at outdoor tables monitored their toddlers playing around a fountain that randomly shot streams of water from jets in the sidewalk. I jogged up the grand staircase near the movie theater, vaulting the steps two at a time.

A string of bells attached to Assurity's doorframe jingled as I entered. The office consisted of a twenty-by-thirty-foot room with two stained oak desks, one on each side of the cream-colored room. Vertical filing cabinets lined the back wall. The other walls featured framed prints of paintings by Monet,

Picasso, and Gaugin. The decor was professional if a bit sterile, making it feel more like an art gallery than a bail bond office.

Sadie Levinson sat at the desk to my left with two faux leather guest chairs in front. She was a slender woman in her forties with a short wedge haircut, red metallic frame glasses, and a no-nonsense expression on her face.

"You got Warren," she said without looking up.

"Told you I would." I unfolded the body receipt and handed it to her. She frowned and flattened out the folds as best she could.

"Is there a reason you were dressed up like a caped crusader?"

"Where'd you hear that?" *When in doubt, play dumb.*

Sadie shot me a don't-bullshit-me look. "Word gets around."

"Technically speaking, 'caped crusader' refers to Batman. I was cosplaying as Wonder Woman."

Not even a chuckle. Tough crowd.

"I was at Winter Con when my skip tracer tracked him to the hotel." I gave her a rundown of my impromptu capture of her prodigal client. "So what else do you have for me?" I asked as she wrote out a check for Warren's bounty.

She pulled some files from the stack on the left side of her desk and handed them to me. "I got two more skips for you."

"Just two? Come on, Sadie! How am I supposed to pay my team with two measly jobs? You giving jobs to other bounty hunters?"

She cocked her head with a look of superiority. "I pride myself on properly underwriting my clients so I don't have to pay you to pick them up for failing to appear. If you need more work, go someplace else."

We both knew she was one of the few bail bond agents who would hire me after my trans status was made public. I let the matter drop and thumbed through the files. "Tell me about these deadbeat clients of yours."

"First one's Robert Rossellini. You've picked him up before."

I chuckled. "Conspiracy Bob! I love him. What's our uber-paranoid buddy done now?"

"Charges are trespassing, causing a disturbance, and violating an order of protection by the office of the Arizona State Mine Inspector. Bail's set at ten thousand dollars."

"The mining inspector has a restraining order against Conspiracy Bob? What in the world for?"

Levinson shook her head. "Mr. Rossellini's been haranguing the mine inspector's staff. Some nonsense about mole people plotting the end of the world."

My chuckle turned into an all-out belly laugh. "Jesus Christ on a surfboard, where's he get this stuff?"

"I couldn't begin to tell you. Just pick him up."

"Bob's bounty is chump change, but I'll take him just for entertainment value." I pulled up the next file. "Who's this Pratt fellow?"

"Rudy Pratt. Charged with murder in the first degree in the death of a coworker. Bail's set at two hundred fifty thousand dollars."

"Now we're talking. I can use twenty-five grand." My bounty rate was ten percent of the bail amount. I flipped through the defendant's application. "What's your take on him?"

"No priors. His demeanor was rather subdued when I met with him. His wife has a bit of a mouth on her. He missed his evidentiary hearing yesterday. Judge wants him picked up and held until trial. I've left messages on his phone, with his wife, and his attorney but haven't heard back."

I stood up. "Okay, I'll track him down."

Sadie leveled her eyes to my chest. "Try not to take so long this time, okay? I want Pratt back in custody pronto. I prefer not to play Russian roulette with my business."

"I'll do my best."

"Oh, and do it dressed in street clothes and not as"—she made a hand gesture as she struggled for the words—"one of the Avengers."

"The Avengers are from the Marvel universe. Wonder Wom—"

"Goodbye, Ms. Ballou." She turned back to her computer and resumed typing.

I saluted with the client folders and walked out.

One of these days, I was going to get that woman to loosen up. Maybe take her out for drinks at Grumpy's and help her get laid.

On second thought, who knew what she'd be like if she loosened up. Might be worse than she was now.

4

It was after one o'clock, so I scarfed down a couple of Chicago hot dogs in Arizona Center's food court while I perused the files for the two fugitives. Conspiracy Bob, I could handle on my own. This Rudy Pratt fellow might be a different story.

Pratt's lack of priors was a good sign he wasn't a hardened criminal. Then again, the man was charged with first-degree murder, and now the judge wanted him remanded. He might not be so keen on going back to jail willingly. So once I took care of Conspiracy Bob, I'd contact my crew for backup on Pratt.

After lunch, I hopped on I-10 to the Loop 101 North and exited west onto Bell Road. Sun City was a retirement community northwest of Phoenix, where golf carts were a common form of transportation and turning left from the right-hand lane was considered going with the flow of traffic.

Conspiracy Bob lived in a small yellow house. A low wall cordoned off a front patio littered with dusty old watering cans and garden gnomes his late wife had collected before she died a few years back. A forest of weeds, some at least two feet tall, poked up from the layer of crushed rock in the front yard.

Bob's forest-green Subaru, a relic from the 1980s, baked in the sunny driveway. From the back, I could hardly tell what color it was painted with all of the conspiracy-themed bumper stickers.

Behind the house, a shortwave antenna rose forty feet

into the air. Bob used an elaborate radio set to communicate surreptitiously with his fellow conspiracy theorists.

I blocked the driveway with the Gray Ghost in case Bob got any ideas of making a run for it. He'd done so once or twice out of the dozen times I'd picked him up. What he lacked in rational thought, he made up for in determination.

My knock at the door triggered a series of barks from inside. Sounded like a big dog and might have been convincing if it hadn't deteriorated into a fit of very human coughing. Conspiracy Bob was up to his usual shenanigans.

"Bob, it's Jinx Ballou!" I hollered loud enough for him to hear me. "You missed your court date."

The barking continued, although with less enthusiasm.

"Sure is a nice door you have here. What is it? Oak? Be a shame if I had to knock it in with my battering ram."

"Bob's not here right now," said a rattly tenor voice, "but if you leave a message at the beep—"

"I'm getting my battering ram."

"Wait! Wait!" Several locks clicked free, and the door opened to a dour little man in his seventies standing on the tile floor in leather Jesus sandals. He stood six inches shorter than me and had a gray beard that hung down to his chest. He wore tattered jeans and a pale-green shirt that read Everything You Know is a Lie.

"We really have to do this?" he asked with hands on his hips.

"'Fraid so. You wouldn't want to lose this, uh, lovely house of yours."

"None of this would've happened if they'd just listened to me." He sighed. "All right. Let me get my coat."

I followed him into his house, past half-empty cardboard boxes, computers in various states of assembly, stacks of newspapers, dirty dishes, and heaps of clothing. Aluminum foil lined the walls and windows.

"You know, you'd save yourself a lot of money and trouble if you just showed up to court." I trailed him into his bedroom.

A bookshelf stuffed with yellowing paperbacks stood next to a bed that reeked of urine.

"Where's the fun in that?" He picked through the crammed wall closet until he found a faded Grateful Dead hoodie. "I'm trying to make people understand what's happening before it's too late."

"And what's going on?" I asked casually, not interested in hearing his latest conspiracy theories.

"The mole people are planning to take over the city, possibly the world." He pulled on the hoodie and held my gaze with fervor in his eyes. "They're planning to detonate bombs at strategic places around the city. The first one's set to go off in a few days near the state government buildings."

I gestured toward the front door, and he led the way outside.

"Have you actually seen these mole people?" I asked.

"You think I'm crazy, don't ya?" He pointed at me as we stopped next to the Gray Ghost.

"Well, Bob, the thought crossed my mind." I unlocked the passenger door, and he climbed in. I hopped in behind the wheel and cruised out of the neighborhood.

"They've been living in the abandoned mines north of the valley and communicating via shortwave," he explained. "I started picking up their transmissions a couple months ago."

"So mole people have shortwave radios, huh?"

"Oh, they've adopted much of our technology. Radios, gene splicing, even video games."

"How do you know they're mole people? Maybe they're just, well, people."

"For starters, they use code names like Lodestar, Grays Gulch, and Crizaba—all names from abandoned mines in the area."

"That doesn't necessarily mean they're mole people."

He got a gleam in his eye. "When you've been listening as long as I have, you can tell. They have a certain way of speaking. And one thing I heard is that the days of tolerance are over. They refer to us as the immigrants because they were here first.

They're tired of how we're polluting the planet. All the drugs and violence and corruption."

"They speak English?"

"Oh yeah, they've been studying us for a long time. Listening in."

"And what do they look like?"

He pulled up a photo on his cell phone. I glanced at it as we waited at a red light. "Isn't that a character from a *Star Wars* movie?"

"That's what they *want* you to think. But they're real. And when they start blowing up buildings in Phoenix, everyone's going to be sorry they ignored me."

"If that happens, you are welcome to tell me you told me so."

Suddenly his glee vanished, replaced with profound sadness. "We'll all be dead or enslaved by then. So what would be the point?"

Conspiracy Bob got quiet for the rest of the trip to the North Phoenix Jail.

As the officer was processing him in, I told Bob I'd put in a good word with Sadie for him and hoped his lawyer could get his bail reset.

I felt bad for the guy. Yeah, he was brainwashed by the talking heads spreading absurd ideas, faulty logic, and outright lies to the gullible masses. But all in all, Conspiracy Bob seemed to have a good heart and never gave me any trouble.

After Bob was back in custody, I sat in the Gray Ghost and studied Rudy Pratt's file in depth. Pratt lived in a single-family residence, not far from Metrocenter mall in Phoenix. He was married with two kids and had worked for ten years as an electronics engineer on rocket systems at SpaceJet America.

More recently, Pratt had worked as a salesclerk at Hardware SuperCenter, where the murder in question occurred. From rocket scientist to cashier to murder suspect to bail jumper. Helluva fall from grace.

No prior convictions. His credit report showed some medical

bills that had gone ninety days before being paid, but whose hadn't these days? He owned three pistols, a revolver, and a shotgun registered in his name. Not unusual for Arizona, but as a bounty hunter, I didn't like taking any chances.

I called my friend Rodeo, who worked for me part-time. His real name was Nathaniel Kwan, but he'd earned the nickname Rodeo during his time in the army due to his fondness for cowboy hats. More recently, he'd developed a fondness for my brother, Jake, who was newly out of the closet.

"Hey, Rodeo, I need your help with a case."

"Copy that. Who's our FTA?" Shorthand for *failed to appear*.

"Rudy Pratt, a former rocket scientist charged with first-degree murder."

"Interesting. You want me to meet you somewhere?"

"The guy lives near Metrocenter. I'll text you the address."

"Meet you there in a couple hours."

"Couple of hours? Come on, dude. Time's money. Whatever it is can wait."

"Sorry. I'm dropping Gwyneth off at her dance studio as we speak. They're rehearsing their Christmas recital."

"Ugh, I'm so tired of this Christmas nonsense."

"Come on, girl. Don't be such a Scrooge."

"Charles Dickens can kiss my skinny white ass." I sighed. "Go do the daddy thing then get your butt over to our fugitive's house. I want to get this job done so I can go back to Winter Con tomorrow."

"Aha! The real motive for urgency emerges."

"Screw you."

"I'll see you in two, boss."

I disconnected and hit another number on speed dial.

"This is Caden." His voice was a youthful tenor, growing deeper each month he was on testosterone therapy.

I'd known Caden Morrow for a few years, having met him at Phoenix Gender Alliance, a local transgender support group. At the time, he was working as a CO at the women's prison in Tonopah. When his employer, Rehabilitation Systems of America, fired him for transitioning on the job, he came to me looking for work. Turned out he was a good fit for the job.

"We got another case, dude. Need you to meet Rodeo and me near Metrocenter in a couple hours."

"Sounds good. Hey, d'you hear someone dressed as Wonder Woman arrested Daniel Warren at a comic book festival?"

"Really? Imagine that," I replied with feigned surprise. "I'll text you the address."

"Oh my God, was that—"

I ended the call and started the Gray Ghost.

5

Caden's cobalt-blue Audi roadster was parked in front of Rudy Pratt's driveway when I pulled up behind him. The setting sun had smeared the western sky with a palette of fuchsia, blood orange, and lavender.

As I climbed out of the Gray Ghost, wind gusts tugged at my ponytail and whipped the bougainvillea bushes in the Pratts' front yard like a flag, sending scarlet petals tumbling down the street.

I hugged Caden as he got out of his roadster. He had a sparse but scraggly beard and wore his hair in a well-gelled fauxhawk. Though a few inches shorter than me, he was ripped from an intense bodybuilding regimen he'd been on lately.

On his left hip, he carried a Taser pistol, similar to mine, as his primary weapon. A twenty-six-inch collapsible baton sat in a holster on his right. I knew he also had a SIG Sauer P229 .40-caliber concealed inside his waistband at the small of his back.

"How's it going, bro?" I asked.

"Kicking ass and taking names. So that was you with Warren?" he asked with a wry smile.

I shrugged and glanced down the street. "Where the hell's Rodeo?"

"Come on, Jinxie. It's cool." He chucked me on the shoulder. "You're a badass. Who else could pull off something like that?"

"Yeah, a badass who prefers to stay out of the limelight if I can help it."

"You going to Juanita's fundraiser next week?"

Juanita Valdez was a trans woman who mentored me when I came out. She currently owned the Main Drag, the most popular queer bar in the city.

"What fundraiser?" I asked.

"The Barbra Shop Quartet. Four queens performing Barbra Streisand songs in a barbershop quartet style."

I shuddered at the thought. "Good fucking grief! That's insane."

"Yeah, but they're raising money to rebuild the Queer Youth Shelter after some asshole torched it last month."

"If it's to support a good cause, I'll be there. Besides, Juanita would have my ass if I missed it."

Caden laughed. "Yeah, she can be scary when she's pissed."

Rodeo's turquoise Mazda Miata turned onto the street and rolled to a stop behind my SUV.

"'Bout damn time," I said as he got out of his car. "Is it New Year's already?"

Rodeo was clean-shaven with an athletic build. He wore mirrored aviators and a Stetson that arched over his head.

"Very funny." From his trunk, he pulled a shotgun loaded with beanbag rounds. "Just wait till you have kids."

"No, thanks."

"Oh, come on," Rodeo teased. "Just a matter of time before you and Conor adopt a few of your own. Gwyneth would love some cousins to play with."

"I can just see Jinx now," replied Caden, "carrying a baby on her hip in a little Kevlar onesie."

"You two are seriously delusional. Let's bag this deadbeat already."

I gave Rodeo and Caden the 411 on Pratt. "He's charged with murder. No priors, but he has multiple weapons registered in his name, so stay frosty."

Rodeo asked, "What's the plan?"

"Standard procedure for now. I'll hit the front door. Rodeo, you cover the back. Caden, stay here by the vehicles and keep an eye out in case Pratt sneaks out the garage or side window."

Caden sighed dejectedly. "Why do I always have to stay by the vehicles? I want to be where the action is."

I patted him on the back. "I need a lookout. You up to the task, or you gonna bitch?"

"I'm up for it." He crossed his arms. "Sometime I'd like to cover the back door and let Rodeo keep lookout."

Rodeo clapped him on the shoulder. "Hang in there, little man. I used to be the newbie. Now it's your turn."

Pratt's house was a combination of white siding and tan brick. A red sign reading "Christ Is Born" stood in the yard, next to an inflatable snowman, currently deflated.

A white Toyota Camry sat parked in front of the two-car garage. The license plate matched the one listed on Pratt's bail application. Between our three vehicles, we had the driveway blocked, but some FTAs weren't above plowing across their own yard to avoid going to jail.

Rodeo scooted around the side of the house.

"Let's get this party started." I strode to the front door. "You ready, Rodeo?" I asked into the walkie.

"Ready and waiting."

"Caden?"

"As ready as I'll ever be."

My pulse quickened. This was the scariest and most exciting part of the job. Anything could happen and usually did.

I drew my Taser and pounded on the screen door. "Open up! Bail enforcement!"

After a minute or so with no answer, I pounded again. "Open the door, Mr. Pratt, or we'll force our way in."

I heard hushed voices inside. I had no way to tell if one of them was our guy or not.

"Last chance!" I shouted. "If we come in by force, you'll wish you'd surrendered voluntarily."

6

The door opened. A woman in an orange cotton dress glared at me through the security screen door. Her face was bony, with eyes the color of steel and every bit as cold. "Can I help you?" she snarled.

"You Mrs. Pratt?"

"Yes, I'm Linda Pratt."

I recognized her name from the application. "Your husband missed his court date. He needs to come with me. Now."

"He ain't here."

"Bullshit. His car's in the driveway."

"My son's borrowing it. My husband's in our minivan."

"And where is your husband?"

"Why should I tell you?"

"Because if the bond is forfeited, Assurity Bail Bonds takes your house and kicks you out on the street."

"This is all such bullshit. My husband was defending himself after that wetback assaulted him."

"Ma'am, I'm not here to try him. He and his lawyer can do that when he shows up in court. So unless he wants to spend the duration of his trial in jail, he needs to come with me."

"They're railroading my husband because he's white. The goddamn Mexicans and blacks and faggots all got more rights than a good white Christian man does."

I so wanted to slap the stupid out of her racist, Fox-News-watching ass. But the last thing I needed was to be charged with assault. "Tell me where Rudy is, or I'll run you in for aiding and abetting a fugitive."

"Fuck you, lady. My husband doesn't tell me where he's going. I'm not one of them shrill femi-Nazi types who has to monitor their husband's every move. You can tell that Jew lady at Assurity Bail Bonds he's not guilty. And if she tries to take our house, she'll regret it." She slammed the door shut. The dead bolt clicked in place.

I heard Rodeo laughing over the walkie. "Wow, she's a piece of work, huh?"

"You can say that again." I holstered my Taser.

"You think he's in there?" asked Caden.

"Hard to tell." We had the right to force our way in provided we had reason to believe he was inside. His truck in the driveway constituted enough reason for me, no matter what his wife said. "Bring me the battering ram!" I shouted to Caden loudly enough for everyone inside to hear.

"Battering ram coming up!" Caden yelled for similar effect.

The front door reopened. Linda Pratt glared at me. Her mouth squeezed tight like a sphincter.

"You break in here, I'm calling the cops."

I put my hand on my cheek and feigned horror. "Oh my, not the cops!"

"You think I won't?"

"Call them, lady. Your husband murdered someone and jumped bail. Now you're hiding him. Who you think they'll side with?"

"I'm telling you, he ain't here."

Caden trudged up the walk while hefting the thirty-pound battering ram, the strain showing on his face. He set the ram on the concrete with a clunk. "Battering ram as requested."

"What the hell you gonna do with that?" Some of the iron was draining from her voice.

"Unless you let us in, I will use this ram to tear your door off its hinges. And then me and my team will search your house room by room, cabinet by cabinet until we find your loser of a husband or determine for ourselves that he's not here. Could take us a few hours." I turned to Caden and nodded.

"At least." He hefted the ram and drew it back for his first hit. "Here goes!"

"Wait! Stop! Stop!" Mrs. Pratt hurriedly unlocked the screen door.

Caden stopped just in time. "Damn."

"Stay outside in case our guy tries to sneak out," I whispered to him.

"Yeah, yeah."

I stepped into the living room as Mrs. Pratt backed up with her arms folded. The room was filled with a combination of antique wingback chairs, a glass coffee table, and an IKEA entertainment center. Walls were decorated with an assortment of religious Christmas decorations, family photos, a picture of white Jesus, and Bible verses stitched in needlepoint.

From my vantage point, I could see through to the kitchen at the rear of the house. Rodeo stood outside the French doors, his shotgun at the ready. A hallway led off to my left.

"Happy now?" she asked.

"Overjoyed. Where's your husband hiding?"

"I. Don't. Know."

"I'm just going to verify that. Open the back door and let my associate in," I ordered.

"Do it yourself, lady."

Movement in the hallway caught my eye. I turned to see a shirtless boy in his late teens holding a Japanese katana one-handed, as if it were a fencing foil. He bore a strong resemblance to the photo of Rudy Pratt but was a couple of decades younger.

I stepped back, keeping both mother and son in my line of sight, and drew my Taser. I was tempted to juice the little juvenile delinquent with a nice jolt of electricity but wasn't sure which direction the katana would fly when his muscles contracted.

"Drop the katana, kid. No one needs to get hurt."

"Leave us alone!" he bellowed as he entered the living room. "Our family's got enough problems right now."

"The sooner I locate your dad, the sooner me and my team will be outta here."

"Fuck you, you goddamn spic!"

"Spic? Seriously?" I rolled my eyes.

Because of my dark hair and tan skin, people often assumed my family was from south of the border. However, my mother's side of the family was Italian, my father's Cajun. Not that I minded being mistaken for Latina. I did, however, object to people using racist slurs.

"Let me rephrase. Drop the katana, or I'll light you up with my Taser and jam that blade right up your ass."

"You don't scare me." He raised the katana as if to strike.

The sound of breaking glass caught the boy's attention as Rodeo busted through the French doors. I kicked the boy's wrist, knocked the katana from his grip, and pulled the trigger on the Taser. The boy shrieked as his muscles seized, and he collapsed to the floor, gasping for air.

"I warned you."

While Mrs. Pratt rushed to her son, I examined the katana. It was a cheap Filipino knockoff, probably bought at a local swap meet. I jammed the tip of the blade into the floor and snapped it in half with my boot.

"Now if you two are quite done with the theatrics, my associate and I will check the house for dear old Dad. Any more bullshit from you two, and I will handcuff you both. Do I make myself clear?"

The two of them huddled on the couch. The kid was still moaning while his mother consoled him.

Rodeo reached through the broken pane on the French door and let himself in. I replaced the Taser cartridge in case mother and son got any other bright ideas.

"Thanks for the distraction." I fist-bumped Rodeo when he walked into the living room.

He grinned. "Hate to see you sliced into steak tartare."

"Ha! Blade was so dull it probably couldn't cut rotten bananas."

We systematically searched the house for Rudy Pratt and didn't bother to be neat about it. We flipped over beds and cleared out closets, cabinets, and any nook where a person could hide. We sifted through drawers for clues that might lead us to Pratt.

In the master bedroom, we found a bookcase filled with Bibles and books by Glenn Beck, Alex Jones, and other ultraconservatives.

A Confederate flag hung from the second bedroom wall. Underneath one of the dresser drawers, I discovered a stack of porn magazines, a box of condoms, and a bag of weed. The Holy Trinity of being an all-American teenage boy.

The third bedroom was decorated in every imaginable shade of pink. A menagerie of plushy animals huddled together at the head of the four-poster bed.

When the main part of the house turned up nothing, I hoisted Rodeo up to check out the attic while I searched the garage. Only thing I found was a workbench with a soldering station and cabinets filled with wires, circuit boards, and other electronic parts.

"Well, what now?" Rodeo asked when we reconvened in the kitchen.

I picked a piece of dusty fiberglass out of his hair. "Let's talk to the wife again." We returned to the living room.

"Didn't find him, did you? Told you he ain't here," the wife said with a sneer.

"Where is he?" I demanded.

She shrugged with feigned ignorance. "How should I know?"

"You're not doing yourself any favors by hiding him."

She crossed her arms and glowered. "If your husband was being framed, you'd do the same damned thing."

"Fine." I pulled out a pair of handcuffs. "But tell me. How can you protect him when you're in jail?" I snapped the cuffs on one of her wrists.

Her son moved to intervene, and Rodeo stepped toward him with the shotgun aimed at the boy's chest. "Sit."

"He's at work, all right!" said the boy.

"Rusty!" his mom scolded.

"I ain't letting them take you to jail too." Rusty's eyes burned into me. "You got the information you wanted. Now leave us alone."

"He's at the Hardware SuperCenter?"

"Yes," he mumbled.

"They didn't fire him?"

"Like I said," the wife piped in, "it was self-defense, and they know it. That beaner attacked him. Rudy said he caught the guy selling drugs. You know how they are. Nothing but drug dealers, rapists, and murderers."

I resisted the urge to give her a jolt from the Taser. "You two have a nice fucking day." I unlocked the cuffs. "Come on, Rodeo."

"Yeah, y'all get out of here, you fucking spic and goddamn chink!" the kid called. "Go back to your own countries."

Rodeo wheeled around and aimed the shotgun at him. Mrs. Pratt shrieked, shielding her son with her body.

I put a hand on Rodeo's arm. "Don't. They're not worth it, dude."

We hustled out of the house and met Caden near the street. "What was all that yelling?"

"Nothing," I said.

"Just putting a little fear into a couple of racist assholes," Rodeo said with a chuckle.

"How come I always get stuck outside while you two have all the fun?" Caden whined.

Rodeo mussed Caden's fauxhawk. "'Cause you're the new guy, little man."

"Cut it out." Caden tried to reshape his fauxhawk, leaving it a bit lopsided.

"Okay, folks, we still have to find Pratt. Wife says he's at work. Next stop, Hardware SuperCenter on Peoria. Let's move!"

7

Hardware SuperCenter was a sprawling big-box store composed of ten-foot-tall shelves stocked with hardware, tools, pool supplies, appliances, and a garden center. And not a helpful hardware person in sight. I'd once accompanied my brother, Jake, to the location near my house. Big mistake. He was like a kid in a candy store. Seriously, how many hammers or saw blades does one person need?

Caden, Rodeo, and I strolled in through the automatic doors, drawing stares from customers and employees alike. Between our ballistic vests, walkie-talkies, and weapons, they probably figured we were a SWAT team.

"Caden, head over to the garden center and cover that exit," I said. "Pratt's file says that's where he works."

"Finally a chance to get in on the action." Caden hustled away past the pool supplies toward another set of automatic doors separating the garden center from the rest of the store.

"Where you want me, Jinx?" Rodeo asked.

"Circle around outside to the back door. Don't need him slipping out through an employee exit."

"Copy that."

I approached the customer service desk. A woman in her midforties wearing a brown employee vest looked up as I came near. Her name tag read "Sylvia" and indicated she was a shift manager. A concerned expression emerged on her face.

"Can I help you?" she asked.

"I'm Jinx Ballou." I held up my badge and ID. "I'm looking for Rudy Pratt, one of your employees."

She shook her head. "What now?"

"He missed his court date. I'm authorized to return him to jail."

"Let me see if he's clocked in." Her mouth was a thin line as she typed on a computer keyboard. "Should be in the landscaping tools section."

"In the garden center?"

"Not quite. I'll show you."

I followed her past bins of Christmas lights and yard decorations. "I'm surprised you didn't fire him."

"We did initially," she said through gritted teeth.

"But what? You thought, 'What the hell, he's only charged with murdering one of our employees?'"

"I got an email from corporate insisting we reinstate him pending the outcome of his trial."

"Corporate office wants an accused murderer working here? Sounds like a lawsuit waiting to happen."

She turned and met my gaze. "I don't disagree."

"What's he like as an employee?"

"All I'm allowed to say is that he works here. For now, at least."

We arrived at an aisle stocked with shovels, pickaxes, machetes, and other implements of destruction. A wiry man with close-cropped hair and a brown vest walked past the other end of the aisle.

"That's him," she said, pointing. "Hey, Rudy! Someone to see you!"

He poked his head back down the aisle. His eyes widened. He took off toward the middle of the store.

"Shit!" I took off after him, dodging customers, carts, and product displays. The guy was fast. It was all I could do to keep up with him. I drew my Taser, but too many people wandering through the aisles made it impossible to get a clean shot.

He cut to the right into the hand tools section. I rounded the corner and just missed getting beaned with a claw hammer he'd thrown. I raised the Taser. "Stop, Pratt!"

He ducked behind a Dremel tool display and took off back toward the garden center.

"Dammit!" I poured on speed, trying to catch him, and spoke into my walkie. "Caden," I said through gasping breaths. "Pratt's headed...your way."

"Copy that."

I gained on him as we blazed through the Christmas decorations area. I aimed the Taser squarely at his back. As my finger squeezed the trigger, a shopping cart appeared out of nowhere. I tumbled headlong over it, ducked into a roll on the bare concrete floor, landed on my feet. A box of icicle lights flickered from the jolt of electricity from the Taser darts embedded in the package.

"You people should watch where you're going!" A pudgy African-American woman with a crown of white hair gave me the stink eye while a store employee helped her to her feet. A load of plastic Santas, artificial garland, and gold Christmas balls lay scattered on the floor next to her overturned cart.

"Sorry." I took off again after Pratt, replacing the Taser cartridge as I ran.

In the garden center, I scrambled down aisles of potted plants, searching for my quarry. My nose filled with the scent of soil and growing things.

I turned in time to see Pratt charge toward Caden with a shopping cart loaded with potted citrus trees.

Caden hunkered down in an attempt to stop the cart and grab Pratt, but the momentum of the cart was too much for him. He fell hard into a row of concrete statuaries. The cart overturned, and Pratt raced out the entrance.

By the time I reached the doorway, Pratt had vanished into the parking lot. "Damn it!"

I returned to check on Caden. He was pulling himself to

his feet. He felt the back of his head and winced. "Mother puss bucket."

"You okay?" I asked.

"Just a bump on the head. Can't believe I let him get past me."

"Don't worry about it. We'll get him."

"What happened to your knee?" he asked.

My jeans were torn and stained with a quarter-sized spot of blood. "I tried vaulting over a shopping cart. Failed to stick the landing, I guess."

"Shopping carts are dangerous," Caden said with a smirk. "They should be banned."

Despite the ache in my leg and my frustration at losing Pratt, I couldn't help chuckling. "Damn straight."

I called Rodeo on the walkie. He showed up along with Sylvia, the shift manager.

"How'd he get past you?" Rodeo asked.

I shrugged. "Home field advantage." I turned to Sylvia. "No offense, lady, but your corporate office was stupid to keep him on."

She looked embarrassed. "I just called HR corporate about Rudy jumping bail. They denied advising me to rehire him after his arrest. Turns out the email was a fake."

"Do yourself a favor and don't take him back." I handed her a business card. "If he shows up again, call me."

"Don't have to tell me twice." She walked away and assisted a fellow employee cleaning up the toppled trees and statuaries.

I led my team out into the parking lot. The sun was below the horizon, and the reds and oranges of the Phoenix sunset were fading to pink and gray. The air had grown chilly.

"Let's check to see if Pratt went home to the wife and kids. I suspect he's in the wind, but since he's a first-timer, you never know."

We piled into our vehicles and returned to the Pratt residence. Nearby street lamps flickered on, and houses glowed from within like a cheesy Thomas Kinkade painting. Except for the Pratt house. It remained dark. The car in the driveway was gone.

I sent Rodeo around one side, Caden around the other, while I crept to the front door, peeking through the side windows. No movement from inside as far as I could tell and no sounds. I pounded on the door and rang the doorbell a few times. "Open up! Bail enforcement!"

I waited a few minutes, but there was no sign of life inside.

"You guys see anything?" I asked over the walkie.

"No lights in any of the bedrooms," replied Caden.

"They put a piece of plywood over the broken door," Rodeo said. "Kitchen and living room are dark. Looks like they bugged out."

"What now?" Caden asked.

I pulled out my phone and called the cell phone number listed in Pratt's file. It went straight to voicemail. "No answer."

"Can you use that tracking app?"

The previous year, Becca had installed an app on my phone that let me instantly track the location of another phone by entering the number. She'd also warned me that the app's legality was questionable.

"I deleted it after Becca said the feds were tracking installations of the app. I'll have her do some skip tracing on Pratt and see where he might be holed up. Let's canvass his neighbors, then call it a day."

Even in this day of internet searches and virtual paper trails, 90 percent of apprehending FTAs was knocking on doors and making phone calls. In short, talking to people who knew the person I was looking for.

I sent Caden east. I took the neighbors to the west. Rodeo knocked on doors across the street. Since it was early evening,

I figured people would be home from work and might know where Pratt was hiding out.

A Latina woman with tired eyes and graying hair opened the first door I knocked on. She looked frail and all of five foot two if she were standing on her tiptoes. The pale-pink-and-gray sweater she wore looked as if it had been knitted sometime before the color television was invented.

"Hi! I'm looking for your neighbor, Rudy Pratt. Would you know where he is by chance?"

"*No hablo ingles.*" She started to shut the door.

"Wait!" I repeated my question in Spanish. The neighbor replied that she didn't know her neighbors well. Just noted that they were rude. She wasn't surprised he was arrested for murdering a Mexican immigrant.

Got no argument from me, sister, I thought.

I gave her my business card and told her I was there to take Mr. Pratt to jail.

"Call me if you see him," I said in Spanish.

The twinkle in her eye told me she'd be happy to help if she could. "Is there a reward?" she asked.

"If you help me catch him, I'll pay you twenty dollars."

"*Cinquenta dollares,*" she insisted. Fifty bucks.

"*¡Demasiado!*" Too much. "*Trenta.*"

She harrumphed and started shutting the door.

"Fine. *Cuarenta,*" I said. Forty.

"Okay. I call you if I see him," she said in English and shut the door.

I continued to the next neighbor but with similar luck. No one knew the Pratts by name, but a lot of people, both Latino and Anglo, held a dim view of the family. Most had seen his picture on the news and weren't surprised he'd been arrested.

When I reached the end of the block, I backtracked and met Caden and Rodeo by the vehicles.

"Any luck?" I asked, trying not to shiver. I was a hot weather girl, so anything below sixty degrees felt like freezing.

They both shook their heads.

"Not exactly a popular guy," said Caden. "I don't think even Mr. Rogers would want to be his neighbor."

"Can't imagine why," I said with dripping sarcasm. "Just because he's a racist charged with murdering a Latino coworker."

"Where to now?" Rodeo rubbed his arms to keep warm.

"Let's call it a day. I'll phone the references on his bail application. See if anyone knows where he might be."

"Okay, catch y'all later," said Caden.

Rodeo fist-bumped him. "Later, dude."

"Take care, Caden." I waved as he climbed into his car.

I turned to walk to the Gray Ghost when Rodeo asked, "Jinx, can we talk?"

He had a pained expression on his face, exaggerated by the shadows cast by the overhead streetlights.

"What's up?"

"I'm planning on breaking up with your brother."

"Why?" I asked. "You two make such a cute couple."

He folded his arms and stared at the pavement. "He's embarrassed to be seen with me."

"Bullshit! Why would he be embarrassed to be seen with you? You're fucking hot."

Rodeo's face colored. "Thanks, but I think he's dealing with some lingering internal homophobia. Absolutely refuses to hold my hand in public. And God forbid anyone sees me give him a peck on the cheek. I'm getting tired of it."

"Have you talked to him about it?"

"Many times. He keeps begging me to give him time, but it's been a year." He adjusted his Stetson. "I know Arizona's not the most gay-friendly state, but dude, come on. We're two tough, masculine guys. No one's going to mess with us. And if they do, fuck 'em."

I sighed. "I don't know what to say. I wish you'd give him

another chance, but I get where you're coming from. Do what you feel's right. It doesn't affect you and me."

Rodeo put a hand on my shoulder. "Thanks, girl. I didn't want things to get weird between us."

"Would it help if I talked to him?" I asked.

"I don't want it to seem like I'm airing our dirty laundry with you."

"Well, you kinda are."

"I know, but for now, let me handle it."

"You got it." I gave him a hug and a pat on the back. "I hope you two work things out. I like having you as family."

8

I called Becca on the way home. "How are you feeling?" I asked.

"Managing."

"Good. When you're up to it, I need you to do some digging for us on an asshole named Rudy Pratt. Phone logs, bank records, credit report, the works."

"I'll run it in the morning if I'm feeling better."

"Great. I'll send you the info I have on him." My phone beeped, showing an incoming call. "That's probably Conor. I gotta go. Take it easy, Becks."

"Say hello to lover boy for me."

"Will do."

I clicked over to the incoming call. "This is Jinx Ballou."

"Where are ya, love?" he asked in his Irish brogue.

"On the way home. Where are you?"

"At your place. Cooking dinner."

"You're cooking?" This was new. He could cook up a decent breakfast, but dinner was a new twist for him. "What's on the menu?"

"Potato leek soup. My grandmother's recipe."

"Sounds delish. I'll be there in ten." I hung up and drove the rest of the way home.

Before we started dating two years ago, Conor had been my boss at Viper Fugitive Recovery. But mixing business with pleasure turned out to be more problematic than I'd expected. So I quit and started my own bounty hunting crew.

I walked through the front door and was immediately drawn to the wonderful aroma in the air. "Smells good."

"Hope ya like it," he replied.

I stopped in the bedroom to pull off my gear. I was tempted to slip into my Wonder Woman costume since he'd mentioned it earlier. But I was too tired and stuck with my T-shirt, jeans, and bare feet.

The kitchen looked as if a monsoon had blown through. Cooking utensils, mixers, dirty bowls, and vegetable scraps were scattered everywhere, including the floor. Conor was wearing a lacy cooking apron over his tan Viper Fugitive Recovery polo shirt. His coppery curls were mussed. "Should be ready shortly. Just needs to simmer a bit more."

I hugged him from behind and was about to kiss him on the back of the neck when he jerked to the side. "Oi! Watch out!"

"What's wrong?" I asked.

"Nothing serious. Things got a wee bit rough when me and the boys nabbed this bloke." Conor tried to put on a brave face, but I could tell from his eyes he was hurting. "How was your day?"

"Two out of three for the day. Captured Daniel Warren, as you noted earlier." A flush of warmth ran up my neck as I thought about images of me in costume all over the news and internet. "Also picked up Conspiracy Bob."

A big grin split Conor's face. "How's our mate Bob doing these days?"

"Convinced that mole people are living in abandoned mines and planning acts of terrorism."

"God love the silly bugger! He's entertaining if nothing else." He scooped up a spoonful of soup from the pot, blew on it, and ate it gingerly. "I think that's bloody well right."

He tossed the apron on the counter. I grabbed a couple of bowls from the cabinet, and we sat down at the kitchen table to eat. I caught him wincing as he settled into the chair next to me. A dark spot on his shirt glistened under his left arm.

"Con, you're bleeding."

Conor looked down at the growing stain. "Jesus bloody Christ!"

I peeled up the bottom of his shirt. A folded piece of gauze was taped to his skin and oozing blood. "Doesn't look good, babe. What happened?"

"Some wanker came at me with a broken bottle to keep me from dragging his mate back to lockup. It's nothing."

"Nothing, my ass. I'm not letting you bleed out on my kitchen floor." I tugged off the tape and revealed an ugly gouge, crusted with dried blood but still seeping quite a bit. "Shit, this needs to be stitched up, hon. We gotta take you to the ER."

"Bollocks! I'm not going to bloody hospital for a wee scratch. All it needs is a little Superglue. That's what they'd use at the ER, anyway. Why hand over a few thousand dollars to those greedy fucks when I can do the same job for a buck ninety-nine?"

His aversion to going to the ER wasn't about money. It was fear. I'd seen the man stare down the barrel of guns, tangle with large dogs, and go at it with some seriously scary dudes. He was no wilting flower. But a brutal experience twenty years earlier had left him with a phobia of hospitals.

He and his father had been involved with a car bombing in the shopping village of Omagh. Shortly before the blast, Conor made a call to the media to warn people away from where the bomb would be detonated. But he was given the wrong location. Local police ended up steering people toward the danger zone. Conor's sister, Bernadette, was among those killed in the blast. When he found her shattered body in the hospital, along with dozens of other casualties, it left a deep and lasting scar of guilt and trauma on his psyche.

"Fine. But just so you know, this isn't how I prefer to 'play doctor.'"

I tried to squeeze the edges of the wound closed, and he yelped. "Bloody fucking Christ!"

"I don't think Superglue's going to close this, Conor. This cut looks deep, and it could get infected. It's not worth the risk. I'm taking you to the ER."

"I'm not going to bloody hospital." His freckled face turned flame red. His eyes grew large, no doubt from a mix of anger and deep terror. "I…I can't."

Our eyes locked. I caught a glimpse of the frightened seventeen-year-old embroiled in the insanity and violence of the Troubles in Ireland. "Oh, come on. You took me to the hospital last year when I got hurt."

He shook his head. "That was for you, love, when ya had a major concussion. I'm not going through all that…"

"Trauma?"

"Whatever ya want to call it, over a fucking scratch. Just put some of that disinfectant on it and pull it shut with a couple of plasters."

I sighed. Nothing I said would convince him to get proper medical treatment. "Fine. I'll do what I can. But I'm telling you now, if it gets infected, I'm going to roofie you, throw you over my shoulder, and drag your freckled Irish ass to the ER." I retrieved my first aid kit from the guest bathroom.

"Before you do anything, can ya give me a little whiskey first?"

I grabbed a sterile pad and pressed it to the wound. He winced. "Hold this in place so my kitchen floor doesn't end up looking like a crime scene."

I grabbed the bottle of Jameson from the pantry. He took it from me and made a face. "Ya trying to be funny, love?"

I glanced at the bottle. It was empty. "Guess you finished it off last time you were here."

"Don't be daft. There was at least a third of a bottle left last Thursday."

"Don't look at me." I shrugged. "I rarely touch the stuff. I'm more of a tequila girl."

"Must've been the dog, then," he said with a half smile.

"I don't have a dog." I playfully chucked him on the shoulder. "Guess you're gonna have to grit your teeth while I deal with this barroom battle wound. You want a wooden spoon to bite down on?"

He harrumphed. "Just bloody do it."

I donned a pair of latex gloves and squeezed antibiotic gel into the wound. He growled when I pulled the wound closed.

"Huh," I said, grinning. "I guess I have a dog after all." I secured the wound with four Steri-Strips.

"Ya done?" His forehead glistened with sweat.

I covered the wound with a sterile pad and taped it in place. "For now. Try not to twist around too much."

"Now what fun is that?" he asked with a mischievous grin. "No need to stop playing doctor now."

9

After dinner, as I was cleaning up the mess Conor had made, he came up behind me and wrapped his arms around me. He planted kisses on the back of my neck, sending jolts of excitement down my spine and an intense heat to my groin. My breath quickened, and my ass curled into hardness. "Oh… sweet mother of bliss…" I hissed with pleasure.

"Now where's this super suit I saw ya wearing on the telly?"

"Silly boy." My head swam as he pinched the hardened buds of my nipples while pressing my hips against the kitchen counter. My body ached to feel him inside me. "You've…you've seen me wear it…a hundred times. Oh fuck, that feels so good."

"What? You'll dress for your geeky mates but not for me?" he teased, pulling my T-shirt up and off and turning me around to face him.

Those emerald eyes coupled with his cheesy grin took my breath away every bit as much as his firm but gentle touch.

"Oh, baby…I'd do anything for you."

He kneeled down, grunting, and began teasing my nipples with his tongue. "Would ya now?"

"Anything, just please don't stop." My hands reached into his ginger curls, pressing him to my chest. Waves of passion, pleasure, and gratitude tossed me around like a ship in a storm.

Slowly he rose to his feet, leaving a trail of kisses up my

neck until I kissed him deeply. When I finally came up for air a moment later, I managed to ask, "You want me in my costume?"

He grinned and shook his head. "Naw, I'd rather us just get naked."

Despite my wobbly knees and the headiness of hormones raging through my system, I managed to lead him to the bedroom, where I peeled off my jeans, then helped him off with his shirt. His torso was pockmarked with scars acquired from his experiences as a security specialist in Afghanistan and Iraq and a few from his work as a bounty hunter. But these marks only turned me on more, reminders of his strength and endurance.

I glanced down at his most recent injury. The Steri-Strips seemed to be holding because no more blood was seeping from his wound.

"You okay to do this?" I asked as I sat on the bed and pulled a bottle of lubricant from my nightstand. "Maybe I should be on top this time."

He studied me for a moment, the wheels clearly turning in his head. His smile deepened. "I think I'd like that."

He lay on his back on the bed, wincing. I helped him off with his jeans and boxers. The sight of his hard cock rising from a nest of coppery hair sent a new wave of chills through me.

I bent down and wrapped my lips around the head of his cock, eliciting a throaty groan from Conor. "Bloody hell, that feels good."

I continued to suck, taking him into my throat as deeply as I could, stroking his shaft with my hand. More groans told me he wasn't feeling too much pain. His hands guided my head in a rhythm with his hips. I would have let him come in my mouth, but my own need to feel him in me grew irresistible.

I sat up and rubbed a spot of lubricant on his cock.

"Oh yeah, love, come here," he murmured.

Gingerly I mounted him, trying not to bump his side with my knee. I rubbed my labia up and down the length of his cock, the head rubbing the nub of my clit. Shock waves of pleasure caused me to gasp. When I could take no more, I let him slip inside me. I gritted my teeth as his cock throbbed and filled me. "Conor, yessss…" I purred.

He leaned up and suckled the bud of my breast as we fell into a natural rhythm, creating our own music of sighs and moans. My pulse raced as I neared climax. We thrust harder, slamming into each other with such force that each beat nearly took my breath away.

His hands tightened around my waist as he neared orgasm. "Oh, Jinxie. I'm so close."

"Yes, yes, yes!" I gasped. A flash of lightning rippled through my brain, sending shock waves of orgasm through every nerve ending in my body. An instant later, a blast of warmth exploded inside of me as he came. I pressed him as deep as he could go.

He eased me on the bed beside him, cradling me in his arm. Waves of ecstasy continued to crash on the shores of my mind, like the aftermath of a storm.

"That was fucking brilliant, love," he whispered into my ear.

"I didn't hurt you?" I asked.

"Don't see me complaining, do ya?"

I pulled him close, breathing in his scent. We'd been together more than two years, and it still amazed me that a guy as sexy and sweet and masculine as Conor could be interested in a trans gal like me—the niggling remnants of internalized transphobia.

"Oh, Jinxie," he said, laying gentle kisses on my shoulder. "Now don't ya think life would be easier without worrying whose house we're sleeping at on any given night?"

I groaned and not from pleasure. "Let's not spoil the evening."

"Just sell your place and move in with me. Make everything loads simpler."

"Or you could move in with me. I've got more square footage. How am I supposed to squeeze all my shit into that matchbox you call a home?"

He made a face. "I'm still paying for the renovations I had

done a few years ago. You've got all that equity in your place. Think of what ya could do with all that money."

I met his gaze. "I'm sorry, but your place is empty and… sterile. It feels like a bunker."

"No one's saying ya couldn't gussy it up a bit, love."

"I've grown really attached to this house. It was the first place that was mine, you know? Besides, where would I put my workout equipment? And my action figures. And my comic books? Also, your kitchen's so tiny, you can't cook a decent meal there."

He shrugged. "I've been eating there quite fine for several years."

"Frozen dinners and mac 'n cheese from a box don't count."

"Oi, I can cook more than that. Didn't ya like the soup?"

Now I felt guilty. I kissed him. "The soup was wonderful."

"This is about your ex-boyfriend, isn't it? Willie Steinwhats-it?"

"His name was Wilson Stametz. And how do you know about him?"

"Your brother mentioned him a couple weeks ago at your parents'."

"Where was I?" It felt weird that Conor and Jake were talking about me behind my back.

"Helping your ma with something in the kitchen, I think. We were talking about his business renovating houses. He mentioned he renovated your place."

"What's that got to do with Wilson?"

"He thought that might be the reason ya didn't want to shack up with me."

"Jesus, fuck!" I rolled over and faced the wall. "Why can't Jake mind his own fucking business?"

"What's the big deal, Jinxie?" He started to massage my shoulder. I shrugged off his hands. "And how come ya never mentioned this bloke before?"

"Because he's ancient history, that's why. I was in the process of moving in with him when I caught him sticking his dick into some bitch from work. In what would've been our bed."

I wanted to throttle Jake so bad I could almost feel his pulse underneath my grip.

"Is that it? Ya think I'm gonna shag some other girl? 'Cause ya know I'd never do that to ya."

"I'm just not ready, okay? Besides, what would my mother think of the two of us living together?"

"You don't think she knows we're shagging?"

"I try not to think about it."

"Is this a backhanded way to get me to marry ya?"

I turned around to see a big grin on his face. "Marriage? What? No...I'm..." My face grew hot.

"I'm just messing with ya, love. We got no need to rush anything." He cradled my head in his hands and kissed me gently on the lips. "Jenna Christina Ballou, I love ya with all my Irish heart. Even if you don't want to marry me."

"I love you too. With all my Italian-Cajun-whatever heart. I just... I never thought of myself as being someone's wife. Sounds so..."

"Normal?" he said with a chuckle. "You're anything but, that's for sure."

"What?" I asked, playing along. "Just because I'm a transgender woman who works as a bounty hunter and dresses like Wonder Woman when I'm not practicing parkour or krav maga? You're saying that's not normal?"

"I think the proper term would be uniquely brilliant." He kissed me. "Besides, normal girls bore the shite outta me."

"Do you hate me for not wanting to give up my little Bohemian bungalow?"

"'Course not. If you're not ready, you're not ready. I just think life'd be simpler if we both lived at my place. And safer."

"Safer? Why?"

"Those renovations I did? Well, I actually did turn it into a bit of a bunker."

I sat up. "What do you mean?"

"The walls are a foot-thick solid brick. The windows are one-inch polycarbonate instead of glass. Steel-reinforced doors. No one's getting in unless I want them to."

"Was this because of that drive-by a few years back?"

"Aye! When I captured a member of the Nineteenth Avenue Jaguars after he jumped bail, some of his mates decided to use their TEC-9s to send me a message. Luckily I was out with you that night."

"Why haven't you told me about these renovations before?"

Conor blushed. "You already called it a bunker. I was embarrassed to admit you were right."

"You think I should do the same to my house?"

"No, I think ya should move in with me. Trust me, love, we can sort out all the details. And if ya decide ya wanna get hitched, then I'm happy to oblige."

"Let me think about it." The afterglow of sex was morphing into fatigue. "It's been a long, weird day. I'm exhausted."

"Sweet dreams, love." He kissed me again on the lips. Passion rekindled, but I was too exhausted to go another round, even with someone as sexy as Conor.

10

I took the next two days to enjoy Winter Con and give Becca time to see what she could dig up on Rudy Pratt. On my way home from the convention each evening, I drove past the Pratts' residence, but the place remained dark and deserted.

On Monday morning, I woke to the sound of someone laying on my doorbell at quarter to six. I usually got up at six, anyway, but those extra fifteen minutes of sleep could make all the difference. Whoever was at my door was going to meet a slow and painful death, unless they had a good reason for being there.

Conor had spent the night on a stakeout for one of his fugitives. I chambered a round in my Ruger and shuffled out of bed in my pajamas. Overly cautious? Maybe. But after finding the body of a dead journalist on my doorstep the previous year, I'd been wary of unexpected visitors.

"Who the hell is it?" I mumbled, too bleary-eyed to make sense of anything through the peephole in my front door.

"Morning, sunshine. It's your favorite brother, Jake," he replied in a tone way too cheerful for that time of morning.

"Oh for fuck's sake. You're my only brother."

I set the Ruger on a side table and opened the door. It was still dark outside and damned near freezing. My brother stood there in a ratty denim jacket over a Stone Temple Pilots T-shirt. His gelled hair was tossed in a devil-may-care style.

"Dude, you're lucky I didn't shoot your ass. You got any idea what time it is?"

"You missed Sunday brunch yesterday. Mom was worried. Didn't you get her voicemail messages?"

Sunday brunch at my parents' house was a big deal in my family. Missing it without a good excuse was a mortal sin in my mother's eyes, especially after I quit accompanying her to Mass several years ago.

A good daughter wouldn't blow off Sunday brunch to cosplay at Winter Con, especially without telling her mother ahead of time. A good daughter would return her mother's calls to keep her from worrying. I was not a good daughter.

But to be fair, several cast members from *Black Panther* had appeared on a panel Sunday morning. I figured it was easier to beg forgiveness than ask permission.

"I was busy. Work stuff." And now I'd lied to cover my ass. I was a bad daughter.

"You couldn't call? Mom's been freaking out. Bad enough you chase bad guys for a living."

"Look, I'm sorry, all right? Things have been crazy lately." I regretted upsetting my mom more than she already was. But sometimes her incessant worrying felt oppressive, dripping with Catholic guilt.

"You're going to be there tomorrow night for her birthday, right?"

Shit. I totally spaced it. "I...uh...yeah, of course."

"You forgot, didn't you?"

"No," I insisted. "I just, well, I'm a little groggy from being woken up early."

"You forgot." He shook his head. "Sometimes I wonder—"

"I'll be there, all right? You want to play the Catholic guilt game, let's talk about..." I stopped myself, remembering that Rodeo had told me to let him handle their situation.

"Talk about what?" His face darkened.

"Nothing." I stared at his dusty work boots as the tension

between us grew. "I'll call Mom in a little while and tell her I'm sorry for worrying her. I'll see you tomorrow night, okay?"

"Yeah," he said without enthusiasm. "See ya." He stormed back to his truck. His tires squealed as he drove off.

I stood there feeling like shit. I was a horrible daughter, a lousy sister, and a rotten girlfriend afraid of commitment. I just felt so smothered by everyone wanting something from me. Maybe that was what family was supposed to be.

A couple of hours later, I called my mom and apologized for missing brunch and not calling. I even admitted that it was to attend Winter Con. Catholic guilt was a powerful weapon, and my mother was a true master.

After a quick shower, I pulled on my bounty hunter gear, determined to track down Rudy Pratt. At eight thirty, I arrived at the Hub, near Grand Avenue and Roosevelt Street.

The old building reminded me of an inverted boat hull, with a broad metal beam that jutted out like a ram bow. A twenty-foot-tall wall of paned glass served as the front of the building, a carryover from its days as a car dealership in the 1940s.

I shuffled across the parking lot, still weary from my early wake-up call. I carried a tray of two coffees from Tres Leches Café in my left hand, with my computer bag slung over my shoulder. I stopped short when a flyer taped to a lamppost caught my eye. Across the top, the words "White Nation" were printed in large block letters with swastikas on either side. "What the hell?"

White Nation was a militant white separatist group that had held rallies across the country, particularly in conservative-leaning states. These rallies often ended in violence. A few people had been killed. And yet somehow these people still managed to get permits to protest.

The text of the flyer announced an upcoming protest at Wesley Bolin Plaza near the Arizona State Capitol complex. It called on "white citizens to show up and take back their city from all the undesirables." It decried the planned removal of the Confederate Troops Memorial in the plaza as symbolic of "the liberal elite's systematic agenda to extinguish the white race and imperil Christianity."

Bile rose in my throat. Since Republicans had taken the presidency and both houses of Congress, white nationalists of all stripes had been emboldened to spew their hate without fear of reprisal. Violence against women, queer people, and people of color was on the rise.

I ripped the flyer from the post and crumpled it in my hand. I was tempted to toss it on the ground, but I tried to avoid littering. Also I didn't want some alt-right neo-Nazi to put it back up either. I stuffed it in my pocket and trudged inside the building.

The Hub's interior was a grungy, open industrial space with a cracked cement slab for a floor, pockmarked with divots from where they'd pulled out the walls. Dozens of collapsible tables served as desks with a wild assortment of secondhand seating ranging from uber-adjustable Herman Miller knockoffs to flimsy plastic folding chairs.

Like Becca, most members of the Hub worked in the tech industry. A few were online entrepreneurs. And then there was me, bounty hunter extraordinaire. As I walked in the door, the hypnotic beat of electronic dance music thrummed from unseen speakers. Overhead lighting was subdued.

Becca sat at the table we shared, staring intently at a trio of flat screens. I set a large latte with almond milk in front of her.

"Good to see you up and about," I said.

"Yay, coffee!" she exclaimed, her eyes suddenly coming alive. "You are a goddess."

"You're welcome." I pulled the crumpled flyer from my pocket and handed it to her. "Can you believe this shit?"

She took a sip of her coffee and uncrumpled the flyer. Her upper lip curled in disgust. "Jeez Louise, what is it with these people? That buffoon gets elected, and suddenly every bigot thinks it's open season on marginalized people. If I weren't so opposed to guns and violence, I'd have half a mind to get a machine gun and mow them all down."

"Good thing I'm not opposed to guns and violence," I said with a smirk.

"Don't! The last thing we need is you in prison. I just get so sick of these assholes."

I sat down next to her. "Speaking of bigoted assholes, what'd you find out about my latest fugitive, Rudy Pratt?"

She took another sip of her coffee and rattled away on her keyboard. "Rudy Pratt. Rudy Tootie Fresh and Fruity. The Rude-ster. Quite a bit, actually."

"Yeah?"

"He was originally from Houston. Got a track scholarship to Texas A&M, where he earned a degree in electrical engineering. Worked at SpaceJet—"

"I know all that. I'm not writing his memoir. I need to know where he is. Who's he been talking to?"

"Most of the recent calls to his cell phone are to his immediate family—wife, son—and to his attorney at the law firm Longstreet, Bragg, and Jackson. I'll send the log to your cloud drive."

"What about social media?"

"He has accounts on Facebook, Reddit, and Twitter. Not very active. He follows a lot of extreme right-wing political and religious groups. The guy's a bigot from the word go. Racist. Homophobe. Transphobe."

"His family's the same way. Any indication where he might be hiding out?"

"No. As I said, he's not real active. Lurks mostly."

"Financial records?"

"He has a checking account and a small savings. He makes small but regular donations to ultraconservative organizations like the Christian Heritage PAC, the Patriots of Liberty Caucus, and the Divine Truth Full Gospel Church. But get this, he has numerous debit card charges from the Pink Pearl Gentleman's

Club and Maggie's Cabaret. Both strip clubs. The guy likes the ladies, despite being married."

"Maybe he's going there to spread the gospel of Jesus," I said in an exaggerated Southern accent.

"Praise Jesus!" Becca said with a chuckle.

"Also a bar called Dixie's but no more than once a month or so."

"Not a lot to go on, but it'll have to do. Thanks."

I opened up the file Becca sent me and perused the most frequently called phone numbers.

"Oh, Jinx. There is something else."

"More info on Pratt?" I looked up, hoping for a clue to track down my quarry.

"I'm afraid not." Her face had an unsettled expression on it. "It's bad, but you need to see it."

11

On one of Becca's screens, a grainy surveillance video began playing. In the video, a burly white guy was holding up a bank while wearing a rubber Halloween monster mask. A tattoo peeked above the collar of his coat, but I couldn't make it out.

"This was taken a week ago at a bank in Casper, Wyoming," she said.

"Why are you showing me this?"

"You'll see."

She pulled up a second video over the first, this one from an exterior camera. "This was taken in the bank parking lot." The same guy was pulling off his mask. The video was less grainy than the first, but I still couldn't make out any details.

"He looks vaguely familiar, but I can't place him. That tattoo on his neck looks like a cartoon. Can you boost the resolution?" I asked.

She enhanced it enough that my subconscious started sending up red flags. The hand holding my coffee trembled. Something I had buried deep in my memory was struggling to surface. Something about that tattoo.

She pulled up a third video. "Another robbery a few days later in Grand Junction, Colorado. Same guy, same mask, same tattoo."

My stomach twisted like a rope. "Becca, I—"

"And this from last Friday at a bank in Kayenta, Arizona."

This time it was clear enough for me to make out the ink—Woody Woodpecker with boxing gloves.

My coffee cup slipped from my hand and hit the floor, but I barely noticed. My whole body was shaking, my eyes fixed on the screen. I knew why.

Someone was calling my name. Someone else was repeating the word "no" like a broken record. I realized the latter voice was mine.

I was no longer the thirty-year-old bounty hunter who could take down fugitives twice my size. I was back to being a shy seventeen-year-old trans girl being bludgeoned in the street by former middleweight boxing champion Barclay "The Beast" Dietz, who happened to be my high school boyfriend's father.

Police arrested Dietz that night, then released him on $200,000 bail. He never showed up to court. He simply vanished without a trace after emptying the bank account he shared with his wife.

Dietz's family lost their house. His son, Peyton, lost his basketball scholarship to UNLV. All because Barclay Dietz couldn't deal with the fact that Peyton and I were dating. Didn't matter that Peyton knew I was trans and didn't care. His father was terrified I'd turn his son gay.

"Jinxie! Look at me, girl." Becca held the sides of my head in her hands, forcing me to look away from the screen and into her eyes. "I'm so sorry. You're safe. You're with me."

"No, no, I…I'm not safe. He's coming. He…he…he's coming after me."

"What the hell's wrong with her, Becca?" asked Troy Reid, a game developer at the next desk.

"Jinx, listen to me. He's not coming after you. He's probably coming back to see Peyton."

I took a deep breath and tried to stuff all of the fear into the furthest reaches of my mind. "How…how do you know?"

"A hunch. It's been what? Ten years?"

"Th-Thirteen."

"He doesn't know anything about you. What you look like. Where you live. For all he knows, you moved clear across the country."

"He might've seen that article in *Phoenix Living*."

"That article was published over a year ago, and he's been living up in Wyoming or North Dakota somewhere."

"Peyton could've sent it to him."

"Why would Peyton do that? He probably hates the guy. The man ruined Peyton's college career."

"Peyton never came to see me in the hospital. You know that? I spent a month in the ICU and not one word from him. Not even a text. He blames me for ruining his family. I just know it."

"Don't be stupid. Peyton probably feels guilty about what happened to you."

I turned away from her and stared at the floor. My pulse was still racing. I felt the need to be very, very violent. "I should go. I've got a fugitive to catch." I stood unsteadily from my chair.

Becca stood up and hugged me. Her arms helped steady me.

"You've got this, girl," she said as she pulled back. "Don't let that piece of shit fuck with your head. Go splash some water on your face in the restroom. Get yourself centered. You're gonna need your head in the game when you go after Pratt."

"You're right." I took a deep breath and walked toward the restrooms at the back of the building.

"And grab some paper towels to clean up the coffee while you're at it," Becca teased.

The two restrooms at the Hub each had four stalls, but they were no longer marked as men's and women's. Both were designated as unisex. It had felt weird the first time I walked in and saw a guy washing his hands at the sink. But since the stalls all had locking doors on them, I figured what the hell. It wasn't that big of a deal. Everyone else adjusted, as well.

I stood for a moment, staring at my reflection in the mirror.

My heart thundered in my chest as I tried to stop the loop of memories playing in my throbbing head.

Someone put a hand on my shoulder. Instinctively, I wheeled around with a palm heel strike. The blow landed on Troy's chin, cushioned by his bushy hipster beard. I stopped myself an instant before years of training drove my other fist into his solar plexus.

"What the hell, Jinx?" he said, rubbing his chin. "Just checking if you're okay. Shit."

"I-I'm sorry. I thought you were...doesn't matter what I thought. You okay?"

He eyed me warily. "Remind me not to pick a fight with you. Damn!"

"Sorry." I couldn't think of anything else to say. He walked out without another word.

"Shit." I turned back to my reflection. One thing I was sure of. Somehow, I was going to track down Barclay Dietz. And I was going to make him wish he'd never laid a hand on me.

12

I sat down at my desk, and Becca gave me a strange look. "You okay?"

"I accidentally punched Troy," I said, staring blankly at Pratt's file.

"What?" She chuckled. "Seriously?"

I shrugged.

"Considering all the times he tried to mansplain IT security shit to me, I'd say he had it coming. What'd he do this time?"

"Put his hand on my shoulder." When Becca raised an eyebrow, I continued. "Not in a sexual way. I think he was checking if I was all right."

"That'll teach him. Seriously, though, you going to be okay?"

"I'll be fine. Especially once I track down Barclay Dietz."

"And then what? You going to arrest him or..." She let it hang, as if uncertain where to go with it. She knew me well.

"I'll decide that when I find him. Would I kill him in cold blood? I can't tell you how many times I've wanted to."

"It might be a tad illegal. I'd hate to see that beautiful bod of yours in a pair of Department of Corrections coveralls. Do they still make prisoners wear pink boxers?"

"Just the guys." I caught her staring at me. "Okay, I wouldn't kill him in cold blood. But you know, a guy like that might easily get provoked. And if I let him throw the first punch..."

"Don't be crazy. The man's a former boxer. Even though

he's older now, he could still knock you out. And then who knows what?"

"I'm not saying he'd *land* the first punch. I've learned a thing or two since high school graduation. I can take him. The fact that he's a boxer plays in my favor. I could claim I was in fear for my life, especially since he nearly killed me the first time."

"I'm not hearing this." She put her fingers in her ears. "Lalalalalala..."

I balled up the White Nation flyer and threw it at her. "Fine. I won't kill him. I'd much rather get the reward money for dragging his ass back to jail."

"That's more like it."

"How'd you put all of this together?" I asked her.

"Back when I was a fledgling hacker, I was experimenting with search algorithms. I used what you'd told me about Barclay Dietz as search criteria to scour the web. Never thought it'd locate him for real."

"Well, it worked."

"How you plan on finding him?"

"As you said, he's probably here to see Peyton. If we track down my ex, maybe we'll find the Beast."

"You want me to skip trace your ex-boyfriend?"

"If you don't mind."

"Will do."

"Now I just need to track down this Pratt fellow." I opened Pratt's file. He'd listed several personal references on his bail application. Always a good place to start. The first name on the list was Jack Stagg, so I called the number.

On the third ring, a gruff voice asked, "Yeah?"

"Oh, hi. Is this Jack?" I cranked up my voice to bubble-headed babydoll stripper.

"Yeah, who the hell's this?"

"My name's Amethyst. I'm a dancer down at the Pink Clam."

Becca glanced up from her Mac and gave me a bemused look.

"How'd you get this number?" asked Jack.

"Well, here's the thing. Last night, this guy Rudy came into the club and asked me for a lap dance. Believe me, I give the best lap dances. Afterward, I discovered he'd left his wallet. Total bummer, right? So I looked through it and found his address. I went by his house, but no one was home. Then I noticed this little piece of paper with your name and number on it. So I figured, like, I'd call, you know, hoping I could get him his wallet back."

Becca started cracking up. I put my finger to my lips so she'd keep quiet.

"Why'd he have my number in his wallet?"

"Honestly, sir, I got no idea. I'm just trying to get it back to him. Especially after he gave me such a generous tip."

"Try his cell." He rattled off the cell number listed on the bail application. No help there.

"Thanks, but do you know where he is? Don't want the missus answering the phone when I call, if ya know what I mean?" I snort-laughed.

Becca turned purple trying to keep quiet.

"Look, lady, I got no idea where he's at."

"Well, if you see him, can you have him call me?" I gave him my number. I'd have to be careful how I answered so as not to tip him off when he called.

"Not planning on seeing him anytime soon. But if I do, I'll have him call you." He hung up.

The moment I put down the phone, Becca burst into a raucous fit of laughter. The other people in the Hub stared at the outburst. "Oh, shit. I gotta say, Jinx, that was the best one yet. When you snorted, I about peed my pants."

"Unfortunately, the dude didn't know where Pratt is and seemed awfully suspicious."

"I know you. You'll track him down one way or another."

"Let's hope." My mind drifted to the events of the night before. "Hey, I meant to tell you. Conor asked me to move in with him. Again."

"It's about damn time you two shack up."

"I like having my own place."

"So have him move in with you."

"He doesn't want to sell his house. Still owes a lot on those renovations he had done." I rubbed my face with my hands, trying to clear my head. "And then he sort of asked me to marry him."

"He proposed?"

"Not exactly. He asked me if I was asking *him* if I wanted to get married."

She shook her head. "Doesn't sound very romantic."

"Speaking of relationships, who's this new friend of yours?"

Her face turned a rosy tan. "Easton. They're nonbinary."

"Yeah? That's cool. And when do I get to meet this Easton?"

"Soon. We're taking things slow for now," she said.

"But they've been helping out when your chronic fatigue flares up?"

"Yeah. They moved in next door a couple months ago. We got to talking and learned we're both ace," she said, meaning asexual. "We've been doing a lot of cuddling but no decisions on whether this is a long-term committed thing."

"Well, I'm happy for you."

"Thanks. Me too."

"Just know that if Easton's ever not available during a flare-up, I'm still here for you." I put a hand on her shoulder.

"Thanks. We're still besties, right?" she asked shyly.

"Absolutely! And if Easton breaks your heart, I'll break their fucking legs."

Becca laughed. "Thanks. Let's hope it doesn't come to that."

I called Pratt's other references and left a few generic voice-mails saying I was a friend of Pratt's and was having trouble getting ahold of him.

From there, I flipped randomly through the documents I had on him. Nothing jumped out at me as an obvious lead.

Using a word processing program, I created a Fugitive

Wanted poster with Pratt's photo and details on it, along with my phone number and a promise of a reward for tips leading to an arrest. The promise of a reward usually generates leads. Most turn out to be bogus, but every once in a while, I get a vital tip when all other leads have been exhausted.

When I was satisfied with the poster, I emailed the file to the GraphX print shop on McDowell Boulevard, requesting a hundred copies.

That was when an idea came to me, and I picked up my phone. "Amber?" I asked when she answered. "It's Jinx."

13

"Oh my goodness! Jinxie!" Amber said in a velvety voice I'd always been envious of. "How the hell are you? I haven't seen you in forever!"

"I'm doing well. And you?"

"School's kicking my butt, but doing well otherwise."

"You still dancing?" I asked.

"How else could I afford ASU? You should drop by sometime. I'll give you a complimentary lap dance."

I laughed nervously. "I think I'll pass on the lap dance, but I would like to get together."

"Aw, what's wrong? You shy? Afraid you might like titties and pussy instead of dick?"

"Funny. No, I need your help with a case I'm working."

"Ooh, color me intrigued. I'm on my way to work, but you're free to stop by. You know where the Arizona Bush Market is?"

"I'm sure I've passed it a time or two, but can't say I've ever been in."

"It's south of Indian School Road on Thirty-Ninth Avenue. I'd love to see you."

"I'll meet you there in about an hour."

Call me a prude, but strip clubs don't interest me. Yeah, the women are hot. But hanging out in a room full of creepy men drooling over the dancers? Yuck! I have better things to do with my time.

Not that I have anything against the women who work there. We all gotta do what we gotta do to pay the rent. And when it came to sizable expenses like gender reassignment surgery and college tuition, sometimes a less conventional approach is necessary.

I hugged Becca and stopped at GraphX to pick up my Fugitive Wanted posters before heading west to the Arizona Bush Company.

The building had an all-wood façade, like a trading post from Arizona's pioneer days. I walked inside and found it wasn't as sleazy as I thought it'd be. I had pictured a smoke-filled room that stank of stale beer and piss. Instead, it smelled more like pine cleaner and reminded me of the Grand Palace Saloon in Old Tucson.

The music was a bit loud and clangy. One of the speakers was buzzing. The girl dancing on the main stage pole moved as though she'd had some serious gymnastic training. The small clusters of men in the audience seemed more interested in their conversations than the female entertainment.

I was scanning the room for Amber when a burly guy with a bad haircut and a tomato for a nose approached me. "Look, Officer, we don't need no trouble."

I realized I was still geared up in my ballistic vest, with my Taser and Ruger holstered at my waist. "No trouble. Just came to talk to a friend."

"Yeah, well, you can take your business outside. Don't need no dyke cops scaring off paying clients."

"Lay off, Lou! She's with me." Amber sauntered over in a see-through top and a sequined thong. A part of me was jealous of her sexy body. I reminded myself that the Barbie-doll figure was a patriarchal fantasy. But still, whew! If anyone could get me to switch to the all-girls team, it'd be her.

"This ain't some kinda sting, is it?" Lou blustered. "I run a legit business. No drugs. No prostitution. So unless you got a warrant—"

Amber slapped him on the shoulder. "Relax, big man. She's a friend. It's all good."

He gave me a stern look and turned on his heel.

"He seems charming," I said.

"Aw, Lou acts all tough, but he's just protective of us girls. But enough about him. How the fuck are you?" She hugged me, and I felt myself getting aroused. What the hell was wrong with me?

"I'm good. You're looking...hot." Embarrassment colored my face.

"You're sweet." She flashed a seductive smile. "Let's go where we can have some privacy." She led me through a door to the left of the stage. We passed through a dressing room and a couple of closed doors until we emerged out the back.

"So what's this case you think I can help you with?"

"I've got a skip that likes to frequent topless bars. Hoping maybe you've seen him." I pulled out my phone and showed her Pratt's photo.

"Doesn't look familiar. He come here often?"

"Mostly at the Pink Pearl and Maggie's Cabaret, according to his bank statements. You ever dance there?"

"Never danced at the Pearl. That place is a real shit hole. Lots of drugs and sleazebag customers. Run by a family of Russian gangsters named Volkov."

"As in Milo Volkov?" I asked.

"Milo ran things till someone killed him last year. His brother Sergei's in charge now. Total psycho. I was warned early on to stay clear of that place." She shivered. "As for Maggie's, I quit there a few months before my surgery. Money's better here at Arizona Bush Company. But I still know some gals working there. You want me to ask around?"

"That'd be great." A thought occurred to me, though it was a long shot. I pulled up an old publicity photo of Barclay Dietz. "How about this guy? He may be a bit older now."

"Looks vaguely familiar. He one of them MMA fighters?"

"Retired boxer. Jumped bail on aggravated assault a while back."

"Haven't seen him in here, but I can check with some of the other girls."

"Thanks! I'll text you their photos. I'm offering a reward if a tip leads to their capture."

"Nice. You sure I can't interest you in a lap dance?" she asked with a wicked twinkle in her eye. "Bring that boyfriend of yours, I'll give you a two-for-one."

My face warmed. "You don't have to."

Her expression grew somber, her voice choked with emotion. "It's the least I can do after you helped me out when I, uh, you know."

"Amber, you're not the first trans girl to attempt suicide. I tried it when I was eleven. We stick together and help each other through." I hugged her again. "Good luck in school."

"Go kick some ass, girl." She kissed my cheek.

From there, I drove by Pratt's house again and pounded on the door. No sign of life inside. No surprise.

I distributed Fugitive Wanted posters in his neighbors' mailboxes and taped them to light poles. I even handed a few to people walking the neighborhood. They grew concerned when I mentioned Pratt was wanted for murder, and promised to keep an eye out.

Clouds were rolling in, threatening a downpour, so I retreated to the Gray Ghost and contemplated my next move. There was one last source of information that might give me a lead I didn't already have. I put the Pathfinder in gear and headed south to downtown Phoenix.

14

Before I was a bounty hunter, I was an officer with the Phoenix PD. I quit after a year because I couldn't take all the regulations and paperwork. Also, not a big fan of uniforms.

Because the desk sergeant was a buddy of mine back in the day, he let me through unescorted with my visitor's badge attached to my shirt. I took the elevator to the third floor and pushed through the glass doors of the Homicide Unit.

My chest tensed as I approached the cubicle belonging to Detective Pierce Hardin, my former training officer. He held rookies to such a high standard that he earned the nickname Officer Hard Ass. On a good day, he'd ream me over the minutest detail on how I handled a call-out. The bad days felt as if I'd showered in hydrochloric acid.

When I left the force to become a bounty hunter, he didn't hold back from expressing his disappointment. "You had potential, Ballou. Would've made a top-notch detective and could've paved the way for other transgender officers. But no, you'd rather play Dog the Bounty Hunter with some limey hotshot you met in a bar." What hurt was the thought he might be right.

Cutting to the present, I found Hardin talking on the phone. His shirt was rumpled and his tie loosened. A pale line on his ring finger told me that his years on the force had taken their toll on his marriage.

"Yes, if you'd come down and tell us what you know, that'd

be a real help. Oh, I realize that, but people often remember more than they think they do. If you'd rather, I can send a uniformed officer to pick you—what? Oh, okay, then I'll see you here at one o'clock. Thanks a lot, Mrs. Reynolds."

"Morning, Detective," I said, peering over the partition of his cubicle.

He leaned back in his chair and put his hands behind his head. "Well, look who it is." He was a dark-skinned black man in his late fifties. His hair was frosted with gray, especially around the temples. His brow hung low over his eyes from years of glaring at witnesses and perps. "Heard you picked up Danny Warren while dressed as Wonder Woman. That's some messed-up shit right there."

"Got the little perv off the street, didn't I? Wonder Woman saves the day." I figured what the hell, might as well embrace it.

Hardin didn't crack even the faintest of smiles. "What do you need, Ballou? I got real cases to solve."

"Rudy Pratt."

He scoffed and looked at whatever paperwork was in front of him. "Can't help you."

"Bullshit. Bail application shows you were lead detective on the case."

"Operative word being *were*. Even if I wanted to, which I don't, I can't help you."

"Why not? Some new Phoenix PD policy?" I snarled. "Or you shaking me down for some spending money?"

"Don't insult me by insinuating I take bribes. I can't help you because we no longer have the case."

"Who does?"

"FBI. Came in a week ago and grabbed all our files and evidence."

"What do the feds want with a simple murder case?"

"Have to ask them. They had a court order. I followed it. End of story."

"Crap." The last thing I wanted to do was talk to the feds.

Bad enough having to deal with Hardin. "Surely there's got to be something in your system about known associates, aliases, anything to help me find him."

"We had him dead to rights on video, committing the murder behind the store where he worked. We found him at home. No priors. Not a lot in our system. Sorry, Ballou."

"Anyone in particular at the FBI I should talk to?"

"Special Agent Tabitha Lovelace served us the paperwork. Start there."

"All right. Thanks."

As I left the precinct, the dark clouds started to unleash their bounty into a steady drizzle. Usually, I cherish the rain since we get so little of it in Phoenix. But I prefer to appreciate it from the dry safety of indoors. Driving in it sucks rocks.

My wiper blades, which I'd used only once since I'd replaced them, had dried out and split into black rubber spaghetti. They turned my windshield into a smear of wet and grime that was impossible to see through.

Between the weather, the ever-present construction zones, and the countless fender benders I squeezed past, it took me nearly an hour to reach the FBI headquarters in north Phoenix. The blocky redbrick building with tall narrow windows overlooked labyrinthine piles of rocks arranged like the loops and whorls of a giant human fingerprint.

In the building's atrium, I passed through security and approached the information desk. "I'm here to see Special Agent Lovelace about a case she's working." I held up my bail enforcement agent badge and ID.

"Is she expecting you?" asked the woman behind the counter.

"I'm a little early, but I hope so." I flashed my most endearing smile but to no effect.

"Just a moment." She picked up the phone in front of her. "Hi, I have a bail agent named Jenna Ballou to see you. Okay." She hung up and gave me a suspicious look. "Special Agent Lovelace will be down momentarily."

I glanced around the lobby for a place to sit, but there wasn't one. Along one wall was a display recounting the history of the FBI in Phoenix, highlighting major cases and agents of note.

Next to that, the FBI's most wanted fugitives glared out from a collection of black-and-white photos. Under each photo was the fugitive's full name, physical description, alleged crimes, and the reward offered. Barclay Dietz was fourth on the list. The reward was two hundred thousand dollars for tips leading to his arrest.

"Ms. Ballou?"

A slender woman with a head of curly sandy-brown hair approached. She was dressed in a gray suit and a pink blouse. With her was a man with a baby face and a pear-shaped body.

"You Lovelace?" I asked.

"Special Agent Lovelace. This is Special Agent Bender." She shook my hand. "I wasn't aware we had an appointment."

"We don't. I've been assigned to apprehend a fugitive murder suspect. The FBI recently took over his case from Phoenix PD."

"I see. Please come this way and let's talk."

I followed them through a secured door, down a corridor, and into an interview room. It was nicer than the ones in the Phoenix PD. I guessed it was designed to put interview subjects at ease rather than on edge, to get them talking.

"Which case is this involving?" Lovelace asked as she and Bender sat on the opposite side of a table from me.

"Rudy Pratt."

Lovelace nodded. "Yes, I'm familiar with it. It's part of a larger operation. What can you tell me about him?"

"I was hoping you could provide some insights as to his current whereabouts. He and his family appear to have vanished. I've canvassed his neighbors. Spoken to his former employer. Called the references on his bail application but haven't turned up much."

"So you are looking for information, rather than providing it?" Bender asked.

"I prefer to see it as us having common goals. I'm here to make sure this mutual suspect is returned to custody so he can stand trial. Wouldn't want him killing anyone else, now would we?" I forced a polite smile, which wasn't returned.

Lovelace crossed her arms. "As I recall, Ms. Ballou, last year, you and a male associate exposed a sting op we were conducting on Milo Volkov's human trafficking enterprise."

"My partner and I were tracking down a young female fugitive we believed Volkov had kidnapped. We had no idea about your sting operation."

"And did you find your fugitive in Volkov's warehouse?" I got the impression she already knew the answer. She was toying with me, and I couldn't do shit about it.

Sweat beaded under my chest. "No, but—"

"Meanwhile, the two agents who arrested you were later murdered in Volkov's corporate office downtown," she pressed. "Is that correct?"

"Volkov killed them. I wasn't there when it happened."

"Were you working for him?" asked Bender.

"No. Look, this was all resolved a year and a half ago. I was cleared."

"Were you?" he asked. "Because we turned up some interesting texts Volkov sent you. Got the impression you two were intimate."

My stomach turned as I recalled his creepy emails. The man was what we in the trans community called a chaser—someone who fetishized trans women as sex objects. "Volkov had some twisted, stalker crush on me. He murdered a reporter and later your two agents, thinking this would somehow get me into his bed. It just made me sick. I killed Volkov and several of his men while rescuing my fugitive. I would think that would put me in the FBI's good graces, not on your shit list."

Lovelace and Bender exchanged a look, but neither responded. The silence in the room became a presence in and of itself.

This was a familiar tactic. People today have a strong aversion to silence and boredom. Give a suspect the silent treatment, and they're more likely to talk.

I wouldn't have played along, but I had a fugitive to find and didn't have all day to play mind games with some fed with a vendetta.

"All I'm asking is for a little help returning one of your suspects to custody. Whatever info you have on possible places he could be hiding out. Other known associates I might not have reached out to. I have no intention of interfering in your larger investigation, whatever the hell it is."

"I'm sorry, Ms. Ballou, but we can't discuss an ongoing investigation. You're simply too much of a liability." She stood and opened the door to the room. I was at once relieved by the inflow of fresh air and frustrated by their lack of cooperation.

"Do you already have Pratt in custody?" I asked. It wouldn't be the first time they'd scooped someone up without notifying the courts or the bail bond agent.

"I'm afraid we can't share that information," replied Bender.

"Fine." I stormed out the door into the corridor. "But if he kills again, it's on you people." I snatched off my visitor's badge and tossed it on the floor on my way out to the lobby.

As I passed the lineup of the Most Wanted list, I thought about Barclay Dietz. I was sure Lovelace and Bender would love to know he was back in town. But fuck them. I'd take him down myself. I deserved that much satisfaction. But first I needed to deal with Pratt before Sadie started breathing down my neck.

15

Frustrated by my lack of progress, I returned to the Hub and resumed looking through Pratt's paperwork. As I thumbed through recent bank statements, I noticed a charge for Arizona Dialysis Solutions. I checked his phone logs, but there weren't any calls to any doctors or medical offices that I could see.

"Hey, Becks? You think you could run call logs for Pratt's wife?"

"Sure. What's the phone number?"

I gave it to her, and she tapped away on her computer keyboard. "Got it."

"Anything for medical offices?"

"Yeah, a shitload. Arizona Dialysis. Thunderbird Nephrology. Mayo Clinic Hospital. Camelback Children's Hospital. Lots of doctors' offices. I'm guessing someone in the family has kidney problems."

I checked Pratt's bail application. Under family, he listed his wife, his son, and his daughter. "I think it's his daughter, Bethany. She wasn't at the house yesterday, and his son looked fairly healthy." Stupid and bigoted but healthy.

I had a hunch and dialed the number for the Mayo Clinic Hospital. When the person on the other end answered, I asked, "Can you tell me which room Bethany Pratt is staying in, please."

"Hold on, let me check. Is that Pratt with two *t*'s?"

"Yes."

"I'm sorry, I'm not showing anyone with the last name Pratt with two *t*'s as a hospital patient."

"Okay, thanks." I looked up the number for Camelback Children's Hospital and dialed it. "Yes, I need to know which room Bethany Pratt's staying in."

"Certainly, let me pull that up." She paused a moment. "Okay, I just need her PIN code."

"Oh, hold on." My mind raced as I scanned his application for possible numbers that they would have used as a PIN code. "Dang it, Linda gave it to me, and I can't find where I put it," I lied. "Can you just put me through?"

"Not without the PIN. I'm sorry. Because we treat children..."

"Yeah, I understand." I hung up. "Becks, Pratt's daughter is at Camelback Children's Hospital. I think he may be hiding out in her room. Think you could locate which one it is?"

"Hold on. I'm trying to hack into one of my new clients' database servers to test the security protocols. I'm on a time crunch."

Her fingers raced on the keyboard, interrupted by the occasional spout of profanity. Her face twisted through a range of emotions from frustrated to determined to angry to sly until she, at last, did a fist pump. "Yes! Broke it!"

"This is a good thing?" I asked.

"I wanted to show them that their previous IT consultant had left some vulnerabilities. And now I can patch them."

"Great. Now, Camelback's Children's Hospital."

"Oh, right. What was the name?"

"Bethany Pratt."

She typed away. "Wow, they have a good system. Let me try...nope, that didn't work. How about this little code injection. Aha! I'm in. Now, Bethany Pratt. Pratt Sprat could eat no... here she is. Room 481. What else did you need?" She beamed with triumph. I loved my hacker bestie.

"That's it. By the way, did you get anything on Peyton or Barclay Dietz?"

She handed me a stack of printouts. "I ran a comprehensive search on Peyton Dietz. He's working at a liquor shop on Baseline in Mesa. Lives in an apartment just off Country Club Drive. No criminal history. Pays most of his bills, though he's sometimes a month slow. MVD shows he drives an eight-year-old Honda Accord. No outstanding traffic tickets. I'm still going through his latest phone bill and social media."

"Thanks," I said as she pulled out another couple of pages.

"As for Barclay Dietz, it's like you said. After June 2005, he dropped off the grid. Emptied his bank accounts, cashed out a CD, and left his family high and dry. His wife, Gloria, who divorced him in absentia a year later, died in 2010 from pancreatic cancer."

"Interesting. Thanks for the info." I pulled out my phone and called Rodeo. It rang four times before he answered. "Hey! You busy?"

"Yeah. Just a bit. Why?" He sounded out of breath.

"I think I know where Pratt might be hanging out."

"Oh yeah? Where's that?"

"Camelback Children's Hospital. Looks like his daughter has kidney problems."

"Ah. Makes sense."

I heard him take a deep breath.

"Unfortunately, I'm with Conor and his team tracking a meth dealer in Queen Creek. May be a couple hours before I can meet you."

"Don't worry about it. Give my love to Conor."

"Copy that. Check with you later."

I hung up and called Caden. "Hey, man. I need your help."

"Please tell me I'm not going to be hanging out by the cars, missing out on all the action."

"Well, if you'd stopped Pratt the first time…" I teased.

"Hey, I tried, but the guy—"

"I'm kidding, Caden. He got away from me too. And this time, you're my main backup. Rodeo's tied up at the moment."

"That's what I'm talking about. Where are we meeting?"

"Camelback Children's Hospital."

"Hospital? Someone hurt?"

"Pratt's daughter. I think that's where he may be hiding out."

"I'll be there."

I hung up.

16

I walked into the lobby of Camelback Children's Hospital in full Bail Enforcement gear minus my weapons. The last thing we needed was to turn this place into a shooting gallery. I could only hope Pratt was similarly unarmed.

Brightly colored murals of flowers and happy children decorated the walls. Christmas lights and greenery hung from the front of the information desk, with a miniature Christmas tree, a menorah, and a Kwanzaa kinara on the counter between the two workstations. Everything about the decor conveyed a sense of hope and holiday cheer. And yet for all the bright colors and happy images, there was no denying the dark truth—children here faced the unimaginable horrors of cancer and other brutal diseases.

Caden walked up and acknowledged me with a nod. He was also decked out in his vest and tactical belt.

"You think he's here?" he asked.

"I hope so."

I studied a sign on the wall to locate the elevator. A woman in business attire approached me. "Excuse me, can I help you two?"

I pulled out my ID and a folded copy of Pratt's bail application. "Bail enforcement. We suspect a fugitive may be on the premises."

"Here? This is a children's hospital."

"His daughter's a patient on the fourth floor."

"Be that as it may, I can't allow you to disturb our other patients and their families."

"We'll do our best not to disturb anyone. But the man we seek is wanted for murder. I'd hate for him to put your patients, their families, or your staff in danger."

She put a hand to her mouth. "A murderer? Here?"

I handed her the bail application. "See for yourself."

She unfolded the paper. "Goodness. Okay, well, please resolve this as quietly as possible. We have some very sick children here."

"You won't even know we're here." I signaled to Caden to head toward the elevators. "Let's find our guy."

"You think he'll come along quietly?" Caden asked as we rode up the elevator.

"Maybe. But be ready for anything."

The elevator door opened. I scanned the hallway. The chilly air held the scent of alcohol gel and floor cleaner. We followed the signs listing room numbers to the ward where Bethany Pratt was being treated. Memories and emotions from the weeks I spent in the ICU as a teen pressed against my mind.

We strolled past a nurses' break room and a cluster of empty wheelchairs lined against the wall. The corridor widened into a circular ward with a nurses' station in the center with rooms like spokes in a wheel along the outer wall. Somewhere, a couple of vital monitor machines beeped incessantly out of sync with each other.

In front of one room, a woman with a Great Dane in a service animal harness stood next to a bald girl in a wheelchair. The girl beamed with excitement as she petted the enormous dog.

"Which way?" Caden asked.

"Looks like Bethany's room is at two o'clock. Stay out here by the nurses' station while I check out the room." I pointed in that direction. "Keep your head on a swivel in case he's out grabbing a cup of coffee."

"Copy that. I got your six."

I cautiously approached the room, keeping an eye out for movement. By the door, the name "Pratt" was written on a whiteboard decorated with shells and starfish. I peered into the room. A lone figure sat hunched over a bed. It had to be Pratt. I tried to ignore the tightness settling in my throat as I got a view of the pale, emaciated child in the bed.

"Rudy Pratt?" I asked in a quiet voice.

He turned. His eyes were red and deeply set in his tear-strewn face. In an instant, his expression turned from sorrow to rage. He wasn't a big guy. But there was an animus about him, a threatening energy that I could only assume stemmed from his daughter's suffering.

"Leave me alone." His voice was both high-pitched and malevolent.

"I'm sorry, but you missed your court date. You need to come with me to get it rescheduled and your bail reset."

"I'm not going anywhere with you. My daughter is dying because those idiots put a bunch of Negroes and illegals ahead of her on the kidney recipient list."

Compassion for his kid tempered my anger at the racist epithets. "I'm sorry about your daughter, but you missed your court date. Don't make this harder than it has to be."

"Daddy?"asked a fragile voice.

"It's all right, darlin'." He patted her arm and picked up a Styrofoam cup from the bedside table. "Daddy has to step outside the room a moment. I'll be right back."

He turned to me. "I'll come along quietly. Just don't cuff me in front of my kid."

I followed him out of the room. He turned. I recognized the fire in his eyes an instant before he tossed the scalding coffee in my face. I shielded my eyes, but my forearm, cheek, and neck started burning. I steeled myself against the pain and took off after him around the nurses' station.

"Caden, cut him off!" I shouted.

When Caden cut off his escape, Pratt pulled a revolver from his waistband and fired. The entire ward erupted in screams and shouting. Caden fell to one knee, still reaching for our fugitive. Pratt fired again and took off down the corridor.

I wanted to follow Pratt, but I had to check on Caden. "You hit?"

Caden was on the ground, moaning. I found two slugs embedded in the fibers of his vest. Even with the Kevlar, the impact of point-blank gunshots could break ribs and cause internal bleeding.

"I...I'm okay," Caden replied through gritted teeth pressing on his chest. "Fuck that hurts."

I reached to the back of his waistband. Sure enough, he had a SIG Sauer in a concealment holster. "Hang tight. I'm going after Pratt." I took off hoping I could stop our quarry without anyone else getting hurt.

I arrived at the elevator lobby with corridors going off in multiple directions. The call buttons were lit, but Pratt was nowhere in sight. The sounds of a child's screams echoed from down one corridor. I charged full speed, narrowly missing a gurney emerging from a room.

Inside the room where the screams were coming from, I found only a family and a nurse huddled around a child's bed. No sign of Pratt.

"Shit!"

The nurse glared at me, then glanced down at the pistol in my hand. "What are you doing with that?"

"Sorry, wrong room."

I tucked the SIG Sauer in my waistband and retraced my steps. Caden sat in a wheelchair by a nurse in blue scrubs. His Kevlar vest was on the floor and his shirt pulled halfway up, exposing his chest binder underneath.

"You okay?" I asked, kneeling beside him.

He nodded. "Started having trouble breathing, but I seem to be in one piece. Did you catch him?"

"Afraid not," I replied. "You okay to head out?"

"You can't leave. Police are on their way," the nurse said. "They'll want to know what happened."

Not wanting to spend the next hour talking to the cops, I pointed at Bethany Pratt's room. "Her father jumped bail after being charged with first-degree murder. We were here to take him back to jail. When we tried to arrest him, he shot my associate here and took off. That's what happened."

Alarm electrified her face. "Murder? Well, what if he shows up again? What do I do?"

I handed her a business card and said, "Call me."

She nodded. I helped Caden to his feet, picked up his vest, and started to walk away.

"Hey," said the nurse. "You look familiar. You with that superheroes group that comes by now and again to visit the kids?"

I stopped and turned back to her. "I'm usually dressed as Wonder Woman."

"Thought so." She glanced at my business card, then back at me. "I'll call you if he shows again. Go on before the cops get here."

I followed Caden trudging out of the ward toward the elevators.

"I can't believe I let him get away again." Caden's shoulders slumped.

"Yeah, what the hell's wrong with you, man? Aren't bullets supposed to bounce right off you?" My comment managed to get him to smile. "Look, we'll get that asshole. Don't worry. You sure you're okay?"

"No, but I'll be better once I get this binder off."

"We just passed a public restroom. You could take it off in there."

He shook his head and put an arm across his chest. "Not here. I'll be okay till I get home."

I understood. Dysphoria could be a bitch. "Suit yourself."

"What happened to your face?" he asked as we rode the elevator down to the first floor.

In the adrenaline rush, I'd blocked out the burning sensation in my face and arm. I felt it now and winced. "The coffee here doesn't agree with me."

He chuckled and grimaced. "Ow! Don't make me laugh."

"Sorry."

"Where to now?"

I had no idea where Pratt would go. "He's probably holed up in a motel room somewhere, maybe with a friend. Becca's tracking his bank card. If he uses it, she'll let us know. I've been putting out feelers with associates and with some of his hangouts. You should head home and get that binder off."

Caden nodded. "What about you?"

"I have a lead on another case I'm working on."

"Who is it? I'd love to help out."

The elevator doors opened, and we walked out. "Just a personal thing. I can handle it."

Wrinkles creased his forehead. "Is this because I screwed up?"

I handed him his vest. "You didn't screw up. This...it's something I have to take care of on my own."

We entered the lobby just as two uniformed guards approached the information desk. Caden and I slipped past and hustled out the doors.

In the parking lot by his car, I handed him back his SIG. "Thanks for the loaner."

"Probably shouldn't have taken it in there, but I feel naked without it."

"No worries. Go take care of yourself. I'll be in touch about Pratt." I hugged him gingerly.

"Be safe, girl. Keep your head on a swivel."

"Always."

"And if you need me, don't hesitate to call."

I forced a smile. "Thanks."

Caden drove off.

I treated myself to a *pollo asado* burrito at Filiberto's and perused Peyton's paperwork—credit reports, bank statements, emails, social media posts, and phone texts.

I discovered he'd recently broken up with his latest girlfriend, was a frequent customer of local dance clubs, and hated his roommate, Hughie, who made their apartment smell like weed. But no indication his father had been in touch. Would Barclay the Beast drive all this way and not reconnect with his son?

After dinner, I headed east toward Peyton's apartment complex in Mesa. As I sat in afternoon rush hour traffic, I wondered if and when I did track down the Beast, I could best him and put an end to my nightmares.

17

A few stars were twinkling above me as I reached the Orange Blossom Apartments, where Peyton lived. The community was gated except for a small lot in front of the office. Not that it presented much of a barrier to anyone determined to get in. It didn't take a genius to realize you could park and wait until a resident opened the gate and follow them in.

I didn't wait long before a green Hyundai drove up and someone punched a code into the keypad. The gate rattled open like a sideways portcullis. The Hyundai drove through. I followed, my rear bumper barely clearing the gate as it closed. Easy peasy lemon squeezy.

The parking lot inside the fence encircled a block of three-story stucco buildings centered around a grassy courtyard. I pulled into an uncovered visitor's spot and geared up with my Ruger on my right hip and the backup revolver in my ankle holster. If Barclay Dietz was here, he was leaving either in my custody or in a body bag. I didn't care which.

According to Becca's research, Peyton lived in building 5, apartment 109. I scanned the sides of the apartment buildings but didn't see any signs. The street lamps were hooded and cast light only along the concrete walkways that ran through the courtyard.

Outside the truck, I aimed an LED flashlight at the nearest

building. A sign near the roof indicated it was building 3. I was close.

I crept through the courtyard, passing only a few people, none of whom were my quarry. With a hand on the grip of my Ruger, I searched the shadows for the monster who still haunted my dreams.

"Building 5." I shined the flashlight's beam at apartment doors, circling the building until I found number 109. My pulse quickened. I pocketed the flashlight and drew my Ruger.

I pounded hard on the door and stepped to the side. Sometimes an FTA's response to a knock at the door was to let their firearm do the talking. I preferred to be out of the line of fire.

When there was no response, I knocked a second time, harder. "Fugitive Recovery! Open the door. Now!"

From inside the apartment, a male voice said, "All right, dammit, I'm coming." Was it Peyton or his father? I couldn't tell. It had been too many years since I'd heard either. My grip tightened, and I readied myself to spring into action.

"Who is it?" asked the same voice, just the other side of the door. Too young to be Barclay. Most likely Peyton.

"Jinx Ballou. I'm looking for Peyton Dietz."

"Why?"

I rolled my eyes. *Just open the fucking door, Peyton,* I wanted to shout. Instead, I played it cool. "We dated in high school."

The door squeaked open. I stepped out of the shadows. The man inside the apartment looked glassy-eyed, with about three-days' worth of beard growth. He was thin and wore a plain white T-shirt and frayed jeans. He smelled of weed and french fry grease. I studied his face, looking for the young man I had once given my heart to. "You're not Peyton," I said.

"Naw, man, I'm his roommate, Hughie." He glanced at my vest, and his eyes popped open wide. "Oh shit, you're a cop." He scrambled clumsily to shut the door, but I held it open with my boot.

"Relax, Hughie. I'm not a cop."

He looked confused. "You sure?"

I nodded. "Unless you've jumped bail, you've got nothing to worry about from me."

"Did I jump bail? I don't think so." He scratched his stubbly beard, as the wheels turned unsteadily in that head of his. "Whew! That was close, huh."

"Where's Peyton?"

"Oh yeah. You're looking for him, right?"

"Yes. Now, where is he?"

"Um…" More beard scratching. "I think he's, like, at work, ya know?"

"San Tan Convenience Liquors?"

"Yeah, how did you know?" Hughie asked. "Are you a psychic? 'Cause that would be too cool. You could, like—"

"When do you expect Peyton back?" I pressed. "I need to speak with him."

"Not till late. But I'll tell him you stopped by."

"Thanks for nothing." I started to turn away but stopped myself. "Hey, has he been in touch with his dad lately?"

"His dad? Not that I know of. Wait, there was that one guy who called. I think he said he was Peyton's dad. Or was that my dad? I can't remember. I forget a lot of stuff. Not sure why. Kinda weird, ya know?"

"Yeah, whatever. Have a nice night."

Hughie closed the door.

I holstered my weapon and slogged back toward the truck. Before I reached the parking lot, I was intercepted by a petite woman in a floral skirt and a fuchsia top, teetering on four-inch heels. Her heart-shaped face wore a stern expression.

"Excuse me. Who are you?"

Aw crap. "Just visiting a friend." I gave her my most charming smile, but she didn't seem to be buying it.

"I'm the property manager. A resident saw your van follow them through the gate. You're not allowed to tailgate someone inside the fence. Who are you here to see?"

"Not important. I was just leaving." I tried to step around her, but Ms. Busybody Property Manager blocked my path.

"If you don't tell me who you're here to see, I'm calling the cops and reporting you for trespassing. Mesa PD has a substation in the strip mall next door." She pointed in the direction of the shopping center next to the apartment complex.

I pointed at the words "Bail Enforcement" printed in yellow across my vest. "Look, lady, I'm tracking a fugitive wanted by the FBI for armed robbery, aggravated assault, and fleeing the jurisdiction. You want to call the local LEOs, be my guest."

"You're with the FBI?"

I smiled but said nothing. Impersonating a federal agent was illegal. Letting someone else make their own assumptions wasn't.

"Why would you be looking for them here? We run background checks on all our residents."

"He's the father of one of your residents."

"Which resident?"

"Peyton Dietz," I said.

"That nice boy? I can hardly believe that." Ms. Busybody looked at me, as if deciding whether I was pulling her leg. "Well, okay. But next time, check in with the office before you go traipsing around the property. We've had some recent break-ins and are trying to clamp down on the situation."

"Office was closed, lady." I pushed past her to the parking lot. It was time to head to the liquor store. I needed to pick up some Jameson for Conor, anyway.

18

San Tan Convenience Liquors was only a few miles away, just off the Loop 202. The store was decently stocked with three long main aisles. Nothing froufrou. No cutesy chalkboard signs advertising the latest microbrew. Just shelves of booze for the not-so-discriminating connoisseur.

The guy behind the counter was ringing someone up when I walked in, so I went searching for a replacement for Conor's mysteriously empty bottle of whiskey. Four other customers cruised the aisles with me, two of them dressed in pajama bottoms and bedroom slippers. In short order, I found the whiskey section and grabbed a bottle of Jameson. A few steps away, I picked up a bottle of Cuervo Gold for myself.

The cashier looked up as I approached the counter. A mix of emotions tore through me as I recognized him. The years had softened his athletic build and widened his face, but it was Peyton Dietz all right. The first boy who said he loved me. The one I believed would be my Prince Charming. The one who never once visited me in the hospital, who didn't so much as text me, who broke my fucking heart after his father shattered my body. It was payback time.

"Hello, Peyton." I slammed the bottles on the counter hard enough to make him jump.

His eyes narrowed as he tried to place me.

"It's me, Jinx Ballou. Remember?"

He stumbled backward into a shelf of high-priced liquor. "Holy shit! Jinx? That really you?"

"It's me, Pey."

"You . . . you look . . . different."

"Maybe because doctors had to rebuild my face after . . ." Hurt and sorrow mixed with the anger. I struggled to keep my composure. This was more awkward than I thought it'd be. What would happen when I confronted Barclay?

"Yeah . . . I'm . . . I'm so sorry. My father wouldn't let me see you. I was afraid to . . . "

"No need to explain." I took a deep breath and stared at the counter. "Your dad was a scary guy. What happened wasn't your fault."

"I should have at least called."

I looked up at him, and our eyes met. "Yeah, you should've."

"So, you're a cop now?" He glanced at my vest.

"Was a cop. Now I'm a bounty hunter." My fury once again surged. "Your dad's a wanted man in several states. Tell me where he is and all's forgiven."

Peyton gasped as if I'd punched him in the solar plexus. "I...I haven't seen him in years. Not since he took off."

"Bullshit! He's in Arizona and was last seen headed toward Phoenix. Don't tell me he hasn't reached out."

Peyton held up his hands in surrender. "He hasn't. I swear."

"You sure? No phone calls? Christmas cards?"

"No," he said firmly, appearing to get a handle on his awkwardness. "Bastard left me and my mom to fend for ourselves. We lost everything 'cause of him." A fire blazed in his eyes. "I never should've asked you out, knowing what you were ... are."

"You knew who and what I was before you ever asked me out. You said you didn't care, that I was a girl as far as you were concerned. He's the son of a bitch who tried to kill me and then jumped bail. His actions and his alone cost you your football scholarship and your house. So don't you dare put that shit on me, Peyton."

Peyton crossed his arms and dropped his gaze. "You're right. I'm sorry."

"So where is he?"

"I told you, I don't know. I haven't seen him. Nor do I want to."

I slapped my business card on the counter along with a couple of twenties for the booze. "Call me if you hear from him. And don't wimp out like last time."

Peyton stared at the card, his face a palette of concern and remorse. "Yeah."

"And FYI, if you don't, that's called aiding and abetting. A felony. I'll take you both in. You two can catch up on old times in a cell in Perryville." I walked toward the door.

"Hey, Jinx!"

I turned. "Yeah?"

"You look good, by the way. Even better than before."

His compliment caught me off guard. For a moment, I was once again that lovesick teenager doped up on estradiol and high school romance. "Thanks, Peyton. You look good too."

All of the memories and emotions swirling round my head left me dizzy. I couldn't tell if he was still covering for his dad or if I was wrong about his father's return to the valley. The only way to know for sure was to watch him.

I drove next door to a QT convenience store and parked so that I had a clear view of the liquor store. Peyton would get off work in a few hours, so I'd hang out until then. Becca had a program monitoring Peyton's phone activity. If anything interesting came up, she'd forward it to me.

Stakeouts are long and boring, so I stepped inside the QT and bought a large cup of coffee, a bag of Sriracha beef jerky, and a bag of hot 'n spicy *chicharrones*. It's hard to fall asleep when your mouth's on fire.

As I settled back in the Gray Ghost, Conor called.

"Hello, love! Ya coming over?" he asked. "I got the new Charlie Hunnam action flick recorded on the telly."

"Can't. I'm on a stakeout." My face still throbbed from the coffee burn Pratt had given me earlier.

"Shite! I already ordered a pizza for us. Barbecue chicken, your favorite."

"No, Conor, that's *your* favorite."

"That's right. You're more the pepperoni and Italian sausage type."

"Actually, I'm more the Irish sausage type," I teased, suddenly feeling frisky. Seeing Peyton again had whammied me good. My emotions were all over the place.

"Irish sausage?" He paused a moment. "Aren't you a cheeky girl! How about some company on this stakeout of yours?"

The last time we did a stakeout together, we ended up making out in the back seat. Our fugitive drove off without us. "Tempting, but I'm way out in Mesa. Besides, I'd hate to get between you and Charlie Hunnam. I know you two have that whole bromance thing going."

"I'm not gonna dignify that bloody remark with a comment."

"'Cause you know it's true," I said with a giggle.

"So who are ya staking out? Anyone interesting?"

I didn't want to tell him I was stalking my ex-boyfriend. Or that I was hunting Barclay the Beast. Not that Conor was the jealous type, but I knew he'd insist on coming out to protect me. I needed to do this for myself. "Just an old assault case. Pretty routine, actually."

"How long you expect this stakeout to go?"

"Late. I'll crash at my place when I'm done."

"This is why we need to combine lots and move in together."

"I'm not doing this, Conor."

"Doing what? I want a real relationship, love. The shagging is lovely, but I need more than that."

"You're such a girl," I said. "You want marriage and children and a fucking white picket fence. Well, news flash! I can't have kids and don't want them even if I could."

"Don't be daft. I never said nothing about kids."

"I…I don't want to talk about it."

"Jinxie, I know you've had some dodgy relationships in the past. I can't blame ya for being squeamish. But ya know I'm not like that. I'd never so much as look at another girl. You know that."

We'd been over this enough, and I fell silent.

"Ya still there?"

"My mother's birthday's tomorrow night. Party over at my folks' place. You in?"

There was a long pause that seemed to stretch for hours. "I don't know. Got a lot to do."

"Fine." I hung up.

A few minutes later, my phone pinged. I expected it to be a text from Conor, sending an apology. It was from Becca instead.

Jinx, this just came over. Thought it might be relevant.

She'd attached a screenshot showing a brief conversation. Peyton had received a message from a nonlocal number.

Hey, I'm in town. You want to meet?

Peyton responded, *Meet me at Vybe at 930pm.*

"Now we're getting somewhere," I said.

Vybe was a dance club a few miles away. I ran a reverse-lookup search for the phone number but found no identifying information associated with it. Possibly a burner phone. The 801 area code, however, was from Salt Lake City, where Barclay had recently robbed a bank.

While tearing into the sriracha beef jerky, I added the phone number to a file I'd been keeping on Barclay Dietz for the past several years—bits and pieces of information that, until now, had never led anywhere. I was finally gonna get this son of a bitch after all these years.

19

I used the time to apply a little makeup and pull on a lacy black blouse I kept in a bag in the back of my SUV for situations where I preferred a stealthy ambush over my usual badass approach. If I was going to take down the Beast, I was going to have to get close before I pounced.

Ten minutes after nine, Peyton turned off the interior lights, locked up the liquor store, and shuffled to a burgundy Honda Accord.

I trailed him as he drove, keeping at least two or three cars between us. I didn't need him getting suspicious, and since I knew where he was going, I wasn't afraid of losing him.

When I reached Vybe's half-empty parking lot, Peyton was approaching the club's front door. After parking the Gray Ghost, I tucked my revolver into a concealment holster at the small of my back and a couple of pairs of handcuffs in my back pocket.

Thirteen years of revenge fantasies flashed through my mind as I walked to the door. I wanted Barclay Dietz to suffer as I had suffered. I wanted him begging me to stop the way I had begged him to stop. I wanted to humiliate him and see the arrogance fade from his beady eyes.

At the door, I handed my ID to a guy with a goat beard and granny glasses. I could feel the steady thrum of the electronic dance music inside.

Goat Boy checked my license and handed it back to me. "Cover charge is ten bucks."

"Kinda steep for a Monday night."

He shrugged. "Go home, then."

I reached into my purse and pulled a ten out of my wallet.

"Have fun," he said.

When I opened the door, a tidal wave of sound washed over me. The entryway was pitch-black. I followed a series of LED lights up a ramp that wobbled like plywood stretched between too few studs, and I emerged on the perimeter of the dance floor.

Across the room to my right, the bar glowed with purple neon. Lights backlit the glass shelves and the bottles behind it. On the far wall, the DJ booth towered above the dance floor. A girl with blue and scarlet hair head-bobbed to the beat with a set of headphones over one ear as she queued up the next song.

I scanned the dance floor for Peyton and his dad. They were both over six feet and should be easy to spot. But I didn't see them among the small, glow-stick-clad group gyrating on the dance floor. I slipped into the shadows, stalking around the perimeter like a panther. But neither were anywhere to be seen.

Does Peyton already have a set meeting spot here? Could they be in the men's room? Are they out back?

I sent a text to Becca asking if there were any other texts from Peyton's phone. She replied there hadn't been.

I was about to give up when a lanky figure emerged from the men's room. Peyton. I sank deeper into the shadows. He stopped near the DJ booth and looked around the dance floor. *Will he spot me? Can he recognize me across the dark room?*

Peyton nodded to someone. A man emerged from the crowd on the dance floor and gave him a bro hug and a pat on the back. The stranger was a white guy, average height, midtwenties. Longish hair. Not Barclay. But maybe the Beast would show yet.

The pair made their way across the room and back toward the entrance. I gave them a few seconds' head start and followed.

When I stepped outside, the sudden silence felt as if I'd gone deaf. The lights over the parking lot seemed almost blinding compared to the club's dark interior. It took me a moment to spot Peyton and his buddy walking between cars in the lot.

"Didn't like the music?" Goat Boy asked with a sarcastic tone.

I gave him a withering stare. "I prefer punk to EDM." When I looked back out at the lot, Peyton and his buddy had disappeared. "Shit."

I wandered through the lines of cars, looking for movement and straining to hear sounds above the thrum-thrum-thrum-ming still in my ears from the club.

"Don't turn around," said a deep male voice with a Texas accent. Something hard pressed against the back of my head. I caught a glimpse of my attacker in the side-view mirror of a pickup truck next to me. The guy Peyton met inside the club.

I whipped around and caught his gun hand in an arm lock. I drove the heel of my other palm into his nose. The gun went off, shattering glass in a car behind me. I plunged my boot into his instep and my knee into his crotch.

As he collapsed into a moaning heap on the ground, I recovered his gun—a Smith & Wesson .38 revolver. I also picked up a plastic bag that had fallen out of his pocket. It contained a multicolored assortment of pills stamped with little pictures—ecstasy.

I pointed the revolver at my attacker. "What's your name, asshole?"

"Mahoney." It was more of a wheeze than a word.

"You shouldn't go sneaking up behind women and putting a gun in their back, Mahoney. Someone could get hurt." I kicked him in the ass. "Where's Peyton?"

"Jinx?" Peyton emerged from the passenger side of a car with dark tinted windows. "What are you doing here?"

"You know this bitch?" asked Mahoney, wiping his nose and leaving a smear of red across his face.

"We dated in high school," Peyton added, a guilty look playing across his face.

Mahoney pulled himself to his feet and put some distance between us. "Shit, the way she was looking inside the cars, I thought she was a cop trying to bust us."

"Why are you following me, Jinx?" asked Peyton.

"You know why."

Peyton stepped toward me, his mouth a thin line. "Look, I told you, if my dad shows up, I'll call you."

"You wouldn't be the first person to cover for a fugitive family member."

"Fugitive? So she *is* a cop." Mahoney pointed an accusatory finger at me.

"What's wrong, Mahoney? I interrupt your little drug deal?" I emptied the baggie on the ground and crushed the pills into dust with my boot heel.

"Fuck you, Five-O!"

"Relax, dipshit. If I were a cop, you'd be handcuffed and in the back of my patrol car by now."

"You ain't a cop, then what the hell are you?"

"Bail enforcement."

"What?"

"She's a bounty hunter," said Peyton. "She's looking for my dad."

"Then you owe me four hundred bucks for that ecstasy you just ruined." Mahoney held out his hand. "And I want my gun back too, bitch."

I studied the revolver. "It is a nice gun. I think I'll keep it."

"Like hell, you will."

"You gonna take it from me, big man?" I aimed the revolver at Mahoney. He wilted like a dying flower in the summer sun.

"I will catch your father, Peyton," I said. "And until I do, expect to see a lot of me."

I turned on my heel and drove home.

20

It was nearly eleven when I walked in my front door. I thought about calling Conor, then decided against it. He'd want me to come over, and I didn't feel like going anywhere. Not after our argument. A restless energy that I couldn't shake flowed through me. I needed some time to process the evening's events.

After stashing Mahoney's Smith & Wesson next to Daniel Warren's Colt in my gun safe, I put on a pair of shorts and a tank top and went into my workout room, where I had a Bodyman II, a man-sized electronic punching bag. I put on the Pink Trinkets' *Orange Menace*—a protest album against the current president—and proceeded to kick, punch, and slam the shit out of the Bodyman.

I pictured Barclay Dietz's beefy face with its misshapen nose on the head of the mannequin. Fury crackled through every nerve in my body. I punched with all the energy I could muster. I kicked so hard every metatarsal in my foot throbbed from the repeated blows.

Faster, harder, drawing on every ounce of strength, my anger exploded onto the rubberized plastic dummy until I was so exhausted that one of my roundhouse kicks missed its target and spun me hard into a workout bench. I landed in a heap and sobbed. Sweat poured off my body despite the coolness of the room. Eventually, I pulled myself to my feet, stepped into the shower, and cranked up the water as hot as I could stand it.

I should've gotten over all this shit years ago. My love for Peyton. His father's brutality. And the deep wounds they both had caused me. It was so pathetic. I thanked the stars Conor wasn't there to see it.

A part of me wanted Conor to hold me. To reassure me that I'd get through this. That I was tough. And yet the thought of moving in with him triggered feelings of claustrophobia. His place wasn't just a house, it was a bunker. A real bunker. A place of hiding. A place where he was hiding. And what was I hiding from?

Why didn't I want to move in with him? Was I worried he'd cheat on me as Wilson had? It made sense, but deep in my gut, it didn't ring true. So why did the thought of moving in with him make me feel as if the walls—those cold, stark walls of his—were closing in on me?

My body trembled. The water had gone cold. I turned it off, pulled a towel over me, and sat on the toilet, letting my mind go blank. I needed to focus on capturing Pratt and Dietz.

As far as Dietz was concerned, I had no hard evidence he was in the valley. Sure, he'd robbed a bank in Kayenta, but for all I knew, he'd continued on to Los Angeles or Mexico or who knew where. It was only my gut that told me he was here. I could feel it in my bones. And when I'd confronted Peyton about it, I could sense he felt the same way. Sooner or later, Dietz would make contact.

I ambled into my kitchen and made myself a bowl of Lucky Charms. It's true what they say—they are magically delicious. But that got me thinking about Conor all over again. My appetite soured, and I dumped the cereal, magical marshmallows and all, down the food disposal.

I was about to turn on the television to watch the latest season of *Jessica Jones* when something went thump.

I told myself it was nothing. A stupid bird crashing into a window. The ice maker dumping a load of cubes in the freezer. The wooden beams in the roof contracting with the evening chill. A furry critter seeking a warm place in my attic. Santa Claus showing up two weeks early to tell me I was on his naughty list again.

Or someone trying to break into my house, said the paranoid voice in the back of my mind.

My experience as a bounty hunter had taught me that a strong sense of caution was a survival skill, not a neurosis. The people I sent back to jail often held a grudge. It wouldn't be the first time someone with ill intent got out and tracked me to my home.

I grabbed my Ruger and a flashlight and crept outside, looking for anything or anyone that shouldn't be there. The street was quiet. No late-night parties. Not surprising for a Monday. I circled the house, checking the roof. But other than a few missing tiles on the back of the house, nothing seemed out of place.

I stepped inside. Room by room, I searched the house. When a thorough canvassing turned up nothing, I put away the Ruger and returned to watching *Jessica Jones*. But I couldn't shake the feeling that I wasn't alone. Or that someone was watching me.

This Barclay crap had me jumpy. Caution was one thing, but this was turning into outright paranoia. I was physically and emotionally exhausted. Perhaps some sleep would get my head right.

I climbed into bed and read the latest Isabella Maldonado novel until I drifted off to sleep.

I woke a few hours later from a nightmare, the details of which eluded my conscious memory. But the sense I was not alone in the house had only grown stronger. I tried to tell myself it was my paranoia kicking up again, but I couldn't shake the feeling.

I opened my eyes and scanned the room without moving a muscle, in case my intruder was in the room with me. I had excellent night vision and could make out the shapes of my dresser, my closet, and the door to the hallway. But no intruder.

I pulled the Ruger out of my nightstand and slipped out of bed. Keeping the lights off, I covertly searched the house again. The voices in my head argued over my state of mind. Was I crazy, or was I in danger?

As before, the search turned up nothing. All doors were locked. All windows intact and secure.

"What the fuck is wrong with you, girl?" I asked myself in the dim glow of my kitchen.

Perhaps a little Mexican sleeping medicine would help. I opened the cabinet and pulled out the bottle of Cuervo Gold I'd bought. Anything to quiet the voices in my head. I stopped short when I saw that the tax label on the cap was already torn and the level was down a bit. I didn't remember opening it.

In my mind, I could hear Conor's voice saying, "Don't be daft, girl."

I must have opened it. No one would break into my house and take a drink of tequila and nothing else. My computer and electronics were all accounted for. The money on my dresser was still there. Clearly, I was losing my fucking mind. I took a long draught of alcohol, enjoying the burning in my throat, and left the bottle on the counter.

I shuffled back to bed, read another chapter in the Isabella Maldonado novel, and was soon in a dreamless sleep.

21

The *Game of Thrones* ringtone woke me at eight o'clock. I must have slept through the alarm I'd set for six. I fumbled for my phone. "Yellow," I mumbled.

"Jinx, I could use some help." The exhaustion in Becca's voice was telling.

"Ye olde chronic fatigue kicking up again?" I asked.

"Yeah. And Easton flew out this morning for Denver on a two-day business trip."

"I'll be right there."

"Sorry to impose."

"Don't be sorry. We're there for each other, goofball. You need me to pick up anything for you?"

"Just a few basics. I'll text you a list."

I poured myself a cup of coffee to shake off the weariness of the night before. The sense that I was not alone persisted despite my getting a few hours of restless sleep. I didn't want to move in with Conor, and now being in my own home had me on high alert. *What the fuck is going on with me?*

I packed up my vest, weapons, and other gear in a duffel and set it on the passenger seat of the Gray Ghost. I didn't need to be shopping at Fry's Foods dressed as if I were ready to take down a drug-dealing bail jumper. Along with the groceries Becca asked for, I picked up some flowers to cheer her up a bit.

When I reached her front door, I let myself in with the key

she'd given me years earlier. The kitchen was cluttered with dirty dishes on the counters, pans stacked up on the stove, and floors that looked as if they'd been dusted with crumbs. She'd never been much of a cleaner, and I never judged her for it. She jokingly called her decorating style "post-disaster." Apparently, Easton wasn't a neatnik either.

"Yo! Becks! You up?" I dumped some empty TV dinner trays and a half-opened pizza box into a garbage bag to make room on the counter for the groceries.

"In here," she said in a voice as thin as paper.

I walked into the living room, where the six-seat dining table was covered with two laptops, three screens, empty food wrappers, and a wide assortment of computer parts I couldn't begin to identify. Becca sat at one of the computers, heavy-lidded, hair mussed, and looking as if she'd been poured into the chair. Her hands alternated between short fits of typing and mouse clicks.

"I figured you'd be in bed."

She took a deep, halting breath and let it out. "I know, but I've got to install this patch for a client by the end of the day."

"You need some downtime. I feel bad for texting you about Peyton last night."

"You find his father?"

"Not yet. Have you eaten this morning?"

"Not hungry." She held up a coffee cup, the outside rim crusted with gunk. "Get me a one-more-please?" Our silly term for another cup of coffee after I'd given her a mug with the words "One More Please" painted inside the bottom of the cup.

I took the cup and set it down on the table. "You're going to bed, Ms. Alvarez."

She leaned back and stuck out her bottom lip in a pout.

I pulled a pair of cuffs from my back pocket. "Look, lady, we can do this the easy way or the hard way."

A wicked yet weary grin creased her face. "Oooh, promises, promises."

"Or I could just tell your mother to drive down from Flagstaff."

"You wouldn't."

"Try me."

Becca's mischievous grin dissolved into an eye roll. "Fine. I'll go to bed."

I helped her to her feet. When she grabbed the laptop in front of her, I shook my head. "Put down the laptop. That's an order."

"You're so damned bossy," she said.

I shadowed her down the hall to her bedroom. Clothes cluttered the floor. The head of her adjustable bed was raised in a reclining position. She rolled into it, slipped under the covers, and clicked on the TV with a remote from the nightstand. She patted the other side of her bed. "Come lay with me."

I was torn. I needed to be out looking for Rudy Pratt and Barclay Dietz, but I had no active leads at the moment. Besides, Becca was the closest thing I had to a sister. "Let me put the groceries away and then I'll hang with you a bit."

A smile reappeared on her face. "You're the best, Jinxie."

Ten minutes later, I climbed into bed next to her. "What are we watching?"

"*Stranger Things*, season two. You watch it?" Becca switched on the television. Eerie music began to play as shimmering red lines of the opening title slid across the screen. It looked like some old sci-fi movie from the 1980s.

"Not so far."

"It's freakin' awesome. You want me to back it up to season one?"

"That's okay. I'm sure I'll catch on."

I tried to follow the story with Becca filling in bits of plot I had missed. It probably would have made more sense if I had watched the previous season, but I was less concerned with the show and more with just spending time with my bestie. Between episodes, I said, "I saw Peyton last night."

Her face got a slow burst of energy. "Seriously? What was that like?"

"Weird. More than a little awkward."

"He still hot looking or has he flabbed out?"

"Still pretty hot. Followed him to a club in Mesa and caught him buying a bag of ecstasy."

"Ugh. What a loser."

"I kinda feel bad for him. He had such potential in high school."

"Not your fault his dad turned out to be a transphobic, psycho bank robber."

"I know. But it wasn't Peyton's fault either."

"So is he in touch with his dad?"

"Didn't claim to be."

"You believe him?"

"Maybe."

She perked up for a moment. "Oh, are you still looking for Rudy Pratt?"

"Yeah. Why? You got something?"

Becca reached over to her nightstand and grabbed her phone. She tapped on the screen and handed it to me. "This might help."

On the screen was an email about a planning meeting for the upcoming protest by White Nation. Among the list of email recipients was one Rudy Pratt. The meeting was scheduled for three this afternoon at Dixie's, a bar Pratt patronized once or twice a month.

"So Rudy's involved with White Nation, huh?" I said. "Why am I not surprised."

"Be careful, girl. Bring lots of backup. Maybe Conor and his crew can help you out."

"I'll call Rodeo and Caden and see if they can help."

"How is Conor, by the way?"

I sighed. "Conor's...Conor."

A chuckle escaped her throat. "What's that mean?"

"We got into an argument last night about me moving in with him."

"Oh, Jinxie, take the plunge already."

"Every time I think about living with him…" I sighed as a wave of emotion washed over me. "I swear I feel the walls closing in."

"Not afraid of commitment, are you?"

"It's not that."

"Afraid he's going to hurt you like Wilson did?"

"Maybe. I don't know. It just doesn't feel like the right time."

"You gotta do what you feel's right."

"There's something else. Last night when I was home, I kept getting this creepy feeling like someone was in the house with me. Then I went to have a drink of tequila from a bottle I'd just bought and found the seal cracked. Becks, I don't remember opening it. I'm seriously losing it."

"You don't have another stalker again, do you? Leaving dead bodies on your doorstep?"

"Nothing like that."

"Maybe it's a poltergeist," she said matter-of-factly.

"Poltergeist?" I scoffed. "Yeah, right. I don't think so. I think this whole Barclay Dietz thing's got my head spinning around in all directions."

"Speaking of which, I've been looking into the bank jobs Dietz pulled on his way south," she said. "In all cases, local police were already responding to an explosion or fire in the immediate area."

"You're kidding!"

"In Wyoming, a cattle feed plant exploded. In Salt Lake City, a plant that prepares emergency rations caught fire. Kayenta, it was a car bomb."

"That's a little disconcerting."

"There's more." Becca continued, "Before Barclay was a boxer, he served in Operation Desert Storm. As a demolitions expert. He knows his way around things that go boom."

"Shit."

"I'm thinking we should tell the FBI what we've found out. Just too risky for you to take on by yourself."

"And tell them what? We know who's setting off bombs and robbing banks based on a Woody Woodpecker tattoo? Maybe it's not even him. Or maybe these explosions and fires aren't connected to the bank robberies."

"Jinx, you know it's him, and they *are* connected."

"Thing is, me and the feds aren't exactly on speaking terms. Not after what happened last year with Volkov. Sooner or later, Dietz is going to contact Peyton. And when he does, I'm going to be there."

"Oh, Jinxie. He nearly killed you last time. And now he's blowing shit up."

"Things have changed. I've changed. If I can handle Volkov, I can handle this."

An awkward silence settled in. Her eyes started to droop. I kissed her on the forehead. "Get some sleep, girl."

"Love you."

"You too. Call me if you need anything else, sister girl."

I walked out to the Gray Ghost and called Caden and Rodeo, giving them the 411 on the White Nation meeting. Both agreed to meet me at Dixie's. But first, I had another stop to make.

22

I passed under an arch of climbing vines and knocked on the front door of an elegant four-bedroom home a stone's throw from North Mountain in Phoenix. The residents of the house tended to be night owls. My watch read one o'clock in the afternoon, so I hoped I wasn't waking anyone up.

The door opened a moment later revealing a dark-skinned, slender, sixty-something woman draped in colorful silk that accentuated her curves in all the right places. If Tina Turner had been transgender and Puerto Rican, she would have been Juanita Valdez.

"Oh my Godiva," Juanita exclaimed when she saw me. "Come here this instant and give your *tía* Juana a hug!"

Juanita had started out as a drag queen back in the day, performing under the name Tía Juana. She later came out as transgender and transitioned to living full-time as a woman. These days she owned and operated the Main Drag, the biggest queer bar in the valley.

We'd met twenty years earlier at the Phoenix Gender Alliance support group. A firestorm of attitude and wisdom, Juanita immediately took me under her wing and declared herself my fairy drag mother. She also bestowed upon me the nickname Jinx, a mash-up of my first and middle names, Jenna Christina.

"How're you doing, *tía*?" I asked as I released her from the hug.

"If I were any better, I'd give birth to myself. Come on in, *mi'ja!*" I followed her down a dark hallway to a large airy kitchen with a great view of the lush courtyard out back. She poured us coffee, and we sat across from each other at her breakfast bar.

"It's been ages since you called," she said sternly. "Shame on you! You know how I worry about my little ones. Especially you, chasing down all those criminal types."

"Sorry. I've been busy."

"Too busy you can't pick up the damned phone, Miss Thang?" She pointed a well-manicured nail at me. "You should treat your elders with more respect."

"I will, I promise." I grinned.

"To what do I owe this unexpected but much overdue visit?"

"Can't a girl visit her auntie without having an agenda?"

She cocked an eyebrow but said nothing. It wasn't exactly the first time I'd shown up asking for her assistance.

I sighed. "Okay, fine. I need your help."

"More fairy drag mother wisdom?"

"Actually, I need to disguise my appearance."

"A disguise? Color me intrigued."

"The fugitive I'm pursuing is expected at a White Nation meeting this afternoon."

"White Nation?" Her posture stiffened. "You're tangling with those *pendejos*? Bitch, are you loco?"

"I don't even know for sure he'll be there, but I don't have any better leads at the moment. He killed someone, and now he's in the wind, most likely holed up with one of his White Nation buddies. I'm hoping to grab him at this meeting."

Juanita shook her head. "You're a braver girl than me."

I shrugged. "Just doing my job."

"Job like that can get you killed," she continued. "No wonder your mama worries about you."

"Problem is, he's seen me before. He's fast and smart. Used to literally be a rocket scientist. So I have to get close to him without him realizing it's me. Thus the need for a disguise."

"To get a racist peckerwood off the street, you can count on my help." She put a hand to my chin and studied my appearance. "Question is how best to disguise you."

After a moment, she said, "I've got an idea, but you probably won't like it."

"If it helps me nail this guy, I'm in."

She met my gaze and said, "We disguise you as a guy."

I nearly fell off my stool. "Oh hell no!"

"Oh, come on, Miss Thang! What's wrong with a little boy drag now and then? Are you so insecure in your femininity that you can't stand to look like a boy again?"

"I tried to be a boy for eleven years. I hated it."

"Bitch, please! I did it for twice that. The point of this is illusion, make-believe. It's an act so you can catch a murderer, right? You dress up as Wonder Woman all the time. Hell, I saw you the other day on TV, arresting a guy in your superhero drag. Just think of it as a little cross-play."

"But I transitioned before puberty. My voice never dropped."

"Oh, well, aren't you the little *princesa*," she said snottily. "Oops, did your tiara fall off? Let me pick that up for you."

"*Tía*, stop. Even if I wanted to, there's no way I could pull it off."

Juanita sighed and lifted up strands of my hair. "There gonna be a lot of fighting?"

"Not if I do it right." I lied as honestly as I could.

"Fine. Come with me."

I followed Juanita past a few closed bedroom doors to her boudoir, which always looked like a set from *Moulin Rouge*. Imperial-red wallpaper accented with gold flourishes covered the walls. A canopy bed with dark wood posts and a plum satin comforter dominated the room. Along one wall stood a vintage vanity table in front of a large mirror bordered with lights. The only modern accommodation was a flat-screen and sound system in an entertainment center opposite the bed.

Juanita led me into her walk-in closet. Shelf upon shelf of

wigs on Styrofoam heads stretched the length of one side. They came in all colors, styles, and lengths. Most were natural colors, though a few were on the wilder side—electric blue or rainbow.

"Put your hair up," she told me, handing me some bobby pins.

I tied my long dark hair into a tight bun while Juanita studied her collection of wigs. After a moment, she took down a short bleached-blond wig from a stand someone had drawn blue eyes on.

"How about Miss Norma Jean here?" She offered it to me.

"A little too fifties, don't you think?"

She huffed and snatched it from me and set it carefully back on its stand. "So goddamned picky! Let's see, how about this one. I call her Ginger Rose." She handed me a strawberry-blond wig.

I tried it on and looked at myself in a mirror on the back of the door.

Before I could say anything, she snatched it off my head. "Nope! Wrong coloring. No one would believe a redhead with tan skin and brown eyes." She was right about that.

"How about that one?" I asked, pointing at a long blond wig with wispy wings.

"Ah, Farrah." She sighed, holding a hand over her heart. "I always wanted to be her."

"Who?"

"Farrah Fawcett! Please tell me you've heard of *Charlie's Angels.*"

"The one with Drew Barrymore? Never saw it."

I thought she was going to give birth to kittens right then and there. "Not that ridiculous movie! The original series from the seventies. I have failed as a mentor and fairy drag mother."

"I promise I'll look it up on Netflix when I get a chance." I held up a three-fingered salute.

"See that you do. Farrah was a goddess." She lifted the wig from its stand and fixed it onto my head with more bobby pins and teased it here and there. "You know, this one just might work."

"What's that one called?" I asked, pointing at a super-campy wig on the high shelf.

"That, my dear, is Hedwig. From *Hedwig and the Angry Inch*."

"Never heard of it," I said with a shrug.

Her eyes widened. "Are you fucking kidding me? I swear, queer kids today have no sense of their own culture."

I broke into a grin. "Relax, *tía*. I'm messing with you. I've seen it. A few times, in fact. A bit campy for my taste, but a good flick."

"*Pendeja*," she muttered under her breath.

She reached onto a shelf full of accessories and pulled out a pair of large rose-tinted glasses and slipped them on my face. "There! With the right makeup, even your own mama won't recognize you. Now, follow me." She led me into another room filled with racks of outfits.

"Damn! I haven't seen so many clothes outside of a department store."

"A performer needs to have the proper costume." She pulled out a lacy top and a pair of cut-off jeans. "Try these on."

"Right here?" I asked, suddenly feeling a little embarrassed. "Can I have a little privacy?"

"You afraid you got something I ain't never seen before? Bitch, please!"

I took a deep breath and released it. "Fine." I pulled off my T-shirt and jeans. As soon as I did, Juanita guffawed.

"What the hell are those? Granny panties?"

My face flushed. "They're comfortable." I snatched the Daisy Dukes from her and slipped into them. "They're a little loose."

"'Cause you got them skinny boy hips."

"Juanita! That's mean!"

"Oh, please. Just put a belt on them. They'll be okay."

I pulled on the lacy top. "Well?"

She handed me a pair of strappy leather sandals with two-inch heels. I slipped them on, hoping I wouldn't have to run in them.

Juanita nodded. "Close, but we need one more thing. Follow me."

She led me to her vanity, where I sat down on the padded bench.

"We need to recontour your face so that redneck rocket man doesn't recognize you."

Juanita set to work like a master artist with me as her canvas. It had been so long since I'd gotten a makeover, it felt weird for someone else to be doing my makeup. But I followed her instructions to look up or open my mouth in an O, so she could achieve the desired effect.

She applied a lot more makeup than I ever did. I favored the minimalist look, especially in the summer. Didn't need makeup melting across my sweaty face after chasing down FTAs. But in this case, I trusted her judgment to get me close enough to Pratt to slap the cuffs on him.

She finished and stepped back. "Well, what do you think?"

I studied my reflection in the mirror. "I barely recognize myself. This might work."

"You look totally fish. Those redneck boys' dicks will be so hard, they won't know what hit them."

"Thanks for your help." I hugged her and kissed her cheek.

"What's a fairy drag mother for?"

"I'll get the wig and the clothes back to you in a little while."

"In the next day or so is fine. And I best see your skinny white ass at my show tomorrow night."

"The Barbra Shop Quartet? Sounds very campy."

"In the very *best* of ways."

"I'll be there."

"Your little boy toy, Conor, too, I hope."

A wave of sadness passed through me. "Absolutely." *Assuming he's still speaking to me.*

"Be careful, *mi'ja*." She shot me a concerned look.

"Always, *tía*."

23

At a quarter to three, I met Caden and Rodeo outside Dixie's. An image of a buxom woman carrying a Confederate flag was painted on the bar's plate glass window, with stars and bars decorating the name above her. Vehicles sporting pro-gun, Confederate, and far right-wing political and religious bumper stickers filled the parking lot.

Rodeo guffawed when he saw me. "Holy shit, girl! Who the hell are you supposed to be?"

I flipped him the one-finger salute. "Pratt's seen me before. I need to get in close without him recognizing me. My friend Juanita helped me out."

Caden joined in the laughter at my expense. "You look like that woman from that poster back in the seventies. I forget her name."

"Farrah Fawcett?" I asked.

"Yeah, that's it. She was on some show, wasn't she?"

I ignored the question. "Look, is it too over-the-top? I was trying for inconspicuous."

Rodeo took a deep breath and regained his composure, but a couple of persistent giggles crept out. "Inconspicuous? Not a chance. More like fuckably hot!"

"Shit." Maybe going to Juanita was a mistake.

"Don't worry." Caden put a hand on my shoulder. "You look sexy but convincing. Pratt won't know what hit him until it's too late."

"So what's the plan?" asked Rodeo.

"Pratt is supposed to be attending a meeting here for White Nation. The plan is I go in like I'm looking to join. When Pratt shows up, I'll figure a way to lure him outside, slap the cuffs on, and away we go."

They both shook their heads.

"A honeypot lure? Spectacularly bad idea, Jinx," Rodeo said. "That same tactic nearly got us both killed last year when you tried it with Freddie Colton."

"As I recall, we caught Colton," I said confidently.

"While also drawing a mob of armed thugs from the bar you lured him out of."

"Hey, I handled it."

Rodeo glared at me.

"Fine," I conceded. "We handled it, even when Fiddler bailed on us. And now we have Caden. We've got our bases covered."

Caden looked a little nervous. "Sounds pretty sketchy, Jinxie. No offense. Maybe we should stake the place out and follow him when he leaves."

"And then what? He's probably staying with a bunch of White Nation thugs. So whether we take him here or somewhere else, the risk's the same."

"You think he's in there?" Rodeo asked.

I scanned the parking lot and noticed a white Camry, like the one listed on Pratt's bail application. I circled around to the rear of the vehicle. "Shit. Plates don't match."

"Could've switched plates," Caden suggested.

"Anything's possible with these guys." I racked the slide of my Ruger and slipped it into the concealment holster at the small of my back. "Rodeo, guard the back door. Caden, you watch the front. I'll draw him out into the parking lot. I won't have my radio with me, obviously, so if I'm not out in thirty minutes, come and get me."

Rodeo nodded. "Copy that." He slung his beanbag shotgun over his shoulder and strolled around to the back of the building.

Caden drew his SIG. "Watch your ass in there."

"I intend to."

I approached the door of the bar. A sign on the outside read "Libtards Will Not Be Served." *Great.*

Inside, the place was empty except for a bartender and one old man who looked as if he had melted into his bar stool.

"Can I help you?" asked the bartender, a beefy guy with a flattop.

"I'm looking for the White Nation meeting."

The bartender fixed me with a look that said he wasn't sure I was the right type. Was there a password or something to indicate I was with the in crowd? If there was, I was shit out of luck. I flashed my sexiest smile.

"To your right and in the back room past the pool tables." He gestured with his thumb and continued wiping down the bar.

"Is Rudy Pratt here yet? He asked me to meet him here."

"Dunno. I stepped out for a cigarette a bit ago. He mighta come in when I wasn't up here."

"Okay, thanks!"

I felt his eyes follow me as I rounded the corner and followed the sound of male voices laughing and shouting, past a room with two pool tables to a wooden door. My heart pounded in my chest, partly from fear, partly from the thrill of the hunt.

I opened the door and found a dozen people gathered around a wooden table topped with pitchers of beer and stacks of flyers for the upcoming rally. A few were women, but most were men. None of them Rudy Pratt.

I expected a room full of stereotypical white supremacists— militant skinheads, neo-Nazis, and good ol' boy, South-will-rise-again types in wifebeaters. But the people here looked like ordinary suburbanites, most in collared shirts and dad jeans.

"Can I help you?" asked a man with an angular face and a distinct air of authority. He wore a white button-down dress shirt. A leather notebook lay in front of him at the head of the table.

I took a few cautious steps into the room. "Hi! I'm looking for Rudy."

"And you are?"

"Liz Windsor." It was an alias I often used. "He asked me to meet him here. Said y'all could use my organizing skills to help with the rally."

"Well, Rudy isn't here right now, Miss Liz Windsor." His gaze made my skin crawl, like a rattlesnake staring down a potential meal. "You look familiar to me. Have we met?"

A shiver ran down my spine. For the millionth time, I kicked myself for having been interviewed by *Phoenix Living* the previous year. Conor had warned me not to do it, saying bounty hunters should keep a low profile. And now people recognized me as the cover girl for the local trans community.

"Naw, I just have one of those faces," I replied nervously.

"Of course." He didn't look convinced but stalked over and extended a hand. "A pleasure to meet you, Miss Windsor. The name's Eric Freytag. I'm the chairman of the local White Nation chapter."

"Likewise," I said. "Is Rudy expected?"

"Hard to say. A lot going on with his family these days, I'm afraid."

I nodded. "His daughter. I know, he told me. Truly heart-breaking." My survival instincts were screaming at me to get the hell out of there.

Pull your shit together, girl, I told myself. *Act like you belong here.* I took a deep breath.

"How long have you known Rudy?" Freytag asked.

"We met a few months ago at the hardware store where he works. He helped me pick out some shrubs for my front yard. We got to talking politics and things."

"Well, do come join us." Freytag shut the door, put his arm around me, and led me to a seat on the opposite side of the room. *"Come into my parlor," said the spider to the fly.* And I'm *in a room crawling with spiders. I fucking hate spiders. But I'm no fly,* I reminded myself. *I'm a tarantula wasp.*

"Why don't we get down to business," Freytag said. "We have a few stragglers, but I'm sure they'll be along momentarily. Until then, Miss Windsor, perhaps you'd care to tell us about yourself and why you chose to join us."

Ugh, this plan is totally going off the rails. Bad enough being in the same room as these people, and now I have to pretend to think like them.

"Well, I, uh…I love America and Jesus, and I just want our country great again, the way it used to be. Where good Christian people have freedom of religion and being white isn't considered a crime." The words tasted like ashes in my mouth. I couldn't believe I was saying this shit. On the bright side, my rambling white nationalist drivel drew cheers from the other attendees.

"Well said, Miss Windsor. You are certainly among friends." Freytag's expression was hard to read. I wanted to believe I was giving a convincing performance, but I wasn't sure I'd succeeded.

"Now, everyone, I have very high hopes for the rally this Saturday. Our website and social media campaigns have been getting a great response. The conservative media has been helpful in promoting the event. If all goes as planned, our protest will make Charlottesville look like a lonely man's funeral. I believe this will be the biggest rally for white pride this country has seen in over a century."

I wanted to punch this guy in the face so hard, my fists were balled up like hammers.

"And there'll be none of that college boy, tiki-torch nonsense. We will have real people. Families. Hardworking men and women who embody the heart and soul of this country, a soul that for decades has been strangled by liberal PC brainwashing. It was white men who made this country what it is, and for all us white men and women, it is long past time we reclaim our rightful place."

A knock interrupted his speech. "Come in."

The door to the room opened. I expected it to be Pratt, so I readied my body to spring into action.

A figure came into view. My heart thundered in my chest. It wasn't Pratt. The face was familiar, though aged since I'd last seen it in person. But the Woody Woodpecker tattoo was unmistakable. The imposing presence of Barclay "The Beast" Dietz entered the room.

24

The Beast sauntered through the doorway as if he owned the place. The years had reduced his eyes to deep-set slits, but he still carried himself with the threatening presence of a rogue bull.

"Sorry I'm late," he said, or something similar, as Freytag stood and shook his hand. It was hard to hear over the roaring of blood in my ears. Deep inside me, a long-dormant fury rumbled forth like magma gushing up the throat of a volcano, erupting into a cataclysm of emotion and violence.

In an instant, I vaulted onto the table and launched myself at Dietz, swinging, kicking, and pummeling. The world spun around the two of us. I drove hard with elbows, knees, and the heel of my palm at every potentially vulnerable spot on the man.

My arms were twisted behind me as I was pulled off of Dietz.

"Miss Windsor, what is the meaning of this nonsense?" asked Freytag.

My chest heaved. I gulped ragged breaths as the fury of adrenaline burned through my bloodstream. The right side of my face throbbed, and my vision in that eye blurred.

Dietz staggered to his feet. His nose dripped blood, and one of Dietz's eyes was red and swelling. "Crazy bitch! What the hell's wrong with you?"

I struggled to free my arms from the men who held me, but they held fast. I drove a heel into the instep of the man to my right. He released my arm, and I drove it into the nose of the guy holding my other arm. I drew my Ruger and backed toward the door. Unfortunately, several others drew guns, as well.

With my free hand, I flashed my bail enforcement badge and ID. "My name is Jinx Ballou. I'm a bail enforcement agent. I'm here to arrest Barclay Dietz for failing to appear on aggravated assault and attempted murder charges."

"Mr. Dietz, is this true?" Freytag asked.

Dietz cocked his head, and his eyes opened wide in recognition. "You filthy piece of garbage!" His face burned dark red, and he pointed a finger at me. "This *he-she* seduced my son when he was in high school, pretending to be a girl. But it ain't nothing but a faggot in a dress!"

Freytag crossed his arms and grinned. "Jinx Ballou! I thought I recognized you. You were on the cover of that liberal rag of a newspaper last year. Well, I am sorry to disappoint you, but this gentleman here is our guest. He's not leaving with you."

"Like hell, he isn't."

"Mr. Quinton," Freytag said with venom in his voice.

"Yes, sir." A man pointing a snub-nosed .38 at me stepped forward. He had the look of a retired cop.

"Would you and Mr. Overcash please escort this intruder off the premises?"

"Gladly." Something in Quinton's gaze suggested he planned to do more than escort me outside.

Overcash, a skinny guy with a .44 Magnum, edged around the table with him. The large-barreled revolver looked as if it weighed as much as he did.

"Not without my fugitive," I insisted.

"Fuck this bullshit!" Dietz thundered. "Shoot that bitch!"

Overcash raised his hand cannon and fired. I put two in his chest and ducked out of the room before slamming the door shut. Several bullets ripped through the door around me as I braced it closed with a chair.

"You okay?" a voice behind me asked.

I spun around and came just short of putting a nine-millimeter hole in Caden.

"I heard shouting. Figured you could use an assist." He stood by one of the pool tables, his SIG Sauer in hand.

The door shuddered as if someone had slammed into it from the other side. The chair gave an inch.

"Let's get out of here," I said.

"What the hell y'all doing?" The bartender appeared in the doorway between us and the main barroom, holding a rifle.

I smiled and pointed over his shoulder. "Ask the guy behind you."

"Seriously, you expect me to—"

Rodeo pressed the muzzle of his shotgun into the bartender's back. At point-blank range, even a beanbag round could be lethal. The bartender laid the rifle on the floor and held up his hands. Rodeo tossed it to me. I was acquiring quite a collection of other people's guns.

Again someone slammed into the meeting room door. On the third attempt, the chair buckled, and the door flew open. The air exploded with gunfire.

"Out!" I shouted.

Caden, Rodeo, and I charged out the front door. My left calf burned with a sharp stinging sensation. I ignored it as we raced through the lot and took up positions behind a Hummer. I kept my Ruger trained on the bar's front door. Caden and Rodeo did the same.

"Anyone hit?" My body trembled in pain, mostly in my head and leg.

"I'm in one piece," replied Rodeo. "Caden?"

"I'm good."

"Jinx, you're bleeding." Rodeo pointed. My left calf was covered in blood.

I gritted my teeth as the sharp pain intensified. "Fuck."

Rodeo crouched down, took out a bandana, and wiped away some of the blood.

"Shhhhiiittt," I hissed.

"Hold still." He snapped open a jackknife.

"Wait! What are you doing?"

I looked down to see Rodeo insert the blade a half inch into the wound and flick out a piece of something I hoped wasn't flesh. I almost bit off my tongue from the pain. "Jesus fucking Christ!" My arms trembled as I held myself up.

"It's okay." He tied the bandana across the wound. "Just caught a piece of a ricochet." He stood up and showed me a bloody bit of metal. "Put a little alcohol on the wound when you get home."

"What happened to your face, Jinx?" asked Caden.

"I'm in fucking pain," I grunted. "This is my fucking-pain face."

"No, your eyes are all dark and swelling."

I felt my face and temple, and a bobby pin came loose in my hand. If it was possible for me to feel worse, I did. "Aw fuck. The wig came off in there."

Caden shook his head. "Juanita's going to kill you."

I took a deep breath, struggling to get a handle on the pain. "She'll have to get in line behind these other fucks." I glanced toward the bar's front door. "This plan went to shit."

"So Pratt's still in there?" asked Rodeo.

I shook my head. "Pratt didn't show."

"Who were you trying to arrest in there?" Caden gave me a confused look. "I heard you say, 'Not without my fugitive.'"

"Barclay Dietz."

Rodeo did a double take. "Barclay 'The Beast' Dietz? The boxer?"

"Damn, girl. Miracle you're still alive," Caden added.

I looked over at my teammates. "Don't tell Conor about Dietz, all right? I don't want him to worry."

"You got it," Caden replied.

"He's bound to find out sooner or later, especially with your face looking like that," said Rodeo.

"Barclay Dietz is gonna have a lot worse before I'm done with him."

We fell silent. Rodeo was right, and Conor would find out eventually. I just hoped I could put Dietz behind bars first.

"Doesn't look like your buddies are coming out any time soon," said Rodeo. "What now?"

Before I could formulate an answer, the wail of multiple police sirens pierced the air. Two Phoenix PD patrol cars pulled into the parking lot. Two more pulled in a moment later and effectively blocked off the exit. The officers got out and approached us with their weapons drawn.

25

"Drop your weapons and get down on the ground, hands behind your head," two of the officers shouted in unison, one man and one woman. Rodeo, Caden, and I complied.

Why didn't I keep my cool in there? I scolded myself. *If I had, maybe I could have somehow lured Dietz outside, and no one would have been shot.* Not that I would have admitted it to the cops.

"I'm a former cop, now a bail enforcement agent," I told the female officer who approached and cuffed me. "I was here to apprehend two fugitives. My ID's in my back pocket."

"Someone will be along to take your statement shortly." She pulled me to my feet and escorted me to a waiting patrol car.

As I sat and stewed in the back seat, resisting the temptation to release the handcuffs using one of the keys I had kept on me, an ambulance arrived, and a medical team charged into the bar. A little while later they exited carrying a draped body on a gurney. Overcash, I assumed.

I should have been worried about getting arrested and possibly facing charges for killing Overcash. I should have been worried about the shit I was going to get from Juanita for losing her precious wig. But what worried me most as I sat in the cramped back seat of the patrol car was the massive guilt trip I was going to get if I missed my mother's birthday party, especially after blowing off family brunch last weekend.

The car door opened. A familiar face beckoned me out.

"Damn, Ballou. What'd you get messed up in this time?" Officer Mitch Evans had been in my squad for the year that I served on the force. He'd hit on me relentlessly until word got around the precinct that I was trans. All of a sudden, all the sexual innuendoes ended. But so did any sense that I was part of the team. I left the force not long after that.

A couple of years ago, Evans had been suspended after shooting an unarmed black man. Six months later, an all-white jury exonerated him, and he returned to active duty.

"Nice to see you too, Evans."

He pointed at my leg. "You need medical attention?"

I looked down at my calf. The bandana was weeping blood. "Yeah."

He pulled me out of the patrol car and called over an EMT who wore her hair in a French braid. "Looks like we got a GSW," he said.

"Hi, I'm Angie. Can you walk?"

I nodded and followed her to an ambulance, where she examined the wound. "What happened here?"

"Not sure, but I think I caught a ricochet."

She poked around the wound. I did my best not to bite my tongue as I tried not to scream.

"I don't see any fragments. I think you got lucky with just a flesh wound. I don't think you need a trip to the ER, but it's your call."

"I'd rather not." I decided not to mention that Rodeo had already dug out the fragment.

She cleaned it with saline, applied some ointment, and bandaged it up. "Keep it clean and dry for the next week and apply an antibiotic ointment a few times a day. If it gets infected, call your primary or go to the ER."

"Thanks."

"If you'd like, I can give you an ice pack for that black eye."

I shook my head. "Naw, I'm good."

"If you start to feel nauseated or dizzy, get yourself checked for a concussion."

"Will do."

I hopped out of the ambulance and was intercepted by Evans. "How 'bout you tell me what the hell happened here?"

"My team and I are currently pursuing two fugitives—Rudy Pratt and Barclay Dietz—both of whom were expected at a White Nation meeting at this bar."

"White Nation, huh?" He wrote it down in a notebook he pulled out of his pocket.

"Pratt was a no-show. When I tried to arrest Dietz, he fought back. Some of his White Nation buddies also intervened. Some skinny guy shot at me with a large-caliber revolver, looked like a .44 Magnum. I was in fear for my life and returned fire in self-defense." Wording was everything if I was to stay out of jail.

"They carried a guy out with two in the chest. That your handiwork?"

"I don't know. It was rather chaotic."

"Then what happened?"

"When it became apparent my team couldn't safely apprehend our fugitive, we retreated to the safety of the parking lot." I might have left out a few things, but it was basically the truth as I saw it.

"Barclay Dietz. Why does that name ring a bell?"

"He used to be a boxer. Jumped bail some years ago on an aggravated assault charge."

"That's right. That was a while ago. How come you're tracking him now?"

"Got a tip he was in town. The FBI's offering a nice reward for his capture. This is what I do."

"Okay, stay put. I'm going to check out a few things. I'll be back in a bit." Evans again escorted me to the back of the squad car. He returned twenty minutes later. "No one by the name of Barclay Dietz is in the bar."

"Well, duh. He's been on the lam for more than a decade.

Probably has a fake ID with an alias. He's a big guy, over six feet and built like a side of beef. You can't miss him."

"No one fitting that description either."

"What?" He must have slipped out the back somehow before the cops showed up. "Damnit. I almost had him."

"Everybody in the bar's saying you assaulted one of their guests. When Mr. Overcash tried to intervene, you pulled your weapon and shot Mr. Overcash. Sounds like second-degree murder."

"That's bullshit, and you know it. I used to be a cop myself, in case you've forgotten. I know what the law is. These people are nothing but a bunch of racist neo-Nazis harboring at least one, possibly two fugitives. They have every reason to lie."

"I follow the evidence." His voice was cold as he recuffed me and read me my Miranda rights.

"You're a real piece of shit, you know that, Evans?"

After I spent an hour counting cockroaches in my holding cell, an officer called my name and escorted me to a room smaller than my walk-in closet. Not the first time I'd been in this interrogation room. Probably not the last.

My attorney, Kirsten Pasternak, sat on the far side of a table mounted to the floor. She was taller than me by a few inches, dressed in a near-black tailored suit and a beige blouse. Yellow-framed glasses brought out the golden highlights in her chestnut hair. Her fingers were long and delicate, and her voice was deep but sultry enough that most people didn't know she was trans unless she told them.

"What did you get yourself into now?" she asked.

I gave her the rundown of the events at Dixie's. She asked a few pointed questions and made suggestions on framing my version of the story so as not to implicate myself. When we were satisfied with our game plan, she knocked on the door. Moments later, Detective Brent Loughlin and Detective Emma Skoglund walked in carrying folders and notebooks.

Back when I was on the force, I had a crush on Detective Loughlin. Square jaw, broad shoulders, and ice-blue eyes. Just the sound of his laugh made me ache to feel him inside me. We'd met only a few times at crime scenes, though I doubted he ever knew my name. If I hadn't been dating Wilson at the time, I might've done something about that.

I'd run into Detective Skoglund a few times over the years. She'd always seemed a bit twitchy to me and hard to read. The overhead lights on her pale skin made her look jaundiced. She wore a pale-pink cardigan over her ballet-dancer frame.

Loughlin gave me a stern look that crushed any lingering feelings of romantic attraction. This guy meant business. He slid a picture of Overcash to my side of the table. It looked like a mug shot. "Just so we're all on the same page, this man, James Robert Overcash, was fatally shot twice in the chest. I'd like to know why."

I glanced at Kirsten. She gave me a nod to proceed as planned.

"I arrived at Dixie's Bar around three looking for one of my fugitives, who was expected at a White Nation meeting being held here. When Barclay Dietz arrived..." A repetitive clacking derailed my train of thought.

"Yes, keep going," Skoglund said in a monotone voice. A vibration in her jacket clued me in that she was bouncing the heel of one foot. From her poker face, I couldn't tell whether she was doing it intentionally to throw me off-balance. Either way, it was unnerving.

"I, uh, I was attempting to arrest Dietz when Overcash and several White Nation members grabbed me. I pulled away. That's when they drew weapons and fired on me. Out of fear for my life, I returned fire in self-defense."

Loughlin gave Skoglund an annoyed glance and shuffled through the papers in his folder. "Barclay Dietz, the former boxer?"

"Yes." I faced off with Loughlin, trying to tune out the clack, clack, clack of Skoglund's shoe heel. "He jumped bail thirteen years ago on aggravated assault charges. He's also involved in several armed robberies across the country."

"Who hired you to apprehend Mr. Dietz?" asked Detective Skoglund. *Clack, clack, clack, clack.*

"No one."

"Barclay Dietz is wanted by the FBI for numerous violent crimes," Kirsten interjected. "My client was acting within her capacity as a bail enforcement agent as she attempted to return a dangerous fugitive to custody."

"How'd you know Dietz would be there?" Loughlin made a move under the table, and the clacking stopped.

"I didn't. I showed up at Dixie's looking for Rudy Pratt, who jumped bail on a murder charge."

Loughlin nodded. "Must have been quite a shock, seeing your childhood bully after all these years."

Shit. How long had he known? "My intel indicated Dietz was in the area. So no, not a complete shock."

Skoglund sorted through her paperwork. "We have witnesses who deny Dietz was ever there. They say you showed up uninvited, assaulted one of their members unprovoked, and then opened fire." The heel clacking started up again.

"That's bullshit. Check the surveillance recordings."

"Unfortunately, the bar doesn't have any interior cameras," said Loughlin. "What footage we do have shows you and your fellow bounty hunters exiting the building while exchanging gunfire with those inside. That leaves us with the statements from witnesses, all of whom point to you as initiating the confrontation."

"What about the statements from my guys? Caden Morrow and Nathaniel Kwan?"

Skoglund's finger trailed a line across a report in front of her. "Per their statements, neither Mr. Morrow nor Mr. Kwan were in the room at the time the shooting began." *Clack, clack, clack.*

"Would you quit clicking your heels?" I snapped.

Skoglund met my gaze for a second and stopped. "Sorry."

"Bottom line, Ms. Ballou," said Loughlin, "no one's corroborating your story."

"Come on, Loughlin," I replied. "I used to be a cop myself. I wouldn't do anything like that."

He tapped the paperwork in front of him. "What I know is that in the years since you left the force and signed up to play bounty hunter, you've been involved in multiple violent incidents, including the deaths of two FBI agents just last year."

"I did not kill those agents. That piece of shit Milo Volkov killed them in cold blood. I did everything I could to save them. When that failed, I took down Volkov and several of his men, getting them off the streets."

"In other words, you killed them."

"Detectives, you have nothing. My client clearly acted in self-defense. And if you think a jury is going to believe the lies of a white nationalist hate group over a former police officer…"

Loughlin turned to her. "Key word being *former*. She hasn't been a police officer for quite some time. Now she's just a vigilante with a fake badge, pursuing her own idea of justice on my streets."

"I'm not a vigilante, you ass—" I took a breath. "I was there to apprehend a fugitive. That's all."

"Unfortunately, Ms. Ballou, the evidence is not in your favor," Loughlin replied.

We went round and round. In the end, Loughlin and Skoglund charged me with aggravated manslaughter, acting as if they were doing me a favor and not charging me with murder one.

I spent another hour being processed and was eventually released on seventy-five thousand dollars bond via Assurity Bail Bonds. Sadie Levinson wasn't thrilled to be posting bail for her own bounty hunter. In short, I was on everyone's shit list.

It was after six before I was released. The Gray Ghost was still parked in front of Dixie's. As Kirsten gave me a ride back, I checked in with Caden and Rodeo. Neither were charged. Thank goodness for small favors.

When we arrived in the bar's parking lot, she turned to me. "I'm assuming you're not interested in a plea if they offer one."

"You got that right, sister. I stand by my story. I was just there to do my job. They're the ones who turned it into a gunfight."

"I'll get ahold of the witness statements, as well as the ballistics and autopsy reports, as soon as they're available. Hopefully, we can find something in there to clear you. If nothing else, I'm guessing we can dig up enough dirt on these good ol' boys to impeach their testimony."

"I hope so. I don't intend to spend the next decade behind bars." I thought about Conor and his vanishing act after the Omagh bombing. Would I give up my family and friends, my whole life, to avoid going to prison? It felt odd entertaining these thoughts when my job had me chasing after people making the same decision.

26

I was pulling out of the bar's parking lot when I remembered my mother's birthday party. *Shit! Fuck!*

I wanted to go home, put some ice on my swollen eye, and chase some ibuprofen down with a few belts of tequila. But I'd promised Jake, and by extension my mother, I'd be there. Bad enough I was late. But if I ghosted again, there'd be hell to pay. Italian Catholic guilt was nothing to sneeze at.

I pulled up in front of my parents' place around seven o'clock. Jake's truck was in their driveway, and Conor's Dodge Charger was parked on the street. My hair and makeup were a wreck. I was still dressed in the revealing blouse and cutoff jeans I'd borrowed from Juanita. I had several messages on my phone from Conor and my family asking where I was. I slipped on a jacket from the go bag I kept in the SUV.

"Sorry I'm late," I hollered as I walked into my parents' house. The dimly lit living room was filled with comfy furniture and a conglomeration of Cajun, Native American, and Mexican artwork. Family photos in brightly colored frames covered the walls. Conor appeared in the doorway to the kitchen as the warm aroma of Italian spices hit my senses.

"Where've ya been, love? We expected ya an hour ago." His face was a mask of concern and anger. "And what the bloody hell happened to your face? Looks like someone's been using you for a punching bag."

I sighed, trying not to react with the anger that boiled just beneath the surface. "Don't start with me, Conor. I've had a shitty day."

He paused for a moment and put a hand on my shoulder. "I'm sorry, love. It's just we've all been worried since ya missed dinner."

"Things sorta went off the rails. I'll fill you in with the gory details later. Right now I just want to eat, if there's anything left."

We joined my family in the kitchen. My mother sat at the table, surrounded by Jake and my dad. Her face was red and puffy.

"About damn time you showed up!" snapped Jake. "What's your excuse this time? Abducted by aliens?"

I ignored him and embraced my mother from behind. "Sorry I'm late, Mom. Happy birthday." I handed her a greeting card I'd picked up on the way over.

She stood and hugged me tightly. "Oh, punkin, I was so worried something happened to you." Her voice was thick with emotion. Guilt welled up in me. I was a horrible daughter.

"Everything's fine." Except for me facing five to twelve years in prison, every trans woman's dream.

"You should have called." She pulled away and held me with her gaze. "And your face. What happened to you?" She touched my swollen eye socket. I tried hard not to wince.

"Just part of the job, Mom. Nothing I can't handle."

"Your job?" She studied my outfit and shook her head.

"Maybe her pimp beat her up," Jake added with a self-indulgent chuckle. "You working as a hooker now, sis? Couldn't cut it as a bounty hunter or a cop?"

"What the hell's wrong with you?" I glared at him. He and I usually got along.

"You're the one dressed like a beat-up crack whore, and you want to know what's wrong with me? That's rich."

I stepped toward my brother, the fire in my gut curling my hands into fists. "You wanna go, big man? Let's go."

"You think you can take me?" Jake shot to his feet and knocked his chair onto its side.

"Someone who doesn't have guts enough to hold his boyfriend's hand in public? You're goddamned right I can." As soon as I mentioned Rodeo, a sharp pang of guilt stabbed me in the gut. I'd promised I wouldn't bring it up. Whoops.

"Stop this right now. Both of you!" My father rose with a stern expression. He was a tall, lanky man who usually had the demeanor of Mr. Rogers. It took a lot to piss him off.

"Sorry, Daddy." I took the seat between him and Conor.

"That's better. I don't know what's gotten into y'all, but it stops now. You hear me?"

Jake and I both nodded, but the heat between us continued to simmer.

"Now, *cher*, there's leftover lasagna in the fridge, if you still want dinner. Although, I was about to serve up the bread pudding and coffee," my dad said.

"Grandma Marie's recipe? With Southern Comfort sauce?"

"It is."

"I'll have some of that, please."

"Very well, then." He sauntered over to the stove and stirred a small saucepot.

The silence thrummed with tension. The antique clock on the wall ticked like a time bomb in an Alfred Hitchcock flick. Just when I felt as if I'd be the one to explode, my father walked in carrying plates of bread pudding on a tray.

"So, Jenna," my mother said softly between bites, "I understand the two of you are moving in together."

I gave Conor the evil eye and clenched my jaw. "We've discussed it. That's all."

"I think it's a grand idea," said my father. "'Bout time y'all got yourselves married."

I choked on a mouthful of bread pudding. "Married? Who said anything about getting married?"

Conor shifted in his seat. "Just speculating about the future, love. That's all."

"Would you wear a white or off-white Kevlar dress?" asked my brother, a snide smile creeping onto his face. "And will you exchange rings or handcuffs?"

"Bite me, asshole," I whispered.

"Language!" my mother scolded.

My father put a hand on my shoulder. "I think you'll be a lovely bride no matter what you wear."

I tossed down my fork, my appetite gone. "We're not getting married, okay? I'm not even sure I want to move in together." I gave Conor a look that said, *See what you started?* "What's next? You going to ask me when we're gonna adopt kids?"

"Oh, punkin." My mother cupped my chin, making me feel like a five-year-old. "No one's saying you have to do anything right away."

I bore holes into the table as I tried to keep my shit together. My head and leg throbbed. I needed to get out of there before I said something I regretted.

"Happy birthday, Mom. But I need to head home."

"But you just got here."

"I'm sorry. It's just my eye hurts, and I'm not very good company right now."

She put her hand on mine. It was warm and brought back a lot of happy feelings from my childhood. "Maybe you should take some time off, punkin. You and Conor could take a trip to San Diego or down to Rocky Point. Spend some time together."

"I'll think about it." I kissed her cheek.

My father stood when I did. "Be careful out there, *cher.*" He kissed the top of my head.

"I will."

"Walk ya out, love?" Conor asked.

I stiffened. "Yeah, I guess."

I followed him out to the street. Even with the jacket, I was shivering. The air was damp and misty, creating halos around the streetlights.

"Come home with me, love. I'll put something on that shiner of yours to bring down the swelling. Take your mind off your troubles."

"Conor, you told them we were moving in together and that we were thinking about getting married."

"I just figured with your mum being Catholic and all, she wouldn't want her little girl living in sin."

"My point is I don't need you airing our dirty laundry with my folks and using them to pressure me. I'm a grown woman. I get to decide who I live with. And when, and *if,* I ever get married. You going behind my back pisses me the hell off."

"Aw, love, I'm not trying to go behind your back. It just slipped out."

"I...I just need some space. Things are crazy now."

"You said ya'd tell me what happened to your face."

I took a deep breath. "Remember me telling you what happened the night of my high school graduation?"

"Aye, your boyfriend's da battered ya near to death."

"Barclay Dietz. Well, he's back in town."

"Jesus fuckin' Christ! He did this to ya? Tell me where he is, and I'll put an end to him straightaway."

"Not that simple. He's mixed up with White Nation." I filled him in on the day's events.

"The bloody cops charged ya with manslaughter? Are ya fuckin' kidding me? This is madness. Can't have ya going to prison for defending yourself against a bunch of racist motherfuckers. How long have ya known this bastard was in town?"

"A couple days."

"A couple days? And you're just telling me now?"

"It's my problem to deal with. Not yours."

"He's a fucking monster. And his mates are right-wing militants. Ya can't go after them alone."

"I had Caden and Rodeo with me."

"You need someone with more experience, love. Someone like me."

"See? And this is why I didn't tell you. I knew you'd want to take charge. I've been a bounty hunter for nearly ten years, most of it working with you. I've learned a thing or two in that time. I can handle myself."

"And yet here ya are with a battered face, a hole in your leg, and charged with murder."

"Manslaughter. But I'll deal with it. Kirsten's good. She'll get the case dismissed." I hoped.

After an awkward moment, Conor took my hand and met my eyes. "Fine. You're a big girl who can handle herself. I won't try to butt in. Just know that I'm here for ya, love."

"I know. That means a lot. It really does."

"Then just for tonight, give yourself a break and let me take care of ya at my place."

It was tempting. "I don't feel like being around anyone right now. Nothing against you, but I need time to process all the shit going round in my head."

He looked like a wounded puppy I'd just kicked. "Are we breakin' up? Is that what this is?"

"What? No. I still love you, you big lunk." I kissed him. "I'll see you tomorrow, okay?"

"All right. Get outta here, ya crazy lass. Before I throw ya over my shoulder and drag ya back to my man cave."

I pulled away from him. I felt torn, longing for his embrace and feeling smothered by it at the same time. I climbed into the Gray Ghost and gave him a finger wave as I drove off.

27

I drove past multicolored constellations of Christmas lights and turned on the radio only to be assaulted by cheesy Christmas songs. I switched the stereo to a playlist I'd created called Bad Girls. Meredith Brooks's song "Bitch" came on—an oldie but a goodie. I cranked it up and scream-sang the lyrics.

Where the fuck does Conor get off telling my family that we're moving in together, much less getting married? As if! Not that I have anything against marriage, but I am so not ready, even though I'm now thirty. Why can't things just stay the way they are?

Gin Wigmore's "Devil in Me" came on as I turned onto my street. But I didn't pull into my driveway. I didn't even stop in front of my house.

Instead, I cruised on past, turned north onto Central, then east on Camelback until I found myself in the parking lot for L Street, a women's bar run by my friends Chelsea and Izzie Quiñones.

If I'd been smart, I would've called a friend, met them for dinner, talked out the shit in my head, and gone home. But I wasn't always that smart. Besides, Becca was dealing with her chronic fatigue. And most of the other people in my life were men. Except for Chelsea and Izzie. So what better place to be but at their bar, right? Drinking on a mostly empty stomach. What could go wrong?

There was only one couple sitting at a table when I walked in. Not surprising, considering it was eight o'clock on a Tuesday. Most of the regulars were probably out Christmas shopping.

Chelsea sat on a stool behind the bar watching a football game. Prominent brow, broad shoulders, and a baritone voice made it hard for her to hide the fact that she was trans. But rather than complain, she just did her own thing. Purple and blue hair, gothy makeup, multiple facial piercings, and a corset wrapped around a billowy, burgundy split-sleeve dress made her a sight to behold. "I don't do subtle," she had told me on more than one occasion.

Behind her, a printed sign mounted on the wall read, "All women are welcome here, regardless of orientation or assigned sex at birth." Someone had written "and nonbinary people" in permanent marker above the word "women."

Chelsea's face lit up when she saw me. "Hey, girl. Didn't expect to see you this evening. How's it going?"

"Don't ask. Gimme a margarita."

She mixed up the drink with the efficiency of an expert bartender. The tequila wasn't top shelf, but I didn't care. "Where'd you get that shiner?"

"Long story."

Wasn't Conor, was it?"

"No."

She placed the drink on the bar. "What brings you out to L Street tonight?"

"Does a girl need a reason to drink?" I downed the drink in a few quick swallows. It burned, and I liked it.

"You and Conor have a fight?"

"Nope." I pushed the glass toward her. "Hit me again."

"What's wrong, Jinxie? You seem wound up."

"Oh, for the love of fuck, why's everyone wanna play armchair psychologist? I just wanna throw back a few without being interrogated. All right?"

She filled my glass without another word and returned to

the game. Deep down, a part of me felt terrible for being rude to her. But I was in a pissy mood, and I was fucking going to let myself be pissy.

I had her refill the glass a few more times. On the fourth request, she said, "Slow down there, sweets. How about some soda or coffee?"

"Fuck that shit. Just gimme another goddamned margarita." The world was starting to feel a little wobbly, but I didn't care.

"I'll give you another, but you'll have to give me your keys. I'm not letting you drive home shit-faced."

"I am not shit-faced. I am comforbly...comfortububbuly...I'm fine, okay. Fine."

Our gazes met. She had gorgeous eyes. Soulful eyes. No wonder her wife, Izzie, was into her. Not that I was attracted to women. But she was adorable. Her lips looked so kissable with the sapphire-blue lipstick. Maybe I was bisexual or pan or whatever. *You never know until you try, right?*

"I'm sorry for being such a bee-atch, Chels! I've had a really, really, *really* shitty day. You forgive me?"

"I forgive you, sweets. Which is why I can't have you driving home in your condition. So fork over them keys." She held out her hand expectantly.

I fished the keys out of my pocket and dangled them next to my face, then beckoned her with a finger. "C'mere. I wanna tell you a little, itty bitty, little shecret...um, I mean, a secret."

She smirked and raised an eyebrow. "What?"

"You gotta come close. I'll whisper it to you."

She bent down. I leaned forward, my lips extended. Her lips were a lot firmer than I thought they'd be and smelled of furniture polish. As she pulled the set of keys out of my hand, I realized she'd backed away. I'd kissed the bar instead.

"Look, Jinxie. I think you're a beautiful woman. And while Izzie and me are poly, I know you and Conor are exclusive. Not gonna let you mess that up over a few drinks. Besides, I've been tending bar far too long to fall for the old 'tell you a secret' trick." Her voice sounded distorted, as if someone had cranked up the reverb or something.

"What? I didn't try to kish you." I kept my hands firmly on the bar as the room gently swayed. "I was just playing around. Gah! You know, that must hurt."

"What must hurt?"

"Having that pool cue stuck up your ass. Seriously, loooshen up."

The jukebox started playing some tired old angsty Melissa Etheridge song. Fuck that shit. "Fuck that shit!" I repeated in my outside voice. "Sappy, pathetic leshbian...shit. That...that's what that shit ish. Where's my drink?"

"Jinx, you've already had six. You don't need any more."

"Shix? Don't you think how shtupid you think I am? I think. I can count, you know. I only had floor of them. Four. Four of them."

"Hello, love." Conor magically appeared in front of me. *How's he do that? Must be some kind of Irish faerie leprechaun magic shit.*

"Heeeeyyy, babeee... What're you doing here? Don't you know boys aren't allowed in here?" I reached out to him and felt myself topple into his arms. His powerful arms. Goddamn, I loved that man. Fuck women, I got me a real man's man.

"Come on, love. Let's get ya home. I'll even hold your hair when ya hurl."

"No, no, no, no. I doan wanna go home. It's haunted."

"Thanks." Conor winked at me. No, not at me. He winked at Chelsea.

"Doan you go winking at her, Mr. Man! She's a married woman." My body was moving, but the room felt as if gravity kept pulling at odd angles. "Ugh, she gave me some bad liquor, I think. Fucking cheap tequila. Tastes like horsh pisses and fire. Maybe she gave me a roofie. Trying to get me in bed with her. Oh, fuck, I think I'm gonna be sick."

No sooner did the icy December night air hit my face than I

was puking my guts up outside the front door. My throat closed up, and I struggled to get air. *Oh fucking shit. I can't breathe. Oh shit. I'm gonna die.*

"Just relax, love. You're hyperventilating." His hand on my back felt good. I pushed against the panic. Air seeped into my burning lungs.

"Breathe, Jinxie. Breathe."

I breathed and stood up. I wobbled only a little bit with Conor holding me up. Damn, he smelled so good. I wanted to feel his warm body against mine.

Puke was splattered all over the rainbow welcome mat by the bar's front door. Served them right for selling such shitty booze. Mexicans didn't know shit about liquor. But the Irish, though, they knew whiskey. Irish. Like my Irish honey.

"Ya gonna be okay, love?"

"Yeah, I think so." My stomach felt better. But the taste of bile remained burning in my mouth.

"Let's get ya home." He opened a car door and was man-handling me into the front seat.

"Keep your man hands off of me, mister. I'm not a child, you know." I bumped my head and tumbled into the bucket seat.

"You're bloody acting like a toddler. Now put on your seat belt, or do ya need help with that too?" He was sitting in the driver's seat already. *Holy shit, how'd he fucking do that?*

"I can do it." I yanked on the seat belt, and it jammed. I yanked it again, but it wouldn't pull. "If it wasn't fucking stuck."

Conor sighed. "Ya got to be gentle with it." He took the buckle from my hand and pulled it out and clicked it shut.

"Yeah, works for you." I folded my arms and stared out at the cars driving past on Camelback Road. In the distance, a siren wailed. Red and blue flashing lights blew past. "Uh-oh."

"What's wrong?" asked Conor, pulling onto the street in the same direction the police cruiser went. "You're not gonna be sick again, are ya?"

"No! Gah!" I sneered at him and pointed at the disappearing

lights of the ambulance. "Someone's having a bad night." It was something my father always said any time he heard sirens or saw flashing lights.

"Yeah," said Conor. "That someone is me."

28

"Wake up, sleepyhead! Time to catch bad guys."

I opened my eyes to a Conor-shaped silhouette in front of a window. His eyes burned like lasers into my skull. Or maybe that was just the sunlight coming through. My mouth tasted of cotton flavored with tequila and cat shit. My body felt as if I'd somersaulted off the top of the Papago Buttes. My hair smelled like puke.

"I…whuh?" My mouth didn't seem to want to kick into gear.

Conor stepped away from the window, pulling a shirt over his ripped body. "Come on, love. We both got people to track down."

I pulled myself into a seated position on the bed and stared at the floor until the room quit spinning. I could tell from the tile we were at Conor's bunker. "What the hell happened last night?"

"I picked ya up at L Street after Chelsea called me."

"Why would Chelsea call you?"

"Prolly 'cause ya were shite-faced, and she didn't want to deal with your drunken nonsense any longer."

I sneered at him. "Rude."

"Aye. That you were." He wasn't smiling much. So not like him.

"Well, thanks for that, I guess."

"Come on. We gotta go."

"Just go on. I've got a key. I'll head out when I'm feeling a little more human."

"Yer lorry's still at the bar."

Vague memories of being at the bar flitted in and out of reach. A deep desire to kiss Chelsea's pillowy blue lips bubbled up, as well. "Oh yeah. Damn, I hope I didn't do anything stupid."

"Aside from dancing naked on the bar while cry-singing 'Total Eclipse of the Heart'—"

"What?" My jaw hit the floor.

"Just funnin' with ya. Ya weren't naked. At least not in the video posted on L Street's Facebook page."

"Fuck." I pulled on my clothes and shoes. My phone showed that Sadie had texted me, asking if I'd caught Pratt yet. *Shit.*

"Let's pick up the Gray Ghost before some wanker takes it for a joyride or uses it as a canvas for a spray-painted public art project." Conor tossed me my keys. "Then ya can go home and make yerself presentable."

"I'm presentable," I protested, trying to finger comb the knots out of my hair.

"Aye! I forgot 'homeless hipster' is the popular new look these days. That shiner ya got makes quite the fashion statement. Purple's a good color on ya."

I flipped him off and followed him out to his Dodge Charger. *Men and their muscle cars.*

A while later, we pulled into the L Street parking lot. Thankfully, the Gray Ghost was still there with all four tires and no custom paint jobs. A piece of paper under the windshield wipers warned me of hellfire and damnation unless I repented of my perverted lifestyle and surrendered to white Jesus. I crumpled it and tossed it into a dumpster.

Conor walked with me to the door of my SUV. "I'm sorry I've been so pushy about moving in together. I know you're working through a lot, especially with that gobshite of a boxer being back in town. But I want ya to know I'm here for ya. I love ya." His voice grew hoarse with emotion. "I don't want anything to happen to ya. So watch your arse."

"I know. I love you too. Once I bring Barclay Dietz to justice, I'll be in a better headspace to figure out this moving-in-together business."

"I'm happy to help ya out with Dietz. Caden and Rodeo only have a couple years of experience between them. You're going to need more than that to handle this bloke."

"I'll take it under advisement. By the way, Juanita's having her Barbra Streisand fundraiser tonight at eight. Will you come with me?"

"If you want me there, I'm there, love. Want me to pick you up? Or will that also be cramping your style?"

I wasn't sure if he was joking or serious. I wasn't sure of much of anything anymore. "Pick me up around seven fifteen."

We kissed, lightly at first and then more intensely.

"Thanks," I said as I pulled away, more than a little breathless. "For picking me up last night. And for being patient with me."

"You're most welcome, love."

I climbed into the Gray Ghost and dove into the morning rush hour traffic clogging Camelback Road. It took me nearly thirty minutes to go four miles. By the time I pulled into my driveway, I was so frustrated with slow, inattentive drivers that I was ready to strangle a small child.

I started the coffeepot, choked down two ibuprofen, and hopped in the shower to wash off a night of shame.

When I reemerged smelling less like a sewer than I did when I went in, I poured a cup of hot bitterness into my favorite Bitch with a Big Ass Gun mug. I opened my laptop at the kitchen table and studied the files Becca had sent me on Pratt's credit card statements, phone logs, and social media activity. There was nothing since he jumped bail, but maybe there was something from the past few months that would point to his current whereabouts.

As my eyes began to cross, I turned to his past emails.

Plenty of forwarded cartoons and jokes rife with racist and homophobic stereotypes. No shortage of newsletters from extremist right-wing organizations.

Becca had also uncovered a subreddit titled Pure Gardening where Pratt posted under the handle Crizaba. The posts seemed to have an aggressive, almost militaristic tone, especially toward weeds and invasive plant species. I guessed some people got rather passionate about their hobbies.

None of the documentation gave me a clue where Pratt might be hiding out.

I was about to pour another cup of coffee when the roof creaked. I nearly jumped out of my skin. Once again, I got a strong feeling I was being watched. Driven by a deep sense of paranoia and a need to figure out what the hell was going on, I scoured the kitchen, looking for hidden cameras or bugs. It wouldn't be the first time a violent criminal had tried to turn the tables on me.

But after two hours of disassembling toasters, light fixtures, and outlets, sifting through flour and sugar canisters, and checking behind the refrigerator and dishwasher, I turned up exactly squat. Clearly, my instincts had gone haywire, probably induced by a combination of past traumas, legal troubles, and a lack of sleep.

If my dad had been there, he'd have told me to spend the day resting. But I couldn't. Not while Pratt and Dietz were walking the streets free as a bird. And not while my own freedom was in jeopardy thanks to the White Nation pricks.

So instead of a nap, I grabbed my gear and did what bounty hunters do. I drove by Pratt's house. When there was still no sign of life in the house, I recanvassed his neighbors, then spoke with Pratt's former coworkers. I called the contacts on his bail application, trying every trick in the book. The contest winner scheme. The lost wallet scheme. Even a promise that an organ donor had been found for his daughter. Not a goddamn thing worked.

Around one o'clock, I stopped by Peyton's apartment. His roomie, Hughie, was unexpectedly coherent but hadn't seen Peyton for the past day or so. The manager at San Tan Liquors said the same thing and was pissed off that Peyton had missed a shift without calling in. Had Barclay reached out to his son? Or had something happened to him?

A call to Becca yielded nothing new on either Pratt or the Dietzes. I reconnected with the nurse at Camelback Children's Hospital, where his daughter was being treated. She told me Pratt was now banned from the hospital. If he showed up, they had instructions to call me, then the police.

By four o'clock, I decided I'd struck out for the day. Such is the life of a bounty hunter. Just as fishing isn't necessarily catching, searching isn't always finding. Some days were spent going through the motions, shaking the trees, hoping something would eventually shake loose.

29

I got home and took a shower, spending way too long trying to style my hair. It refused to hold a curl or do anything but hang stick straight. As a last resort, I put it up into a French braid.

The swelling in my face had gone down a bit, but no amount of makeup would hide the black eye. Instead, I went heavy on the eyeliner and some dark-purple eye shadow to even things out.

With that done, I stared blankly at my closet. I couldn't remember the last time I'd worn anything even close to formal. I don't usually hang with the evening gown crowd. Galas, fundraisers, and holiday soirees aren't my scene. I prefer to be low-maintenance and casual, for which Juanita gives me no end of grief.

After twenty minutes, I settled on an indigo dress that hadn't seen the light of day for years. I used a lint brush to remove the layer of dust on the shoulders. The collar was cut low and fringed with lace. The bodice was shaped to give the illusion that I had hips. The hem came to midcalf with a slit up one side. I paired it with a cute pair of filigree tights to hide the large bandage on my calf.

I accessorized with midnight-blue three-inch heels, a pair of diamond stud earrings my mother had given me, and a small skull cameo pendant on a white gold choker.

I studied my reflection in the full-length mirror. I was a dime-store diva at best. Oh well. If Conor or Juanita didn't like it, tough. I was there to enjoy myself and to donate two hundred bucks for a rubber chicken dinner and a campy performance of Barbra Streisand numbers by a foursome in drag.

"Don't *you* look deadly," said a deep voice behind me.

I whirled around, grabbed a plaster statue of Wonder Woman from my dresser, and prepared to throw it at my intruder.

Conor stood in my bedroom doorway looking like James Bond in a tailored tuxedo. That is, if James Bond had red curls and freckles. Suddenly I felt very underdressed.

"You think so?" I gave him an insecure smile.

"Absolutely smashing, love." He kissed me. "Ya gonna bludgeon me with that Wonder Woman doll?"

"What?" I looked at the statue in my hand and set it down. "Sorry, I've been a bit jumpy today."

"Didn't get much rest after I left, eh?"

"You look great." I gave him a hug. "Smell great too. I have half a mind to throw you down on my bed and have my way with you."

"Not that I would object, love, but I think we best get going or we're gonna be late."

I was tempted to say screw the event, but I was already going to be in hot water when Juanita learned the wig she'd loaned me was now in Phoenix PD's property room. I grabbed my clutch purse and followed Conor to his car.

When we arrived at the club, a large sign at the entrance of the parking lot read "Lot Full."

"Damn, I had no idea this was going to be so popular," I said.

Conor pulled into the small shopping center on the other side of the club and found a spot. I stepped out and felt exposed and vulnerable, in part because of the dress and heels but mostly because I was unarmed. I'd considered stashing a subcompact semiauto in my clutch, but it would have been too heavy and just felt wrong. I wasn't on the job, hunting some scumbag bail jumper. I was here to celebrate queer culture and raise money for the youth community center.

The speakers outside the club were playing high-energy, EDM versions of Barbra Streisand's more upbeat songs like "The Main Event" and "No More Tears." At the door, a familiar burly man in a white tux and glittery eye shadow stood collecting tickets. His face lit up when he spotted me.

"Oh my Gloria Estefan! Could it be? The one and only Jinx Ballou? How the hell are you?" He hugged me so hard I swore I felt ribs cracking.

"Good to see you too, Mace." I gasped as he released me.

"And in a dress? I never thought I'd see the day."

"Yeah, well, it's kinda hard to chase down fugitives in a ball gown and heels." I gave his bushy beard a playful tug. "Nice man-moss, by the way."

"You like it? My boyfriend says I look like a hipster wannabe. Though he doesn't complain when I go down on him. He likes the way it tickles his jubblies."

"Ew, TMI!" I said with a smirk.

Conor cleared his throat and gave me the side-eye. "Sorry! Mace, this is my boyfriend, Conor. Babe, Mace here is one of the Main Drag's top performers."

"My, my, my!" crooned Mace, sidling up next to Conor, who blushed bright red. "You are one fine hunk of man meat."

I put up a hand between them. "Hands off, bitch," I teased. "He's mine, and he's straight."

"Ha! That's what they all say."

"Pleasure to meet ya, Mace." Conor offered his hand to shake.

Mace took it and kissed Conor's knuckles. "Oh my, what an accent. I'm verklempt. Is it hot out here or is it you?"

"Yo, Mace!" called someone behind me. "You taking tickets or staging your own sex show? We're freezing our nuts off out here."

"Shut it, bitch!" Mace replied while taking our tickets. "These young queens are so rude. Y'all have a good time at the show. And thank you for supporting the Phoenix Queer Youth Center."

"Thanks, sweetie."

Conor's face was still glowing red as we walked into the nightclub. "Well, he…or she was interesting."

"Yeah, he can be a bit of a cliché, but he's a sweetheart. He and his boyfriend, Chad, let me crash on their couch for a while after I caught Wilson fucking around on me."

We stepped through the lobby into the main hall. I'd been to the Main Drag dozens of times and almost didn't recognize the place. The mismatched garage sale tables were now draped in elegant white cloths and set with candles and holiday greenery. The scent of pine and pumpkin spice replaced the usual reek of cheap cologne and beer.

"Wow, you'd never know what a shit hole it usually looks like," I whispered to Conor, who chuckled in response. "And if you ever tell Juanita I said that, I will kill you in your sleep."

"Duly noted, love."

We threaded our way through the candlelit tables until we found Rodeo sitting with an Asian-American woman I didn't recognize. He wore a lavender tux with a matching cummerbund and a white ruffled shirt. Her dress glittered as if woven of diamonds.

"Mind if we join you?" I asked.

"Not at all. Guys, this is Nicole." Rodeo gestured toward us as we sat. "Jinx and Conor are fellow bounty hunters."

I was surprised to see Rodeo with a date so soon after dumping my brother. Of course, considering what an asshole my brother had been lately, it'd serve him right to see Rodeo hook up with someone else so fast.

"Pleasure to meet you." Nicole's eyes sparkled in the flickering candlelight.

"Likewise," I replied.

Caden and Kirsten walked up holding drinks. Caden's face brightened when he caught my eye. "Look who I found by the bar."

"Hey, I'm an attorney. Where else would I be?" Kirsten

snorted at her own joke. She and Caden took the two remaining chairs at the table. "Seriously, though, since getting surgery a few years ago, I've drifted away from the queer community. Figured it was time I show up and give something back."

Nicole started to say something, but half the lights overhead blinked off. "Ladies, gentlemen, and the rest of us," came Mace's voice over the sound system, "please take your seats. Tonight's entertainment is about to begin."

A moment later, the remaining lights went out, replaced by a spotlight blazing on the center of the stage. The crowd hushed in a rustle of people finding their seats. The clack of high heels echoed in the large room, and Juanita stepped into the light in full Tía Juana regalia. "Hello, bitches!"

"Hello, bitch!" the drag bar's well-trained regulars replied in unison.

"Damn straight!" Juanita strutted across the stage. "For those who don't already know me, my name's Tía Juana, and I will be your Monster of Ceremonies."

"You better work, bitch!" yelled someone from the audience.

Without missing a beat, she snapped her fingers and said with a wry grin, "I always work, motherfucker!"

The crowd roared with laughter.

"However, this is a special occasion. Tonight we are here to help fund the rebuilding of the Phoenix Queer Youth Center that was damaged in a recent fire. And I want to thank each and every one of you bitches for your generous support."

The crowd erupted again in applause so thunderous I feared the roof would collapse.

"So without any further ado, I want to introduce four fabulous ladies who have taken the musical stylings of Saint Barbra of Streisand to a place no one ever dared. And Goddess willing, no one will again. I give you, the Barbra Shop Quartet."

The spotlight vanished. The opening notes from *Yentl's* "Papa, Can You Hear Me?" began amid a final surge of cheers. When the spotlight returned, a façade of a barbershop had been lowered to stage. Four of the campiest Barbra ever impersonators appeared in skimpy barbershop quartet costumes.

As bizarre as it was to hear Streisand tunes performed in four-part harmonies, I had to admit the performers were remarkably talented. I found myself entranced in this mishmash of genres. Songs from my childhood were transformed into something oddly mesmerizing.

Just as the quartet finished singing "Somewhere" from *West Side Story*, a man shouted, "Fucking fairies!"

I turned to see three dark figures standing in the aisle fifteen feet away. The place erupted in automatic gunfire.

30

The four drag queens fell, their bodies ripped apart in sprays of blood and gore. Audience members screamed and ran in all directions.

I dropped to the floor, peering above the table toward the thunder of the automatic weapons. I counted muzzle flashes from three automatic weapons held by the strangers in the aisle. I reached for my sidearm only to find the fabric of my dress and nothing more. *Shit!*

I slipped off my heels and gripped one of them like a weapon. Whoever these fuckers were, I wasn't going to let them hurt my friends without a fight.

Keeping low, I hustled between the tables and toward the gunmen. Conor and Rodeo appeared next to me amid the strobe light of muzzle flashes.

I paused a few feet from the shooters. When the rifle of the gunman nearest me ran empty, I pounced before he could reload. I drove the three-inch heel into the back of the attacker's head. When he stumbled, I reached for his rifle and blistered my left hand on the barrel.

The gunman struggled to his feet. I adjusted my grip and drove the butt of the rifle into his head and torso repeatedly, driven by pent-up rage.

Overhead lights blazed on, blinding me for an instant. I squinted, adjusting to the glare.

A hand clasped my shoulder. "Jinxie, ya can stop now. It's over."

Instinctively, I whipped around and nearly took off Conor's head before I recognized him.

"Shit." I lowered the AR-15 in my hand.

Conor was holding the Walther PPX he usually carried on one of the other gunmen, who lay cuffed facedown on the floor. Like the other two gunmen, he was dressed all in black with a balaclava over his face. When Conor unmasked him, I recognized him as Quinton, one of the guys from Dixie's.

I turned back to the gunman I'd disarmed. I pulled the balaclava from his head and felt my gorge rise. His face had been reduced to a pulpy mess.

Spent bullet casings, empty magazines, and two other AR-15s littered the floor. As my ears recovered from the deafening roar of the gunfire, I noticed the dozens of people crying and screaming in agony. The air was sharp with the taste of spent gunpowder and spilled blood.

"Are ya hit, love?" Conor stepped in front of me, inspecting me for wounds.

My legs and dress were splattered with blood. Angry blisters bulged on my palm from grabbing the hot rifle barrel, but that was the worst of it. "No, no, I don't think so. You okay?"

"Nary a scratch."

"What happened to the third shooter?"

He grimaced. "Bloody wanker got away."

"Jinx." A strained voice caught my attention.

Rodeo lay on the floor, his face twisted in pain. A woman in an emerald gown knelt over him, using his cummerbund as a makeshift compress on his shoulder. His once bone-white shirt was now a study in scarlet.

I crouched down next to them. "Shit! How bad is it?"

"This?" He scrunched his face, trying to smile. "Just a skeeter bite. Had hickeys worse than this."

"Liar," said the woman treating him. "Looks like he took

a small-caliber round to the shoulder. Doesn't appear to have hit a major artery. But the slug's still in there."

"You a doc?" I asked, hoping.

"Trauma nurse. Maricopa Medical. Treated more than my fair share of GSWs."

"What happened?" I asked Rodeo.

"One of the shooters dropped his AR-15. Jammed or something. I thought I had him, but he pulled out a pistol. Shot someone on stage and then nailed me."

"Well, sounds like you're in good hands, Rodeo. I'm going to check on the other wounded."

"Find Nicole," he grunted. "My aunt'll kill me if something happened to her."

"Your aunt?"

"She's my cousin. Came out last summer." He took a deep breath, obviously trying to control the pain. "Begged me to come to this shindig."

"I'll keep an eye out for her."

I took a deep breath myself and tried to clear my head from the jumble of sharp emotions. I surveyed the chaotic scene around me. Numerous tables and chairs lay on their sides. A nearby tablecloth had caught fire from a capsized candle.

Broken bodies lay scattered across the room like carcasses in an unruly slaughterhouse. Survivors struggled to save the injured, while others trembled under the imagined safety of their tables and chairs. Across the aisle, Mace sobbed and pleaded on the phone with a 911 operator.

I turned toward the carnage onstage. Caden was kneeling over someone. I pushed people out of my way and vaulted onto the stage to where Juanita lay on the floor near the other drag queens. Caden's hand pressed against her blood-smeared forehead. My knees buckled, and I knelt on the other side of her.

"Juanita! Shit! What happened?"

"They...they shot her," he said in a choking voice. "They fucking shot her."

Panic threatened to undo me. I channeled the rush of adrenaline to keep my anguish in check and focus on the situation. "Is there an exit wound?"

Caden shook his head. "Don't think so."

"Keep the pressure on," I told Caden. "Don't let her bleed out."

I turned to the other drag queens. Three of the Barbras were dead from multiple gunshots that left baseball-sized exit wounds. High-velocity rounds tended to have that effect.

A nearby whimpering caught my attention. Behind the barbershop façade, I found the fourth Barbra—a short African-American drag queen named Blake Washington—in a fetal position, clutching his wig, mascara streaming down his gore-splattered face.

"Blake, are you hit?" I knelt and put a hand on his trembling arm. There was blood on his bare shoulders and his dress, but no visible wounds.

"Why?" he squeaked in a trembling tenor voice. "Why'd they do this?"

"Blake, look at me. Are you hurt anywhere?"

His face was that of a terrified child. His pupils were wide as saucers. He was in shock. I examined him as best I could. No physical wounds that I could find. Just emotional trauma. I sat next to him and held him close. "Hang in there, Blake. We're going to get through this."

31

By the time the police secured the area and medical personnel arrived, I had counted at least fifteen people dead. Dozens of others were severely wounded and traumatized. Rodeo had been transported to the hospital, with his cousin Nicole trailing after the ambulance. Those of us with noncritical injuries were herded into the club's lobby to await questioning.

Conor, Caden, Kirsten, and I huddled together in a far corner. An EMT had treated my burned hand and loosely wrapped it in gauze. Despite Conor's jacket draped over my shoulders, I shivered from adrenaline withdrawal and the chill of the December night air blowing through the lobby's open doors.

As we waited, I consulted privately with Kirsten, giving her my account of events. She made some suggestions on wording and on specific questions she didn't want me to answer.

When my father called, having seen the reports on the ten o'clock news, I assured him I was okay and would talk to him in the morning.

Around midnight, a familiar figure stepped through the front doors, carrying a case file. Detective Hardin looked grim and exhausted. "Ballou." He beckoned me with a finger.

"Detective." I pushed myself to my feet. My legs felt unsteady, my mind a scorched wasteland of exhaustion, sorrow, and anger.

Kirsten stood. "I'll join you two, if you don't mind. I'm her attorney."

"I know who you are, Ms. Pasternak. You're also a witness."

"While I was in the audience when the events transpired, I'm afraid I wasn't close enough to see the assailants. When the shooting began, I helped people nearby take shelter behind one of the tables. That is the entirety of my statement."

Hardin regarded her for a second. "Very well." He led us out the front door and into a small room in a Tactical Command Center van parked on the street.

"Can I get either of you anything? Coffee? A snack?" Hardin asked as if we'd just dropped in for a casual chat.

I shook my head as we sat. "No, thanks."

Hardin set down the case file and opened a notebook, with pen at the ready. "What can you tell me about this evening's events?"

Kirsten nodded before I spoke. "During the performance, three men entered the club dressed in all-black and wearing balaclavas. Each carried an assault rifle full-auto. At least two were white, average height and weight. I didn't get a good look at the third. He escaped before the lights went up."

"And what happened?"

"One shouted the words 'Fucking fairies' right before they opened fire. First at the performers on stage, then spraying the audience."

"What did you do when the shooting started?"

"My crew and I disarmed two of them. One got away."

"Your bounty hunter crew?"

"Yes."

"Were any of you armed?"

"I was not armed, no."

"How about your crew?"

"You would have to ask them."

"What happened to your hand?"

"Burned it on the barrel of one of the attackers' rifles when I attempted to disarm him."

"Did you recognize these men?"

"The two we captured are members of White Nation. I recognized them when I crashed one of their meetings looking for two fugitives."

"That when you shot the guy at Dixie's?"

"In self-defense."

"Is that why they attacked the club? Retribution?"

Pangs of guilt constricted my chest as I thought about the shootout at Dixie's. *Was this retaliation?* "Have to ask them."

"One of the suspected shooters suffered a massive head wound." Hardin held out his phone with a photo of my guy's bashed-in head. "What can you tell me about this?"

I resisted the urge to glance at Kirsten. We'd discussed this. "All I know is that my crew and I acted to disarm the assailants in an attempt to save lives. It was dark, and everything happened fast. I don't recall a lot of details."

Hardin eyed me warily. If he persisted in this line of questioning, Kirsten would step in.

"After the suspects were, uh, disarmed, what did you do?"

"I assisted in helping the injured and the traumatized."

Officer Evans popped his head in the room, gave me a quick look, and whispered something to Hardin while handing him a piece of paper.

Hardin thanked him, and Evans stepped out again with a sneer. *What the fuck was that about?* I wondered.

"Ballou, do we have some sort of gang war going on?"

"Detective, my client is not a member of any gang," said Kirsten. "Her actions at Dixie's Bar were well within her lawful duties as a licensed bail enforcement agent. The fact that your department is charging her with manslaughter for defending herself from a room of armed racist militants is a travesty of justice."

"Counselor, your client—"

"I'm not finished, Detective. If the violent nationalists of White Nation are seeking payback for my client's attempt to return to custody a fugitive whom they are illegally harboring, then that is on them."

Go, Kirsten! I was so wiped out emotionally and physically, I almost stood up and gave her a woop-woop!

Hardin flipped a page in his notebook. "Anything else you can tell me about this evening's events?"

"No."

Hardin reviewed his notes and scribbled a few more as if we weren't there. If he was hoping to get me talking to fill the silence, it wasn't working.

"Detective Hardin," said Kirsten. "Unless you have further questions for either myself or my client, we will be going."

Hardin leaned back and crossed his arms. "Whatever's going on between your *crew* and White Nation, it stops now. You got me, Ballou?"

"I'm merely tracking down fugitives and returning them to custody. I got no interest in anything else White Nation or anyone else has going on."

"I don't want any more bodies dropping on my streets because of this." Hardin closed his case folder. "Call me if either of you remembers anything else to assist us in our investigation."

"Yeah," I said. "I'll do that."

After thanking Kirsten for her help, I found Conor standing alone inside the lobby. He looked like I felt. His eyes held the haunted look of past traumas. "How ya holding up, love?"

I hugged him. "I've had better days."

"Aye. It's a bloody pisser. At least we stopped the bastards when we did."

"I want to go to the hospital," I said. "Need to check on Juanita and Rodeo."

"Jinx..." Conor's face darkened. "I...I can't."

"Dude, seriously, it's been, what, twenty years? You need to get over your phobia of hospitals."

"It's not that simple. Bernie...she was my fucking sister."

"Yes, and Juanita is my family. So's Rodeo." My voice choked with emotion. I couldn't get the image of Juanita's bloody face out of my mind. "I know you were traumatized by your sister's death. And I know you blame yourself. But that was a lifetime ago."

"It's gonna be a madhouse, love. We'd just be in the way."

"Being there for family isn't being in the way. But if you're too chickenshit to help me…" I pulled off his jacket and threw it at him.

"Jinx!"

"Go home, Conor." I slipped off my heels and started fast-walking barefoot down the ice-cold sidewalk in the direction of the hospital.

"Jinxie, stop!" He grabbed my arm and wheeled me around.

"What?" My eyes burned into him. My head felt as if it would explode.

"I can…"

"You can what?"

He took a deep breath and released it. "I can at least give you a ride."

"Oh gee, thanks! Don't do me any favors!" I pulled away, but he held on.

"Don't be daft. Ya can't walk all the way to hospital in your bare feet. Look, I…" His eyes closed and jaw tensed. "I will come in with you. And when it gets too much, I'll…step outside for some air or something. Do you know where they took Juanita? All these casualties, they probably took people to several different hospitals."

"I got a text from Rodeo. He and Caden are at John C. Lincoln, where Juanita's in surgery."

In an awkward silence, we drove to the hospital in Conor's Charger and parked in the nearby garage. I led him through the glass doors of the ER. "Fuck me," I muttered under my breath.

32

The waiting room was wall-to-wall people. Interspersed among the usual crowd of flu sufferers, home accident casualties, and car crash victims were the survivors from the Main Drag shooting in bloodstained formal wear.

People squeezed onto crowded waiting room benches and huddled together on the floor. The more severely injured lay on gurneys stacked two deep against the walls. Medical personnel hurried about, leaving shoe prints on the blood-speckled linoleum.

The sounds of sobbing melded with muffled voices from the televisions mounted on the wall. The tension and trauma was so palpable I could literally taste it—a metallic, bitter flavor that cut through me like a Japanese blade.

Conor stopped abruptly, as if his feet were cemented to the floor. He looked like a man walking to his execution. "I'm sorry, love. I…I thought I could stay here, but I can't." He backed away toward the door, and I followed.

"Why not? You did when I got hurt last year. And when Deez was shot the year before that."

"I know." He swallowed hard, his chest heaving. "But it wasn't like this. This…this is Omagh all over again. Bodies and blood everywhere."

I held his trembling, tear-strewn face in my hands. Instead of a badass bounty hunter, I saw a terrified boy, haunted by shame for a crime he could never make right. I wanted to sympathize, to tell him I understood. But I didn't. People I loved were here, clinging to life if they weren't already dead. I couldn't be there for them and play nursemaid to Conor as well.

"Look, I get this is hard for you. But our friends need us. And I need you. I can't do this alone."

"I'm sorry. I just can't." He started to pull away, and I grabbed his arm.

"Conor, stop! Yes, you can."

He shook his head like a dog shaking off water. "I can't. I just. Fucking. Can't! Every time I walk into a hospital, I keep seeing Bernie's blood-splattered face. Her broken body. And I know it's my fault. I never should have made that phone call. I never should have...I don't know."

I thought of Juanita, lying on the stage. Caden desperately pressing against the head wound. A flood of memories filled my mind. Juanita teaching me how to walk like a girl, how to do makeup, even all the times she teased and taunted me in her sassy, drag queen way. She was my fairy drag mother. Anger, sorrow, and abandonment wrapped together into a single, raw emotion, which I directed at Conor.

"Do whatever the hell you want." I stormed away and searched the waiting room for Caden and Rodeo.

I found them sitting on a bench underneath one of the televisions. Caden scooted over and let me squeeze in. Rodeo's arm was in a sling. A large bandage was wrapped around his shoulder and upper arm. His eyes were glassy, and he had a dopey grin on his face. Clearly not feeling any pain.

"Hey," I whispered. "How's the shoulder?"

"Fucking awesome," said Rodeo.

"Aside from the painkillers they gave you."

His smile cooled. "They say the bullet tore through my upper arm. Nicked the humerus, but no damage to the shoulder joint. They patched me up, told me to take it easy for the next six weeks, and wrote me a script for some good drugs."

"I'm surprised the hospital didn't admit you."

"Short on beds. I was noncritical."

"Where's your cousin? What's her name? Natalie?"

"Nicole. I gave her the keys to my Mazda and told her to go home. This shit messed her up bad."

I hugged him and turned to Caden. "Any word on Juanita?"

Caden's eyes bubbled with tears. He still had dried blood on his arm. "Still in surgery. It's not good, Jinx. Even if she lives, there's a good chance she could become a vegetable."

I didn't want to hear this. "Yeah, well, she's tougher than ten-year-old beef jerky. She'll pull through," I said as much to convince myself as anyone else.

"Where's Conor?" asked Rodeo.

"Doesn't matter."

Rodeo nodded. He'd worked with Conor enough to know about his deep-seated fear of hospitals. "This must've really freaked him out."

"We're all freaked. The important thing is you guys are here."

"Any IDs on the shooters?" asked Caden.

"I recognized two of them from Dixie's," I said.

"Shit," said Caden. "You think it was retaliation?"

I didn't want to admit it, but I feared it was. Guilt twisted my insides like a corkscrew.

I should have kept my cool and waited to grab Dietz when he wasn't surrounded by a room full of allies. I could have tailed him to wherever he was staying. But no, I had to act like an impulsive teenager. And now my lack of self-control had cost the lives of more than a dozen members of my own community.

I shook my head. "I don't know. White Nation's planning a rally on Saturday to protest the city removing the Confederate Troops Memorial in Wesley Bolin Plaza. Got a feeling it's going to be bigger than the Charlottesville protest. And possibly deadlier."

"We gotta do something to teach them a lesson." Caden's voice crackled with anger.

I put a hand on his shoulder. "No. We do our job. When we get a lead on Pratt or Dietz, we go after them. But that's it. They already charged me with manslaughter. Don't need you two getting in trouble too."

The conversation dwindled. I tried to catch some z's while sitting on the bench, but after a couple of hours, my butt ached. I wandered outside for some fresh air and called Conor. I was pissed at him for leaving, and at the same time, I still needed him.

"How is everyone?" he asked.

I wanted to get snarky with him, but I held my tongue. "Rodeo'll survive, but he's out of commission for a month or so."

"And Juanita?"

"Still in surgery last I heard."

"Tell everyone I'm pulling for her."

"Yeah, yeah, thoughts and prayers and all that shit."

"Even if I was there, there's not shite I could do for her, love."

"No, but you could be here for me."

"I wish I could, love. I thought I'd have a heart attack in that waiting room. Bodies lining the wall. Blood on the floor. Smelling like a goddamned slaughterhouse. It was just like hospital in Omagh."

"You can't run from the past forever, Conor. Sooner or later, you gotta face it and move on."

"I'm trying, love. Truly I am. I'm at home, trying not to watch the telly. But I can't stop myself."

"Oh, so you can watch it on the news, but you can't be here for me? That's such bullshit, Conor." I hung up and walked back inside.

"Is Juanita Valdez's family here?" called a pear-shaped white guy in forest-green scrubs and a matching surgical cap.

"I'm her family." I rushed over to him with Caden and Rodeo right behind me.

"And you are?"

"I'm her daughter, Jenna." Close enough to the damned truth.

He gave me a disbelieving look. "But he's—"

"She!" I corrected.

"She's black and you're…"

"Adopted. How is she?"

"I'm Dr. Linden. I'm one of the neurosurgeons on the team. She came in with a gunshot wound to the right frontal lobe." He pointed at the right side of his forehead. "We managed to remove the slug, but we've had to temporarily remove a portion of the skull to alleviate the pressure on the brain caused by swelling."

"Fuck." Caden covered his mouth with his hand.

I felt sick to my stomach, but I had to be strong for Juanita. "What's her prognosis?"

"There are a lot of variables that can affect both short-term and long-term outcomes. On the one hand, the slug appears to be a small-caliber bullet from a handgun. Much less damage than from the high-velocity rounds we've seen a lot of this evening."

"Thank the stars for small favors," I muttered.

"Also, the bullet only penetrated about three millimeters from the entry wound, confining the injury to a single lobe in the right hemisphere. The human brain can often compensate when the damage isn't too extensive."

"So she'll recover?" asked Caden.

The doctor's expression darkened. "Maybe. She lost a lot of blood. Her being HIV positive also complicates matters. While her viral load is very low, her compromised immune system means the risk of infection is high."

Just when I was starting to have hope.

"A neurosurgeon by the name of Dr. Lisa Wolfe is en route from Seattle. She specializes in this type of traumatic head injury with patients who are HIV positive. When she gets here, we'll assess Ms. Valdez's condition and formulate a game plan."

"What're her chances?" I asked, trying to ignore my heart going full throttle in my chest. I couldn't get the image of Juanita's blood-smeared face out of my head.

"Best-case scenario, once she's stabilized, we'll transfer her to a rehab facility where she'll receive physical, speech, and occupational therapy. The part of the brain in question handles certain types of memory, spatial reasoning, and some motor functions, including speech. We won't know how significantly she's been affected until she regains consciousness. If she does."

"You're saying she might not wake up?" Caden asked, his voice breaking.

"We simply have to wait and see. We'll know more once Dr. Wolfe has had a chance to evaluate her."

Caden looked as though he was about to collapse. Rodeo and I put our arms around him. If I couldn't have Conor with me, at least I had my crew.

"I want to see her," I said.

"We're transferring her to the critical care unit right now. She'll be in room 524. Family only at this time." He said it as though he doubted my veracity.

I looked him dead in the eye. "Like I said, she's our mom."

"Thanks for your help, Doc," Rodeo said.

"You're welcome. Now if you'll excuse me, I have other patients waiting." Linden walked away.

"Fuck," I cursed under my breath. "Let's go up and see her."

We followed the signs to the main elevators and rode up to the fifth floor. In the critical care unit, Rodeo pointed at the small CCU waiting room. "I don't really know her. You two go on in. I'll be in here when you're done."

"Go home, if you want," I replied. "Get some rest."

"I would, but Nicole's got my car."

"Conor dropped me off." I slapped Caden on the back. "Guess you're our ride, bro."

Caden and I strolled into the ward and made a beeline to the room, avoiding anyone who might try to keep us from seeing Juanita.

At first I wondered if we were in the wrong room. Her face was so pale and waxy, I mistook her for a white person. A thick crown of bandages encircled her head. She had more wires and tubes coming out of her than a Borg queen.

Anger, sorrow, and guilt constricted my chest. I collapsed into a wood-framed chair, struggling to suck in enough air so I wouldn't pass out. One thought dominated all others. I wasn't going to let these bastards win.

Caden and I sat staring at Juanita's broken body for what felt like days. Only the wheezing from the ventilator and an occasional alarm from the vitals monitor disturbed the grave silence.

I caught myself starting to fall asleep and scolded myself for being so insensitive when one of the most important people in my life was so close to dying.

Caden must have noticed, because he said, "Why don't I take you home? We could all use some rest."

I wanted to argue, but I knew he was right. I wasn't any good to anyone like this.

We picked up Rodeo on the way out. "How is she?" he asked.

"She…" I didn't know how to finish the sentence.

Rodeo put an arm around me.

33

I woke to a garbage truck rumbling through the neighborhood at nine the next morning. The blisters on my left hand looked red and angry. Possibly infected. But I was too numb to care.

I was halfway through a dreary-eyed breakfast when my phone rang.

"Good news," said Kirsten when I answered it. "The Maricopa County Attorney's Office has dropped the charges against you."

"Really? Why?"

"Honestly, I'm not sure. Deputy County Attorney Perkins was unusually abrupt. He said the charges had been dropped and hung up. Maybe he thought it'd look bad to be prosecuting one of the heroes of the Main Drag shooting."

"Heroes! Like hell." I scoffed. "Suppose I should take good news wherever I can find it. When will I get my pistol back?"

"I'll look into it, but considering it was seized as evidence in a homicide case, I wouldn't hold your breath."

"Crap." Considering I'd picked up a Colt M1911 from Danny Warren and a Smith & Wesson revolver from that punk Mahoney, I guessed it was a net plus. Still, I hated losing the Ruger. A good firearm cost money.

"How's your friend Juanita?"

"Alive but still critical."

"I'll keep her in my prayers."

"Thanks." Not that I put much stock in prayers.

"And just so you know, last night's legal representation was on the house."

That woke me up a little. "Dare I ask why?"

"You and your friends saved a lot of lives taking down those shooters. Least I could do."

"Thanks."

"Take it easy, Jinx."

I hung up and decided to go for a parkour run along McDowell Road—shimmying up walls, leaping trash cans, and somersaulting across bus stop shelters. Anything to generate endorphins to help me cope with the current shitstorm and figure out what my next move should be.

While I bounced and ricocheted off of various structures, my subconscious sorted out issues I was struggling with. How to track down Pratt and Dietz, ideally without getting anyone else killed or injured. What to do about Conor. And trying not to think about Juanita being at death's door.

When I was a block from home, my phone rang. To my surprise, it was my brother, Jake.

"Calling to yell at me again?" I slowed my run so that I could maintain a conversation.

"Jinx, I'm sorry. I know I've been an asshole lately."

"Yeah, you have."

"I heard what happened at the Main Drag. You okay?"

"Physically, yeah, more or less. Emotionally, I…shit, I don't know."

"Rodeo called, told me about Juanita. I'm so sorry. I know she's been your mentor and all."

"Thanks." Grief wrapped its tentacles around my chest.

"If you got time, I'd like to buy you lunch."

"Wow. To what do I owe this sudden generosity?"

"I could use your advice."

"Damn, bro. You must be desperate. You usually go to Dad for advice."

"If you don't want to meet…"

"No, that's fine. Where and when?"

"Firebird Cantina at Desert Ridge. Say around one."

"You're on."

At home, I took a shower, went back over everything I had on Rudy Pratt, and made some more phone calls. So far the nurse at Camelback Children's Hospital hadn't called. Neither had any of his neighbors or the references on Pratt's bail application, despite all the messages I'd left.

It didn't help that I couldn't get Juanita's deathly pale face out of my mind or the images of the carnage at the nightclub. *This is what Conor's dealing with*, said a little voice in my head. *Only more so.*

I hated to admit it, but it was true. He was no doubt reliving the trauma of the Omagh bombing and the death of his sister. And in response, I took my frustrations and anger out on him. I owed him an apology. But it would have to wait.

My phone had several text messages from Sadie Levinson asking where I was on the Pratt case. I ignored them and called Becca after I got dressed. I filled her in on the previous evening's chaos.

"Listen, Becks, I need to see if there's been any activity on Pratt. Credit cards, phone calls. Him or his wife."

"Hold on a minute." A voice in the background said something I couldn't make out. A door closed. "Okay, let me take a look. Nope, no recent activity. Wherever he is, he's laying low."

"Damn. Was that Easton I heard?"

"Yeah, just got back from their trip. Said they froze their ass off in Denver."

"Glad they're back." An idea popped into my head. It was a long shot, but at this point, long shots were all I had left. "Who's been paying Pratt's daughter's medical bills?"

"Do you have a provider name?"

"Start with Camelback Children's Hospital."

The clicking of her fingers on the keyboard was so fast it almost sounded like static over the phone. "Bills paid by someone named Eric Freytag. Wow, to the tune of about four hundred thousand dollars. Must be nice to have a sugar daddy like that. The name's familiar, though I can't place it."

"He's in charge of the local White Nation chapter. A real snake. I met him briefly a couple days ago at that White Nation bar."

"Sounds like a real charmer. Think he's hiding Pratt?"

"Possibly. Pratt's case has been taken over by the feds, so something big's going on."

"I'll see what I can dig up on Freytag and let you know."

"Okay, thanks."

"Be careful, Jinxie. I mean it."

"Always."

I hung up and checked my watch. "Shit!" I was going to be late.

I pulled on my body armor, slipped the Glock into a holster on my hip, and raced the Gray Ghost north up I-17 to the Loop 101 until I reached Desert Ridge Marketplace on Tatum. The parking lot was packed with snowbirds, holiday shoppers, and the late lunchtime crowd. I snatched a parking space just as someone pulled out.

As I closed my door, I came face-to-face with a forty-something white guy in a polo shirt and Titleist ball cap. He held himself like a frat boy turned corporate executive. "I was waiting for that spot, lady!"

I flipped out my badge, rested a hand on the Glock, and tilted my head. "We gonna have a problem?"

His jaw tightened visibly. "You bitches think you're so smart!" He hopped back into his Tesla roadster and flipped me off as he burned rubber down the lane.

I hustled across the parking lot and into a sprawling outdoor mall filled with overpriced shops and trendy restaurants. Good thing I knew where I was going. Last time I was there, the maps lacked those You Are Here markers, rendering them all but useless.

I charged into the Firebird Cantina, scanned the room for Jake, and joined him six tables in with a morose look on his face.

"Sorry I'm late. Parking's a bitch."

Jake sighed and picked disinterestedly at his focaccia sandwich. "No big deal."

The server came, and I ordered a burger bloody and fries.

"So you gonna tell me what the hell's going on with you these days?"

He looked up. My ordinarily too-cool-for-school brother looked like a whipped puppy. His eyes were bloodshot and rimmed with tears. "Rodeo dumped me."

I tried to act surprised. "Why would he do that?"

"He was always pushing me to hold hands and stuff. In public. I wouldn't."

"Holding hands? In public? What a perv!" I couldn't hold back the sarcasm any longer.

Jake threw a bit of sandwich at me. "I'm serious. I told him it was going to take time."

"And to think you've only been going out with him for a year and a half. What's his rush?"

"Hey! I'm hurting here. If you're just going to make fun of me..."

I held up my hands in apology. "Sorry. I know it hurts."

The server brought my lunch, and I dove into it with gusto. The run earlier had fueled my appetite.

"I loved him, Jinxie." A tear dripped onto his plate. "I thought he loved me."

I clasped Jake's hand. "I'm sure he did. You two were great together. I guess you're just at different levels of...outness? Is that a word?"

"He says I've got internal homophobia."

"Ooh, sounds serious. Have you seen a doctor about that?"

He glared at me, and I apologized for making light of the situation.

"Maybe I do have some issues, but I'll work through them

eventually." He surreptitiously wiped his face with a napkin, clearly trying to make it look as though he was wiping sauce from his mouth instead of tears from his cheek.

"Why won't you hold Rodeo's hand, Jake?"

"I do. Just not when there's people around."

"Why not?"

"I don't want anyone thinking, 'Hey, there go a couple of faggots.'"

"Why do you care what anyone thinks? The whole town knows I'm trans, thanks to that *Phoenix Living* article last year. Yeah, I got some shit for it, but I'm still living my life."

"You were always the strong one."

"Oh, please. Says the guy who can bench-press a Toyota."

"You know what I mean."

"Here's what I know. You're a fucking idiot."

"What?"

"You heard me. Jake, you're prioritizing the imaginary opinions of faceless strangers over the one man who truly loves you. He wants to show you affection, and you're rebuffing him."

"I have the right to determine when and how I'm touched."

"Yes, but this isn't about consent, and you know it. You're worried about people finding out you're gay. You're riding on your perceived straight privilege. Well, guess what? That shit's over."

I stood up and turned to the restaurant. "Attention, everyone!"

The place grew quiet.

"Jinx, don't do this," Jake muttered.

"I would like to inform you all that my big brother is gay. He's a big ol' fairy with six-pack abs and a heart of gold. And I think he's awesome, and I love him."

To my surprise, about half of the patrons and servers in the crowded restaurant applauded. I sat down, supremely satisfied with myself.

Jake was covering his face. "I truly hate you."

"Oh, come on, you big baby. Did you hear that applause? They love you."

"Bullshit, they love *you*. The saintly sister who loves her queer brother."

"You want me to tell them that I'm transgender?"

"No!" He grabbed my hands to keep me from standing up again.

"Hiding is no way to live."

"You sound like Dad."

"Dad's right. I tried to hide who I was when I was a kid, and it nearly killed me. I was always worried people would figure out I was trans, and about what would happen when they did. It's like a fucking cancer that eats at you all the time. Sound familiar?"

"Maybe."

"Fuck all the haters. Just be your own goddamned gay self. And if anyone gives you shit, call me. I'll kick their ass."

He laughed. "Just what I need—my baby sister fighting my battles for me."

"On the other hand, if you continue this bullshit of pretending to be straight when you're not, refusing to hold the hand of the man who's crazy about you, I swear to fucking God I will kick you into next Tuesday."

I held his gaze for a moment before he looked away. "You're right. I've been a wimp."

"Yeah, but you can change that. Find some *cajones*, man. Go fight for the man you love."

"It's too late. He broke up with me."

"Then call him up, tell him you've seen the error of your ways, and beg him to give you another chance."

"You think he will?"

"Never know until you try."

"Thanks, sis. I can always count on you not to sugarcoat it for me. How are things with you and Conor?"

It was so much more fun bagging on his love life. Why'd he have to bring up mine?

"Complicated."

"'Cause you don't want to move in with him?"

"Among other things."

"See, that's what I don't get. You two are crazy about each other. Why not move in together?"

"I like having my own place. Besides, you worked so hard to renovate my house. Why would I give it up to live in that reinforced bunker of his?"

Jake held my gaze until I looked away, distracted by someone or something or whatever. "Is that what it is?"

"What else would it be?"

"I think you're commitment-phobic."

"Bullshit." I sat back and crossed my arms.

"Ever since things went bad between you and your high school boyfriend, you've never gotten serious with a guy."

"That's not true."

"No? When your ex-boyfriend Wilson invited you to move in with him, you dumped him."

"I dumped Wilson because I caught him in bed with some skank." I rolled my eyes. "And when I asked him why, he said there was no spark between us anymore."

"Shit, that must've hurt. What'd you do?"

"What any self-respecting woman would do. I Tasered his ass and said, 'Here's your fucking spark, asshole!'"

We both burst out laughing. Holy hell, that felt good. It rippled through my body, shaking loose all of the crap I'd been feeling.

"Is that why you don't want to move in with Conor? You think he's going to cheat on you?"

It was an easy excuse, but it wasn't the whole story. Before I could answer, my phone rang. "I gotta get this. It's Becks."

"I found your guy Freytag. He lives in a gated community north of Scottsdale. Very tight security."

"Damn, how's a weasel like that get all this money?"

"He's the CEO at Suma Financial, an investment firm in north Scottsdale. The guy's got money all over the place. I've turned up numerous offshore accounts. Major shareholder in beaucoup businesses in high tech, aerospace, and advanced weapons manufacturing. Makes a lot of donations to far-right organizations and politicians. His phone records are extensive, but nothing connected to either your guy Pratt or to...uh... you-know-who."

"Barclay Dietz."

"Yeah, him. Not that I have a number for Dietz, but his name doesn't show up anywhere."

"Thanks, Becks. Text me Freytag's work info. I'm going to pay him a visit. Email the rest to me."

"You're not going there alone, are you?"

"Listen to you. You're as bad as my mother. I'll be fine."

"Be careful."

"Yes, mother." I hung up. "Well, bro, duty calls."

"What's going on?" Jake looked worried.

"What do you mean? Becca's just getting me information on one of my skips."

"You mentioned Barclay Dietz just now."

"He's in town. I almost bagged him the other day. Feds are offering a big reward for his return."

"Damn. After all these years. And this Freytag? He involved with Dietz?"

"Maybe. It's just a lead for now."

"You need me to tag along? Since Rodeo's out of commission for a while."

"No, I need you to go play nursemaid to Rodeo and have some hot makeup sex."

He blushed. "You sure? Barclay Dietz nearly killed you way back when. He could still be dangerous."

"My job's all about the dangerous. If it wasn't, I'd be in danger of falling asleep on the job." I stood up and hugged him. "Now quit being such a pussy and tell the world that you're here, you're queer, and anyone who doesn't like it can just fuck off."

I pulled out my wallet and dropped a ten on the table.

Jake snatched it up and stuffed it back in my hand. "No, this is my treat."

"Wow! You *have* turned a corner. See ya soon."

I left him at the table to settle up the bill. When I reached the front door, Jack shouted, "I'm here, I'm queer, and anyone who doesn't like it can fuck off!"

The restaurant responded with another round of applause. I gave him a thumbs-up and hurried out of the restaurant and back to the Gray Ghost. After punching Freytag's business address into the GPS, I headed out.

34

Suma Financial was located on the top floor of a three-story glass building on Northsight Boulevard north of Raintree. As I parked, I thought about how to play this. Freytag had already seen me, so there was no point trying to pretend I was anything other than what I was—a bail enforcement officer pursuing fugitives wanted on multiple violent criminal charges.

I strolled into the building in full gear. I wanted Freytag to know I was all business and that if he stood in my way, he would be hurt. White-collar bigots like Freytag were always pussies, anyway, getting their underlings to do the dirty work. With enough pressure, they always folded like a lawn chair.

The elevator opened to a glass-enclosed office with the company logo etched on the door. I stepped inside. The receptionist looked like a seasoned gatekeeper, fiftyish with a helmet of dark hair and a shrewd expression.

"I'm here to see Eric Freytag." I flipped my badge and ID.

"You got a warrant?" she asked without breaking her professional façade.

"Odd question. I'm not here to arrest him. Just have a few questions."

"Is he expecting you?"

"He'll know what it's about."

"Your name?"

"Jinx Ballou."

She picked up the phone handset and dialed an extension. "Mr. Freytag, there is a Jinx Ballou here to see you. Yes, sir."

Without a glance at me, she turned back to her work. "He'll be up momentarily. You can have a seat."

"I'll stand, thank you very much."

"Suit yourself." She tuned me out.

"Momentarily" apparently meant thirty minutes. No doubt a power move intended to intimidate me. Freytag opened the door to the back offices. His aquiline features were so snakelike, I half expected him to flick his tongue.

"Ah, Ms. Windsor, isn't it? No, wait. It's Ballou now. That's right. How can I help you this afternoon?"

"I'm looking for Rudy Pratt. He skipped bail on a murder charge. I believe you know where he is."

"I see. Why don't you and I discuss this in my office."

Into the serpent's den, I thought, as he led me to a roomy, well-appointed office. Everything looked very corporate. No signs of his connections to White Nation. No swastikas. No Confederate flags.

He coiled up behind his desk with a look on his face that told me he wasn't intimidated at all. I'd have to do something about that.

"So tell me the name again of this person you're seeking?"

"Rudy Pratt. He was scheduled to be at that meeting at Dixie's. It's why I was there."

"Huh, well the name does ring a bell, but I can't say I know the man. White Nation's such a large organization. Thousands of members in the Grand Canyon chapter alone."

"Really? You don't know him? And yet you've been paying his daughter's medical expenses to the tune of hundreds of thousands of dollars." I pulled out Pratt's photo and set it on his desk. "This refresh your memory?"

He gave it the briefest of glances and returned it. "Not really. No. I donate to numerous charitable causes, you see. My way of giving back to white society."

"The man's a murderer and a fugitive. Your protecting him makes you an accessory after the fact. Ever been to prison, Mr. Freytag?"

"Can't say I have. And your little threats do not intimidate me. Should you display the same type of uncontrolled behavior you did the other day, I will have you arrested. *Again.* I am a busy man with important matters to attend to."

"Like rallying your violent little band of neo-Nazi white nationalists?"

"Violent? You're the only one I've seen use violence. You attacked one of our out-of-town guests without any provocation."

"I attempted to capture a man wanted by the FBI for aggravated assault and armed robbery. And in retaliation, you sent your thugs to murder people in a gay club last night."

"That is a slanderous accusation. We are not thugs, Miss Ballou. White Nation is a peaceful organization fighting for the rights of God-loving white Americans. Right now illegals, Negroes, and homosexuals have more rights than we do. It's a disgrace. And if someone did shoot up one of your queer sex clubs, well, then, it must be God's will."

It took all of my self-control to keep from putting a nine-millimeter hole in Freytag's skull. "You're so full of shit. Poor persecuted white men." I stood and leaned over his desk. "You have no idea what persecution feels like. But before this is all over, you will. I guarantee it."

"Is that a threat?"

I smiled. "Take it however you want, asshole. I will drag both Rudy Pratt and Barclay Dietz back to jail. And then I'll take you down for protecting them."

I turned on my heel and slammed open his office door so hard it smacked the wall. I stormed past the receptionist and charged down the staircase rather than waiting for an elevator.

When I reached the Gray Ghost, I put Freytag's home address in my GPS and drove northeast to where the posh golf-centric communities of Scottsdale embedded themselves in the desert foothills. Clouds were rolling in, giving the desert landscape a dreary, desolate feel.

Becca wasn't kidding about the security at the gated community. Multiple surveillance cameras mounted around the entrance left no square inch unmonitored. Two security guards stood in a guard shack alongside a wrought-iron gate that connected to an eight-foot border wall that I assumed ran around the entire property.

I pulled up to the gate. A man who carried himself like a military veteran, complete with a high and tight haircut, approached the Gray Ghost. "Can I help you, ma'am?"

I flashed him my badge and handed him photos of Pratt and Dietz. "I'm looking for these two violent fugitives. Rudy Pratt and Barclay Dietz. I have reason to believe they are holed up in a house on the grounds."

"What are they wanted for?" asked the guard as he studied the photos.

"Murder, aggravated assault, and armed robbery." I pointed at my black eye. "Dietz did this to my face when I tried to arrest him at a local bar. Believe me, you don't want them going after any of your residents."

"They don't look familiar to me." He showed the photos to his associate, who shook his head. "We haven't seen them. Do you know which house they're supposedly in?"

"The one belonging to Eric Freytag." I gave them the street address.

"Mr. Freytag *is* a resident here. Do you have a warrant?"

"I don't need a warrant. I'm a bail enforcement officer. By law, I can enter any home where I believe my fugitives are hiding."

"Well, I'm sorry, but I can't let you inside the gate without a warrant."

I considered pushing it, but I didn't get the impression he would budge on the issue. And honestly, I had no proof they were staying at Freytag's house.

After taking back the photos, I handed him one of my

business cards. "Call me if you see them. Hopefully, they won't murder any of your residents before then."

I turned around and headed down the two-lane side street that bordered the complex. The eight-foot block wall might intimidate the casual intruders. I was not giving up so easily, however.

As I parked the truck on the street, I scanned the area. No security cameras and very little traffic as far as I could see in the late-afternoon gloom. I made a running jump at the wall. I grasped the top and used my momentum to propel me up and over.

The homes in the community, at least those I could see, were five thousand square feet or more, set on sprawling lots that butted up against a golf course. The lawns were mostly crushed rock planted with a variety of palm and citrus trees, cacti of all types, and heat-tolerant shrubs.

Using the maps app on my phone, I followed the directions to Freytag's place a mile and a half away. With my body armor and holstered weapons, I stuck out in this refuge of wealth and tranquility. But most residents were either at work or safely tucked inside their desert castles.

Thirty minutes later, I was standing in front of Freytag's mansion. A wide driveway led up a slight hill to a four-car garage. A blue light on a security camera above the garage flickered to life when I came within range of its sensor. I suspected all the entryways were similarly monitored.

With the darkening overcast skies, I could see through the windows with relative ease. Rooms were lit, and there was movement within. I decided to try a little social engineering.

I stashed my body armor and sidearms under a large ole-ander bush and rang the doorbell.

A moment later, a towheaded boy about seven years old opened the door, followed by a frazzled-looking woman with long dark hair. "Leonard, how many times I tell you," she said in a thick Latina accent. "Don't open the doors to strangers."

I didn't know if she was the housekeeper, nanny, or both. Couldn't be the wife, could it? Still, it surprised me that Freytag would have an immigrant working in his home. Or that this woman would willingly work for a scumbag like Freytag. The world was weird.

"*Buenas tardes, señora,*" I said.

"*Buena tarde,*" she replied. From the way she used the singular, I guessed she was from Chile or Argentina.

"I apologize for disturbing you," I continued in Spanish. "Señor Freytag asked me to deliver an important message to his guests."

"His guests?"

"Yes, Señor Pratt and Señor Dietz. Are they here?"

She got a confused look on her face. "I'm sorry, but you are mistaken. No one is here by those names. Señor Freytag's guests usually stay at the ranch."

I popped my forehead with the heel of my hand. "Of course. Silly me! Do you have the address? I seem to have misplaced it."

Her eyes narrowed with suspicion. "Who are you?"

"Liz Windsor. I work with Señor Freytag at Suma Financial. Do you have the address for the ranch?"

"Maybe I should call Señor Freytag."

"Wait, you know what? I remembered I have the address in my phone. No need to bother him. You have a nice day, señora."

I hurried away and picked up my gear once I was out of sight of the front door. So much for social engineering.

I retraced my steps and hopped the wall, the wind gusts tugging at my hair and clothes. The Gray Ghost was farther down than I remembered. I must have crossed one house early. And mine was no longer the only vehicle parked on the street. A dark-blue Caprice sat a half block behind me.

I'd had enough unproductive fun for the day. I turned the key and pointed the Gray Ghost toward home.

❋

As I drove toward the main road, the Caprice's headlights blazed to life behind me. The car followed me at a distance through three turns. When it remained behind me after I completely circled the block, I knew I had a tail.

I suspected the driver was one of Freytag's goons. He wasn't hiding the fact that he was tailing me, so I figured he was trying to intimidate me into backing off.

But I don't scare easily. I'd gone toe-to-toe with crazed meth dealers, serial rapists, and sadistic Chechen mobsters. An investment banker with a Hitler complex barely moved the needle.

He changed lanes whenever I did, never more than a car or two behind me. At times, he crept so close to my rear bumper I thought he was going to ram me. Traffic was getting heavier as the afternoon rush hour began. Losing my shadow was going to be a challenge. I'd taken strategic driving courses designed to lose a tail. But I was in a top-heavy SUV, not a supercharged sports car. Another tactic was needed.

I turned south on the Piestewa Freeway and worked my way over to the carpool lane. Driving solo in that lane was illegal after three. If I got pulled over by a cop, it could earn me a hefty fine. But it might also shake loose my pursuer.

The Caprice joined me in the HOV lane, staying hot on my bumper, as I whizzed past the slower lanes. Ahead of me, a Prius nosed into my path. I swerved to avoid it. The Gray Ghost lifted onto two wheels and slammed down hard enough to rattle my teeth. Behind me, tires squealed. I glanced back, hoping for a collision. No such luck! The Caprice whipped around the Prius and once again bore down on me. I had no hope of outrunning him.

I dashed into a gap in the lane next to me and forced my way back across the interstate until I cut off the gore point at the Cactus Drive exit and screeched to a stop in the pullout lane designed for minor accidents.

I scrambled out of the truck, drew my Glock, and squatted

behind the Ghost's front grill. Icy, fat droplets of rain fell, hitting the pavement with a smack-smack and sending a chill down my back. The wind whipped up, blowing wisps of hair in my face.

A moment later, a Caprice cruised up the exit ramp. I caught Special Agent Bender glaring at me as he drove past and turned right onto Cactus. *Goddamned feds.*

My hands trembled as the cold rain came down harder. I hopped back into the Gray Ghost. Since I was already on the east side of town, I decided to reach out again to Peyton, see if he'd heard from dear old Dad. Along the way, I kept a wary eye on my rearview mirror in case anyone else decided to play follow the leader.

35

It was early evening when I pulled into parking lot of San Tan Liquors. Rush hour traffic had made the drive all the more unpleasant. Even listening to the Pink Trinkets' *Singing Mammogram* album couldn't free me from my worries. It felt as if the world was coming to an end. Everything was so fucking upside down. I was determined to make it right again if it killed me.

The bell over the door jingled as I walked in. A hulking guy in a red flannel shirt stood at the counter, ringing up a couple of college kids in ASU sweatshirts. Maybe Peyton was stocking the shelves or in the back somewhere.

I wandered aimlessly through the aisles. I needed to call Conor and apologize for getting angry at him. But with everything going on, I couldn't bring myself to do it. I didn't even know what to say to him. I still didn't want to move in with him and wasn't sure why. Not wanting to give up my house and old baggage from an ex-boyfriend sounded like legit excuses, but there was something deeper. I just didn't know what.

"Let me know if you need any help," called the lumberjack behind the counter. There was a warning in his voice, as if he thought I planned to slip out without paying. Last time I shoplifted, I was a closeted eleven-year-old and got caught stealing a dress for my secret stash.

I wandered over to the cooler, grabbed a six-pack of Four

Peaks Ale, and carried it to the counter. "Peyton here?" I asked
as the lumberjack rang up my purchase.

Lumberjack shot me a look. "Why?"

"He's a friend of mine."

"Your *friend* stopped showing up for his shifts. I fired him."

"Any idea where he might be?"

"Don't know. Don't care."

I paid for the beer and cruised over to Peyton's apartment,
where I nabbed a visitor spot outside the gate. When a resident
drove through, I slipped inside the rattling gate on foot, keeping
an eye out for the property manager.

I pounded on Peyton's door. When there was no response
after a few minutes, I knocked again. Still no response. Where
was he? It was only a little after six. Too early to hit the clubs.
*Could he be hiding out with his father somewhere? Or just out
running errands?*

I weighed my options and decided to let myself inside to
look for clues to Peyton's whereabouts. After a quick glance
around for possible witnesses, I pulled out a set of lockpicks
and went to work on the door lock. It took me a few minutes
and a few false starts before I defeated the security pins in the
dead bolt. As soon as the cylinder turned, I was inside in a flash.

The sweet haze of weed hung in the air. A wooden trunk
with circular watermarks served as a coffee table between a floral
upholstered couch and the flat-screen TV. The blue glass of a
bong glinted in the dim light next to a PlayStation controller.

I pulled out a flashlight and thumbed through a loose stack
of papers on a side table. Just a few unpaid bills, a postcard
advertising solar panels, and a *High Times* magazine for Hughie.

I moved on to the bedrooms, bypassing the one with the
sour smell of smoked ganja in favor of one that was relatively
tidy. I searched through the drawers of a black laminate desk.
I found the usual bank statements, appliance warranties, and
health insurance statements. A ream of printer paper and a stack
of blank envelopes. An external hard drive and a Bluetooth

keyboard lay on the edge of the desk, but there was a blank spot where a laptop might go.

I dug through the wastebasket, finding mostly crushed beer cans, used tissues, and the remains of a padded mailing envelope with no return address. Further digging turned up a handwritten note that read, *Meet me at Lodestar Ranch. Address in the phone. I'll explain everything.* It was signed "Dad."

I was about to search a little further when I heard voices and laughter outside the apartment. I glanced out the bedroom window but couldn't see anyone. Time to get out.

I crept to the front room again and checked the window there. A straight couple shuffled drunkenly along one of the paved walks. It wasn't Peyton or his roomie. But it was time I cleared out.

I slipped out the front door, leaving the dead bolt unlocked, and shuffled past the couple, who were too wrapped up in each other's affections to pay me any mind.

It was only seven thirty when I got home, but I was exhausted. I called the hospital to check on Juanita only to learn she was still in a coma with no change in condition. The texts from Sadie asking for an update were piling up, so I told her I was close. Of course, I felt closer to having a complete mental breakdown than finding Pratt, but she didn't need to know that.

Something about Barclay Dietz's note to his son was pricking the back of my mind, but I couldn't fit the pieces together. Maybe a little libation would take the edge off enough for me to sort it out. I opened one of the bottles of Four Peaks and took a long pull. I was putting the rest of the six-pack in the fridge when I heard a thunk and a muffled voice say, "Damn it to hell."

"What the fuck?" I hunched down and drew my Glock. Someone was in my house.

I listened further. Shuffling sounds in the attic. The feeling of being watched rushed back. I wasn't crazy. Someone had been watching me. And whoever it was, was still here.

I crept to the hallway and gingerly pulled down the trapdoor to the attic. The ladder creaked as I unfolded it and placed my foot on the first step. More shuffling from above. Go time!

I vaulted up the ladder and turned on the light. The bare bulb threw harsh shadows across the stacks of my stored possessions. I scanned my surroundings, finger on the trigger of my Glock, but didn't see anyone or anything out of place. "I know you're here. Whoever you are, you best surrender now. Or so help me, I will end you," I said in my most threatening voice.

On the far side of the attic, from behind a stack of old suitcases, a pair of dark arms rose. "Please, ma'am. Don't shoot me. I don't mean no harm." The voice was male and frightened.

"Come on outta there. I won't shoot as long as you do as I say."

A gaunt figure stood unsteadily. He wore a green US Marine Corps utility jacket. His hair was an untidy nest of silver, matching his scraggly beard. His skin looked like dark leather.

"Who are you?" I eased my finger off the trigger but kept the gun trained on my intruder. "And what the hell are you doing in my attic?"

"Reginald Campbell, ma'am. Just needed a warm place to stay. I'll be on my way. Won't be no more bother."

"How'd you get up here, Mr. Campbell?"

He stared at the floor. "There was a loose board under the eaves. I climbed up your air conditioner and shimmied up inside. I'm real sorry."

Once my sense of alarm had subsided, I found myself feeling sorry for the man. He looked to be in his sixties. From the condition of his clothes, I guessed he'd been homeless a while. "You hungry?" I tucked the pistol into my waistband.

He looked at me with lifeless eyes. "A little."

"Come on, then. I'll fix you something."

"Don't wanna be no bother. I just get my gear and go."

"No bother. Long as you don't do anything crazy."

"Won't have no trouble from me."

I stepped down the ladder, and a moment later, he followed suit. In the full light, his face had a skull-like quality, his eyes deep-set and sunken. His cheekbones poked out like knives.

I folded up the ladder and nudged the trapdoor closed. He looked up at it worriedly.

"Don't worry," I said. "I'm not going to steal your stuff."

I led him to the kitchen. He sat down at the heavy wooden table my grandmother, Marie Lafitte, had given me a few years back. She claimed it was originally from the ship captained by our ancestor, the pirate Captain Jean Lafitte.

"You allergic to anything, Reginald?" I asked. Last thing I needed was poor Reginald going into anaphylactic shock from something I gave him.

"Not that I know of. And my friends call me Reggie."

"All right, Reggie. My friends call me Jinx."

"Mighty odd name."

"Well, I'm a mighty odd woman."

He smiled as I cooked up some scrambled eggs and bacon.

When I served his plate, I asked how he came to be homeless. Reggie explained he was originally from Snellville, Georgia, just outside Atlanta. "Weren't much of a town when I grew up there. Last time I was back, though, it was so growed up I didn't recognize the place. Atlanta done swallowed it whole. Cut down all the forests to put up Starbucks and Costcos and office parks. Never went back."

He'd served as a corpsman in the Marine Corps during Vietnam. When he returned to the states after the war, he moved to New York and struggled to find his footing. A drug problem kept him from becoming a paramedic.

He kicked the habit after a few years and worked as a super for a while, then got his hack license and started driving a taxi. After ten brutal New York winters, he moved to Arizona and continued to drive a taxi for twenty years. When Uber and Lyft got in the game, the taxi company he was with folded.

Eventually, he lost his house and spent a few months living out of a twelve-year-old Lincoln Town Car parked in a vacant lot. Then his car disappeared. Whether stolen or towed, he never found out. He'd been on the streets ever since. Until a week ago when a cold snap led him to crawl into my attic.

"You been drinking my whiskey and eating my food this past week?"

He looked humiliated. "Yes, ma'am."

"You haven't been spying on me, have you?"

A wounded look crossed his face. "No, ma'am. Wouldn't never do nothing like that."

I believed him. "Well, what're we gonna do, Reggie?"

He was wiping his face with a napkin after finishing the last of the eggs. "I'll gather my belongings and be on my way. I thank you for the hospitality."

"No, you don't have to go. It's Christmas, for fuck's sake. Not that I'm all that religious. But it don't feel right to kick you out with it being cold as it is." I thought about my options. I didn't want to be taken advantage of, but at the same time, I couldn't turn him away. "For tonight, you can sleep on my couch. We can figure out the rest tomorrow."

"I ain't got no money to pay you back, understand. Don't qualify for social security for a few years yet."

"Maybe you can do some chores around the house, starting with the loose boards around the eaves."

"I can do that."

After dinner, Reggie went to the attic to retrieve his belongings. I called Conor. The call went straight to voicemail.

"Hey, babe. Sorry for getting upset at you last night. Give me a call when you can."

I got Reggie settled on the couch, showed him how to use the remote, and reminded him that I tracked down and arrested people for a living, just in case he got any ideas about pawning any of my belongings.

After that, I turned in for a fitful night of disturbing dreams.

36

When I stumbled out of bed the next morning, I noticed a Caprice parked in front of the house. No sooner had I thrown on a T-shirt and sweatpants than three people emerged. Agents Lovelace and Bender marched toward my front porch. Trailing them was a grim-faced man with a bad combover and wearing a long, black woolen coat. They pounded on my door a moment later.

I walked into the living room. Reggie looked worried.

"Relax, I don't think this is about you," I said.

He nodded warily and made tracks to my guest bathroom before I opened the door and crossed my arms.

"First you refuse to help me track down wanted fugitives, then Tweedle Dee here starts tailing me. What gives?"

"Ms. Ballou, we need to speak with you," said Lovelace.

"I'm kinda busy at the moment," I replied. "So unless you two have a warrant—" I started to shut the door.

"Ma'am, if you please," said Black Coat in an Irish accent with a hint of British posh. He held out a photo. "We need to speak with you about this man. Do you know him?"

The photo was of Conor. He was a teenager in the photo, but I'd recognize his face anywhere. "Who the hell are you?"

"Detective Chief Inspector Matthew Collier of the Police Service of Northern Ireland, ma'am. I'm following up on a cold case."

"What's this about?" In my gut, I already knew the answer.

"Can we come in?" asked Lovelace. "Or do we have to freeze to death on your doorstep?"

My instinct told me to tell them to take a hike, but I doubted it would do much good. "Yeah, come on in."

I led them to the kitchen and started a pot of coffee. Reggie poked his head in as my guests sat down. "Everything okay, Miss Jinx?"

"For now. Thanks."

"Would you mind too terribly if I used your shower?" Reggie looked embarrassed to ask.

"I'd mind if you didn't. Towels are in the linen closet in the hall."

He shuffled off to the bathroom. I poured myself a cup of coffee and sat at the table. "I'd offer you all some coffee but you won't be staying long. Now, what's this about?"

"You're still dating Conor Doyle, are you not?" asked Lovelace.

"Yeah, why?"

"When did you last speak with him?"

"Night before last at the Main Drag. He and I helped take down the shooters. Why?"

Lovelace pulled out a notebook and flipped it open. "Where did you go afterward?"

"To the hospital. John C. Lincoln on Dunlap. A friend of mine was shot in the head."

She scribbled some notes in her notebook. "And Mr. Doyle was with you?"

"Why? What's going on?"

"Answer the question, Ms. Ballou," said Bender. Despite his baby-face look, his voice had some steel to it. Maybe he wasn't quite the doofus I'd originally taken him for.

"Conor dropped me off at the hospital. From there he went home."

"He didn't go in with you to the hospital? Seems odd," Bender pressed.

"I'm not answering any more questions until you people tell me what the hell's going on." I glared at Lovelace.

"Miss Ballou, are you familiar with the name Liam O'Callaghan?" asked Collier.

Fuck. It was Conor's birth name. "Don't know anyone named Liam."

Collier continued. "Liam O'Callaghan was involved in a bombing that took place twenty years ago in Northern Ireland. Nearly thirty people were killed. Countless others severely injured."

"What's this got to do with Conor?"

"We believe Conor Doyle is an alias O'Callaghan assumed after the bombing."

"Conor's not a terrorist. He's a bounty hunter. He puts criminals away for chrissakes." Suddenly I sounded like the family members of the bail jumpers I went after.

"I'm sure this is all just a misunderstanding. As soon as we can speak to him, I'm sure we can clear it up in no time." Lovelace patted my hand, as if to reassure me. It didn't work. How many times had I said those same words to coerce someone connected to one of my skips?

"I don't know where Conor is. I left him a message last night. He hasn't called back."

"So he's not here?" pressed Lovelace.

"Why would he be here?"

"Don't bullshit us, Ballou." Bender was looking less like a man-baby and more like a schoolyard bully.

"He lives a few streets south of here on Almeria. I suggest you try there."

"We have," said Bender. "He's not there."

"Then I don't know what to tell you."

"Does the word 'Freebird' mean anything to you?" asked Collier.

"Freebird? As in the song?"

Collier nodded. "Someone sent your Mr. Doyle a text at

one o'clock this morning that said 'Freebird.' Nothing else. We were hoping you could tell us what it means."

"How the hell should I know? That someone's a fan of moldy oldies? Who sent the message?"

"The sender is as yet unidentified," Collier said. "It was sent from a prepaid phone."

"You have no idea what it means?" Lovelace tilted her head, giving me a disbelieving look.

"Not a clue." I shrugged. "You'll have to ask Conor or whoever sent the message."

Bender leaned toward me and growled. "Where is Conor?"

"Aww, having trouble following the grown-ups' conversation, Bender? Let me use small words so you can catch up. I. Don't. Know."

"So you don't mind us looking around?" Lovelace asked.

"Show me a search warrant, and the place is yours. Until then, the answer is no. You may not look around." I drained the last of my coffee.

"Miss Ballou, if you're harboring Mr. Doyle…" warned Collier.

"I'm not. And this discussion is over."

"You mind if I use your restroom?" asked Bender.

"Nice try, Bender. Either hold it or go in your diaper." I pointed toward the front door. "All three of you, out! Now."

"We'll be watching this house," Bender replied as the three of them stood.

"Good. I've heard there've been a few break-ins in the neighborhood. Nice to know you'll be here keeping an eye on things when I'm out."

When they left, I locked the door behind them and leaned my back against it. *Jeezus, Conor, what've you got me into?*

I stepped back into the kitchen, needing something to settle my nerves.

"They gone?" asked Reggie. I poured him a cup of coffee and a second for myself. I resisted the temptation to add a little Jameson to it.

"For now."

"You in some sorta trouble, Miss Jinx?"

"When am I not in trouble?"

Reggie raised an eyebrow.

"I'm fine. It's my boyfriend, Conor, I'm worried about. Brits and the feds have him confused with someone else. I'm sure it'll work out." I just had no idea how.

I grabbed my phone and called him. Again it went straight to voicemail. "Conor, call me. We need to talk."

I made breakfast for Reggie and myself and told him he could use my washer and dryer to clean his clothes. He thanked me and agreed to do some repairs and other chores around the house that I'd been putting off for a while. The drip from the showerhead. Dusting. Trimming the hedges. Pulling weeds. Replacing several light bulbs that had gone out in the house, including the one in the fridge. And of course, the loose boards that had allowed him entry in the first place.

After breakfast, I showered, put some burn cream on my left hand, gathered my gear, including my laptop and files, and headed over to the Hub. I picked up a couple of coffees from Tres Leches along the way.

Becca was already hard at work. I set her quad shot vanilla latte in front of her.

"How's Juanita?" she asked.

"Caden's hanging out in her hospital room, reading her trashy romances while she lies in a coma. We're still hoping she comes out of it soon."

"And how are you doing?"

"Managing." I didn't want to discuss Conor's legal troubles in the open room of the Hub. Too many nosy people.

"D'you get anything from that Freytag guy?"

"Nada. Claims not to know Pratt. My gut's telling me differently. I think something big's going down. Maybe this weekend at the rally White Nation has planned." I pulled out the note I'd found in Peyton's trash can and handed it to her.

"What do you make of this? Ever hear of a Lodestar Ranch?"
She studied the note. "Doesn't ring any bells."

I opened my laptop and did a search for Lodestar Ranch. The only significant results were for a couple of horse ranches—one in British Columbia, one in Zimbabwe. Nothing in Arizona. I refined my search and added the word "Arizona" to it.

Top result was the Lodestar Mine, an abandoned copper mine north of Cave Creek. Something triggered in my brain. I pulled up the subreddit I had found that Rudy Pratt had been on, talking about gardening. He'd used the handle Crizaba. I ran an online search for that word. It too came up as an abandoned mine in Arizona.

"Holy shit!" Fear crackled down my spine. I pulled out Agent Lovelace's card and dialed the number.

"You calling to tell us where your boyfriend's hiding, Ms. Ballou?"

"I have no idea where he is."

"Then we have nothing to talk about."

"Wait! I've stumbled on something I think you should know about White Nation."

"Oh? And what is that?"

"I think they're planning to set off a bomb at their protest on Saturday."

"And what makes you think that?"

"A fugitive I know has intercepted shortwave radio transmissions from people planning to detonate bombs in Phoenix. He thought they were mole people, but I think it's White Nation."

"Mole people?" Lovelace laughed. "Are you calling to mess with me, Ballou?"

"He's a bit of a conspiracy nut, but I think he may have stumbled onto something real."

"Fine, who is this conspiracy nut of yours?"

"Robert Rossellini." I gave her Conspiracy Bob's contact information. "I returned him to custody a few days ago, but he may have renewed his bail bond."

"I'll look into it."

"You do that." I hung up. Becca was staring at me.

"What?" I asked.

"You think White Nation's going to set off a bomb at the rally?" She looked worried.

"Maybe not at the rally itself. But think about it, what better time to set off a bomb than when a significant portion of the police force is trying to maintain order between a bunch of neo-Nazis and counter-protesters."

"No offense, Jinx, but you're starting to sound like your buddy, Conspiracy Bob."

"I know it sounds crazy. But Bob claims he's intercepted radio transmissions from people using the names of abandoned local mines. Several people on that subreddit we found were using handles that are also the names of abandoned mines. Then in that note that Barclay Dietz wrote to his son, he mentions Lodestar Ranch. Lodestar is an abandoned copper mine near Cave Creek, not far from Freytag's home. It can't all be a coincidence."

"Seems a bit of a stretch. Like Conspiracy Bob's theory that jackalopes and chupacabras were extraterrestrial beings that built ancient stone temples in Latin America."

"Maybe you're right." But I wasn't going to let it go. There was a connection here. I just had to find it.

I went through the information that Becca had dug up on Freytag. His business, Suma Financial, held a number of assets, but they were all commercial properties, including payday loan businesses, nail salons, shopping centers, and a small timeshare resort. Nothing residential.

I dug deeper and found he was on the board of several other businesses, but still nothing that might be this Lodestar Ranch. At times I felt like a rat running through a virtual maze of nested shell companies, many of them based in the Caymans, Turks and Caicos, or some other ridiculous tax haven.

From time to time, I called Conor. Same results. Didn't

bother leaving a message, though I was getting seriously worried. Was he laying low to avoid the feds? Or had something happened to him?

Around four o'clock, I packed it in and drove north to the hospital. Juanita's condition hadn't changed. Caden was looking and smelling awful. The staff had allowed him to remain after visitors' hours. I told him to go home and take a shower while I kept an eye on Juanita. He resisted, but I threatened to fire him if he didn't.

"Doc says her vitals are improving," he said on his way out the door. "Mild infection, but the antibiotics appear to be working."

"Best news I've heard all day. Now get the hell outa here, Stinky! And get some fucking rest."

With Caden gone, I sat listening to the wheezing of the respirator. I wanted to believe Juanita was looking less ashen than when I saw her last, but in the dim light of the room, it was hard to tell. Her hands were cooler to the touch than they usually were.

Memories of the shooting flashed in my mind. I kept hearing the one shooter shout "Fucking fairies" before the turmoil began. His voice sounded familiar. I'd heard it before and recently. I just couldn't place it.

Caden returned around eleven. I was struggling to stay awake when he walked in looking more like his old self.

"Any change?" he asked.

I shook my head and hugged him. "'Fraid not, bro. You get any sleep?"

"A little. Thanks for spotting me."

"I'm sorry I haven't been here more," I said. "But time's running out on getting Pratt."

"Keep your head on a swivel, girl." Caden sat down in the chair next to Juanita. "And if you need me, call. I'll be there."

"I will."

37

The cold air outside woke me up enough that I wouldn't fall asleep on the drive home. The strings of holiday lights decorating homes and businesses didn't help my mood. I couldn't shake this chilling sense of foreboding. Maybe it was just lingering trauma from the shooting. Or unresolved anxiety from my bitter history with Barclay Dietz.

I walked in my living room and nearly jumped out of my skin when I flicked on the lights and found Reggie lying on my couch. I'd completely forgotten about my houseguest.

"Didn't mean to scare you, Miss Jinx," he said as I sat and let my heart rate return to normal.

"It's okay. I'm actually glad to have a little company." Especially since Conor was incommunicado.

Reggie and I talked for a while. I should have been uncomfortable having a complete stranger sleeping under my roof, but he'd been doing it for a week, and nothing bad had happened.

I woke the next morning to the smells of breakfast. Coffee. Bacon. Eggs. My first thought was that Conor had returned and was making me breakfast. I walked out in a tank top and a pair of his boxers only to find Reggie at the stove. He wore a faded Rolling Stones T-shirt and a ragged pair of jeans.

"Morning," I said, feeling a bit awkward.

"Morning, Miss Jinx. You hungry?"

"Starving. What's cooking?"

"Eggs, grits, and bacon. You like grits?"

"My father's from Louisiana. It's one of the major food groups there."

"Here you go." He dished us each a plate and poured cups of coffee to go with it. "Been a while since I cooked, but it shouldn't be too bad."

"Looks great." I dug in. It was.

"Got the drip in your showerhead done and the boards under the eaves. Won't nobody be sneaking in that way no more. However, while I was up there, I noticed some roof shingles missing. I can fix that too, if you like."

"Happened during the monsoons last August. If you think you can repair it, I'd appreciate it, Reggie. I'll give you the cash for the replacement shingles."

"My pleasure, Miss Jinx."

"There's a ladder in the garage. If you need anything else, let me know. You have a phone?"

Reggie pulled a silver flip phone from his pocket. "Got a prepaid. Not sure how many minutes left on it, though."

I opened his phone and put my info in his directory. "Now you got my number. Call if you need anything."

"'Preciate that. Where you headed today?"

"That big protest that White Nation's got going."

Reggie stopped with a forkful of grits halfway to his mouth and gave me a look. "You with White Nation?"

"No! I'm not *with* them. But the fugitives I'm chasing are. I'm going on the slim chance that they'll show up."

Reggie shook his head. "Them's some bad folks, hating on people for being different."

"Tell me about it. My gut tells me they were behind the shooting at the Main Drag."

"Main Drag? Whassat?"

"You didn't hear about it on the news?" I asked.

He shook his head.

It had completely escaped me that Reggie didn't know

about me being queer. And despite being out to my friends and family for most of my life, coming out to someone new never got easier. "It's a club where drag queens perform."

"Like men in dresses?"

"Pretty much. Friend of mine owns the club. She was shot in the head."

I could see the wheels turning in his head, but I wasn't sure which way. "Sorry to hear 'bout your friend. She gonna be okay?"

"Not sure. She's in a coma."

"Terrible thing to happen during the holidays. Your friend, she a girl, right?"

"Yes. She's transgender. I am too."

"Transgender? What's that?"

"Started out as a boy on the outside, but on the inside I was a girl. When I was eleven, I transitioned to living as a girl."

He studied me for a moment. "You look like a girl."

I couldn't help laughing. "Well, yeah. That's 'cause I am one."

"You got girl parts? Down there I mean?"

"That's an awfully personal question to ask a relative stranger, don't you think?"

"Welp, I suppose it is. But since you're—"

"A human being," I said. "Just like you. Just because I let you stay doesn't mean I don't value my privacy."

He was quiet for a moment. "You're right. Ain't none of my business what you got between your legs."

"Now you're catching on."

"That boyfriend of yours. The one the feds are looking for. He a gay man?"

"Nope. He's straight as they come. Strictly attracted to women."

"And you a woman."

"Bingo!"

"You shore gave me a lot to think about, Miss Jinx. I ain't never met a transgender before."

"That you know of. There's a lot more of us than most people realize."

"I suppose you're right." He finished his coffee. "You best be careful at that rally. Them White Nation folks be crazy and fulla hate."

I gave him a wink. "I'm tougher than I look." I took my plate to the sink, went to my bedroom, and geared up. When I walked out in my Bail Enforcement body armor and tactical belt, Glock at my hip, and wraparound shades tucked into the collar of my shirt, Reggie gave me a whistle. "You look like you mean business, Miss Jinx."

I smiled. "See you after a while, Reggie."

An hour later, I parked in a surface lot on Adams and Twelfth Avenue and walked a few blocks to Wesley Bolin Memorial Plaza between the Arizona state legislative buildings and the state supreme court. The usually empty plaza was now a roiling mass of humanity. Streets were cordoned off for a half mile in every direction.

The plaza contained a dozen different memorials, ranging from an enormous anchor from the USS *Arizona* to a recent memorial for the Granite Mountain hotshots, nineteen firefighters who lost their lives fighting a blaze up near Yarnell.

The White Nation crowd was easy to spot with their Confederate and Nazi flags as well as a few flags I didn't recognize. I estimated the group size to be about a hundred, holding their ground around the main circle of memorials. A large portion of them wore black uniform shirts with white nationalist patches, assault rifles slung over their shoulders. Others were skinhead biker types with bomber jackets and chains. Klan-type hoods in a variety of colors poked up among the crowd. Some members stood with shields and helmets similar to those carried by police working riot control. Ninety percent of their ranks were men between the ages of thirty and fifty.

A sea of counter-protestors surrounded them, holding

banners supporting diversity and denouncing racism. Uniformed patrol officers manned barricades that created a twenty-foot gap between the opposing sides. The air vibrated with the beating of drums, chants, and random shouts rife with profanity and threats.

The news media also got in on the excitement. Armed with video cameras and large microphones, they wandered the crowd to capture the dark carnival-like atmosphere to be repackaged as infotainment for hungry viewers.

My chances of finding either Pratt or Dietz in this angry sea of humanity were low. I didn't have either the time or energy to waste on this. I turned on my heels and pushed my way through the park.

Under the shadow of the colossal USS *Arizona* anchor on the east end of the plaza, I spotted a familiar figure. "Peyton!"

He turned as I rushed toward him. "Jinx! Wh-What are you doing here?"

"Oh, you know, fighting bigots. Punching Nazis. The usual. Where the hell's your dad?"

"I...uh...dunno."

"Bullshit! I know he reached out to you. Staying at the Lodestar Ranch, right? Where is that?"

His expression hardened into a warning. "Jinx, you should go."

"Why? Whose side are you on?"

"Doesn't matter. Get outta here. It's not safe. I-I don't want you to get hurt, okay?" The tone of his voice triggered a sense of foreboding.

"What's going to happen, Peyton? What's White Nation planning?"

His face turned to stone. "My father was right. I never should have dated you. You ruined my life."

"The fuck I did. You knew about my history before we ever dated. You told me it didn't matter."

"I was young and impressionable. You seduced me."

"I what?" I almost laughed at the absurdity. "You asked me out, remember? Everything was fine until your father tried to kill me."

"My father only tried to protect me from your depravity. You were nothing but a trap."

His vicious words cut me to my core. I felt as if I'd been sucker punched. "You're a piece of shit, you know that? Just like your dad. I'm going to put him behind bars if it's the last thing I do. And if you don't tell me now where he is, I'll send you there too."

"Go home, Jinx. Last warning."

I grabbed him and threw him against the base of the platform on which the giant anchor rested. Despite him being several inches taller than me, I had him off-balance. "This is your last warning. Tell me where he is right now or—"

Someone seized the back of my collar and yanked me away from Peyton. I whirled around, pinwheeling my arms to break my attacker's grip. I was about to go at him when I recognized Officer Evans—the same one who'd arrested me for shooting the guy at Dixie's.

"What the hell you doing, Ballou? How many times I gotta arrest you this week?"

I pointed at Peyton. "This man is protecting two wanted fugitives. It's my job to return them to custody."

"You lay one more hand on him, I'm arresting you for aggravated assault."

"Oh, so you *want* violent criminals walking the streets of Phoenix. Good to know! Fine cop you turned out to be, Evans."

"I'm warning you, Ballou. Walk away or I'll drag your faggoty little ass back to jail."

I glared at him. I needed to locate Pratt and Dietz, but I couldn't do it from a holding cell. I turned to Peyton and pointed at him. "You're gonna wish you talked."

"Come on, Peyton." Evans put his arm over his shoulder. "Don't know what you ever saw in that fucking fairy."

I stopped in my tracks, feeling as if someone had struck my chest with a hammer. *Fuck me. Evans was the third shooter at the Main Drag.*

I pushed my way through the raucous crowd, trailing Evans and Peyton and unsure of my next move. At the barricades for the counter-protest, Evans flashed his badge to an officer keeping the two sides separated. Evans and Peyton continued into the White Nation area.

If I reported what I knew to Detective Skoglund, would they do anything? I had no proof other than a vague memory of Evans's voice that night. And eyewitness accounts were unreliable. For all I knew, my mind could be filling in details just because Evans and the shooter both said, "Fucking fairies."

"Jinx! Jinx!"

I turned around, looking for who had called my name. Chelsea and Izzie from the L Street bar were pushing their way through the crowd.

"Hey!" I hugged them. "Crazy scene, huh!"

"I know, right?" Izzie's head was shaved on the left side, while the right side flowed in shoulder-length purple locks. "D'you hear what happened at the Main Drag last night?"

"I was there."

"Shit," said Chelsea. "You all right?"

"Better than most who were there. I…" I couldn't finish my sentence. And judging from their faces, I didn't need to. "Hey, sorry for getting trashed at the bar a few nights ago."

"No worries." Chelsea winked at me. "Lotta people in a funk this time of year."

Someone in the White Nation crowd began launching smoking canisters into the air.

"What the hell?" shouted Izzie.

One landed at my feet, spewing white smoke. The acrid scent of tear gas stung my eyes. I covered my nose with the inside of my arm and looked toward the source of the projectiles. Most of the counter-protesters backed away from the barricades.

A few others picked up the canisters and threw them back at White Nation.

"Let's get out of here," I yelled to Izzie and Chelsea over the din, pointing toward the *Arizona* anchor. Coughing and wiping their eyes, they nodded.

Before we could take two steps, an explosion shook the air, nearly knocking me off my feet. Screams erupted as dark smoke rose from the now blackened and shattered USS *Arizona* anchor. Caught between the tear gas and the explosion, the crowd flowed north like a powerful ocean current. I moved with them to keep from getting trampled, losing Izzie and Chelsea in the process.

My mind raced with questions as I tried to make sense of what was going on. Was this what Peyton was warning me about? What had his father gotten him mixed up in? Conor's face appeared in my mind. Was this how he'd gotten involved with the IRA?

And why hadn't the feds believed me when I tried to warn them? Yes, my evidence was flimsy, but now people were dead. I took no joy in being right. Instead, I just felt sick and angry.

The panicked crowd snaked between buildings and began to thin around Monroe Avenue. I hustled east and crossed back to Adams on Fifteenth Avenue, where I'd parked.

I sat in the Gray Ghost, staring at the black column of smoke rising over the downtown area. Police sirens screamed like a chorus of coyotes.

What the hell was this world coming to? All the hope I'd once had of a kinder, safer world during the Obama administration had been crushed with the new politics of cruelty, apathy, and bigotry. Outright lies and absurd conspiracies were trotted out as truth. Stalwarts of journalism had abandoned investigation and objective reporting for an endless parade of political consultants and biased talking heads.

And now my high school boyfriend blamed me for his father's brutality. My current boyfriend was being hunted by the Northern Ireland police for the crimes of his youth. The world was upside down. I didn't know how to turn it right side up. But that didn't mean I wasn't going to try.

38

Too numb and shaken to drive, I dialed Detective Hardin's cell phone.

"Not now, Ballou," he said sharply. "Shit just hit the fan downtown."

"I was there, Hardin. That's why I'm calling."

"Where are you?"

"In a parking lot. Monroe and Fifteenth Avenue."

"Stay put. I'll send a uni to pick you up."

As I waited, I texted Becca and my brother to let them know I was okay.

Thirty minutes later, I was sitting in an interview room in the Phoenix PD Homicide Unit with Hardin after a patrol officer picked me up. He pulled out his notebook and asked me what I saw.

"When I was at the protest, I ran into an old friend. Peyton Dietz."

"Why's that name sound familiar?" Hardin asked.

"His father's Barclay Dietz."

He paused a moment, then nodded. "Barclay the Beast. He's the one who assaulted you when you were a teen. Peyton was his kid, whom you were dating."

"I'm surprised you remember."

"I remember you had a lot of potential when you were a boot. I was disappointed when you quit the force." He looked up from his notes. "Is this Peyton kid connected to the bombing?"

"He told me to leave the protest, said he didn't want me getting hurt. When I pressed him why, your buddy Officer Mitch Evans intervened. Threatened to arrest me for assaulting Peyton."

"Had you assaulted him?"

"No. But Evans and Peyton seemed awful chummy. The two of them went over to where White Nation was staging their white nationalist temper tantrum."

"Seems a little thin, Ballou."

"There's something else. As the two of them were leaving, I heard Evans call me a 'fucking fairy.' It was his voice I heard the night of the Main Drag shooting. He was also first on scene when I tried to apprehend Barclay Dietz at that meeting at Dixie's Bar, where a White Nation meeting was being held."

"You're saying Evans was involved in both this bombing and the shooting? Those are some serious accusations with very little proof."

"Hey, I'm trying to help you out, doing my civic duty and all. If you don't want the info, fine by me." I stood up to leave.

"Hold on, Ballou. I'm not saying I don't believe you. But if you're going to be pointing fingers at a law enforcement officer—"

"An officer who's already shot an unarmed black man."

He held my gaze for a few minutes. The wheels were turning in his head.

"Look, Hardin, you know him better than I do. Is it really a stretch to believe he's involved with White Nation? I've given you a few leads you might not get anywhere else. Do with them what you want."

He called after me as I walked out. I didn't care. I'd done what I felt was right. Now it was on him.

I barely noticed the cold as I walked the mile back to where the Gray Ghost was parked. I was about to call Caden for a status update on Juanita when my phone rang. It was Becca with what I hoped was a new lead on either Pratt or Dietz.

"Becks, what've you got for me?"

"Jinx, you need to get home now."

"Why? What's going on?" Had Reggie fallen off the ladder trying to fix my roof? Would my homeowner's insurance cover that?

"I can't say over the phone." Her voice had an odd quality to it.

"You're freaking me out here. I barely survived that explosion downtown. Just tell me what the hell's going on." I had a flashback to when Milo Volkov had left the body of a dead journalist on my porch in a sick attempt to woo me. "Is my house on fire? Was there a burglary? What?"

"I...I can't say. Just trust me. Get home now."

A sick feeling spread through my body. Whatever it was, it sounded bad. But why couldn't she tell me? "Fine. I'm on my way. Are you there now?"

"No, but someone else is."

"Who?"

"Go."

I hung up and raced the Gray Ghost north along Seventh Avenue. No sooner had I crossed Fillmore Street than I noticed that damned Caprice tailing me again.

"Mother-goddamn-fucker, can't those feds leave me alone for once?" I swerved into a convenience store parking lot, tired of playing these silly games. The Caprice followed suit before parking a few spaces to my left.

I jumped out of the Gray Ghost and slammed the door shut. Time to give Special Agent Baby Face a piece of my mind.

As I approached, the Caprice's passenger window lowered. The barrel of a gun emerged from the dark interior. I ducked behind an ice machine as two rounds ripped through the air.

"What the fuck?" *When does the FBI shoot at people they're tailing? Answer: they don't.*

I drew my Glock, peeked around the ice machine, and

unleashed a barrage of nine-millimeter rounds into my attacker's car. The Caprice's wheels smoked as it whipped around in reverse. I had enough time to put another two rounds into the trunk and read the license plate before it peeled out and disappeared down the street, tires screaming, engine roaring.

I looked around to see where the shooter's bullets had gone. Clouds of steam billowed from under the hood of a nearby Toyota.

A black man jumped out of the car. "What the hell? I just bought this car."

I wrote the Caprice's license plate on one of my business cards and handed it to the guy. "Call the cops. Tell them this is the car that the shooter was in. I'm going to go try to catch them."

"Hey, wait a minute, lady," he called as I hopped in the Gray Ghost.

There was no way I was going to catch the Caprice. It was long gone. But I still had an unknown emergency at home to deal with. So I floored it, honking for the slower cars to get out of my way. What the hell was going on? A house fire? Had White Nation attacked my house and hurt Reggie?

When I pulled onto my street, I looked for emergency vehicles, but there weren't any. No crowd of onlookers gathered in their yards. In fact, the street was as quiet as it usually was on a Saturday afternoon.

I pulled into my driveway and rushed in my front door to the sound of raised voices.

"For the last time, Miss Jinx's letting me stay here while I do a little repair work around the house." This was Reggie.

"If she needed repairs done, she woulda hired her brother to do it." *Fuck me.* Conor'd shown up finally. "So put down that whiskey bottle or I'll put a hole in ya."

"What the hell's going on?"

"Finally!" Conor said, holding a gun on Reggie. "Took yer bloody time gettin' here."

"I had stuff to deal with. Now what the fuck's going on, Conor?"

"Found this creepy bloke lurking in your yard, helping himself to my whiskey."

"Miss Jinx, would you tell this gentleman you asked me to fix your roof and that I could help myself?"

Good grief. Men. As if I didn't have enough shit to deal with.

I pointed at Conor. "You! Put away the gun." I turned to Reggie. "As for you, I said help yourself to food, not booze." I grabbed the bottle from him.

To Conor, I said, "You and me need to have a serious talk, mister."

Reggie guffawed, and both Conor and I told him to shut the hell up. I led Conor down to my bedroom and slammed the door shut.

39

"What the bloody hell's going on, Jinxie? Ya taking in strays and lodgers now? When I said you should get a pet, I didn't mean a scraggly git like that dodgy bloke."

I took a breath. "First of all, my house, my rules."

"The guy's a drunk."

"The guy has a name. It's Reggie. And just because he takes a drink doesn't make him a drunk."

"Oh yeah? And who's Reggie when he's at home? Or your home, I should say."

"I found him camping out in my attic. He's homeless." I held up a hand before Conor could interrupt. "He's been living here for a week already with no harm done."

"'Cept drinking my whiskey."

"For the record, it's my whiskey. I bought it just the other day. And I asked him to do some repair work on my house."

"And how long is he staying?"

"I don't know. But enough about Reggie. Let's address the real elephant in the room. Where the hell have you been? I haven't seen you since the shooting at the club."

His demeanor changed. In an instant, he looked like a deflated balloon. "They're onto me. The PSNI and the feds."

"Yeah, I know. They showed up earlier this morning asking where you were. I didn't tell them shit."

"I'm so bloody sorry, love." He hugged me. It felt so good to be in his arms again.

"Any idea who tipped them off? It wasn't Sadie, was it?"

Conor shook his head. "I talked to one of my mates from Dark Horse Security. Apparently PSNI's working cold cases. Something to do with Brexit and wild rumors of Irish unification. Somehow they got hold of surveillance footage with me in it. Face recognition pulled up a possible match."

"After all these years? Damn." I shook my head. "So what's your plan?"

I didn't like the idea that I was harboring a fugitive wanted for an act of terrorism.

"Been staying with someone from way back who happens to be local."

"Who?"

"Best ya didn't know, in case they question ya again."

"Maybe you should come clean. You've been running for most of your life. Explain you never meant for anyone to get hurt. That you were told the wrong information. Besides, you were just a teenager at the time."

"I was seventeen, love. And they don't care what I was trying to do. That bloody phone call…" His words caught in his throat. "On the other hand, I don't want you gettin' messed up in this nonsense. I just…I hate to think I'd never see yer gorgeous face again."

"I could visit you in prison, maybe. They have bounty hunters in the UK?" It was a feeble attempt at humor, but it beat crying, which was what I felt like doing.

Conor's face turned deadly serious. "Traitors and terrorists aren't exactly greeted with open arms over there. Assuming they don't execute me, I probably won't last long in prison. But maybe that's what I deserve."

"No," I said, choking back tears. "I'm not going to let anyone hurt you. But you shouldn't be here. They've been watching the house. They've been tailing me."

"I know, but I had to see ya. I've been shite without ya, love."

"I've missed you too." He smelled of body odor and sweat. Nothing ever smelled so good to me. "I'm sorry for all the crap I said to you about not coming into the hospital."

"How's your mate, Juanita?"

"Not good. Still in a coma."

"I'm so sorry."

"Sometimes I wish I could just chuck it all and move away. Like to Canada or the UK. Some place where people aren't trying to kill each other all the time. Maybe Scandinavia. But I'd probably miss the sun too much. And I don't do real well in the cold."

"What about Spain?"

"Spain?" I looked to see whether he was kidding. But his face was serious, if a bit earnest.

"It's a warm, relatively dry climate, not that different from Arizona."

"You serious? Just pack up and leave?"

And that was when it hit me—why I didn't want to move in with him. We were bounty hunters, bound to return fugitives to custody. And yet he was a fugitive. If I moved in with him, I'd be no different than the people hiding their bail-jumping loved ones. I couldn't live with myself.

"Why not pack up and leave? It'll be an adventure."

"Adventure, my ass. Conor, that's crazy. What's to keep the Northern Ireland police from coming after you there?"

"Picardo can set us up with new identities. A whole new start." Picardo was a document forger who sometimes helped us with fugitives trying to leave the country. In exchange, we didn't turn him in to the cops.

"What will we live on?"

Now he grinned. "I have a sizable nest egg I set aside a while back in case I had to run."

"Like how big a nest egg?"

He shrugged. "Three, four hundred grand. Maybe a little more now. Been a while since I checked the balance."

"Three or four hundred grand? For doing what?"

"Combination of things. I made some good investments early on. I did some private bodyguard work for some Arab royalty after Iraq. They pay rather well, it turns out, especially when you're watching their kids."

"You're just telling me this now. I feel like I don't even know you."

"I'm someone who wants to live the rest of his life with the woman he loves."

"Conor...What about my family? My friends?"

His enthusiasm waivered. "Unfortunately, ya wouldn't be able to contact them. Not ever."

"Fuck." I sat on the bed, my head spinning.

"I realize it's a tough choice, love. I know how close ya are with your folks. But I can't stay now that they're onto me."

"I'm going to have to give this some thought." I looked into his eyes, as green as the first buds of spring. I felt I was being torn apart, forced to choose between the people I loved the most. "How long do I have to decide?"

"A couple days at the most."

"That's it?"

"I'll need some time to arrange documents, transport, and lodging, so the sooner you decide, the better. I don't know how long I can keep dodging that inspector from PSNI."

"I love you so much, Conor. But this is the hardest decision I've ever had to make."

"Maybe this will make it easier." He reached into his pocket and got down on one knee. "This isn't how I meant to do this, but now's as good a time as any."

He held a black velvet box that he opened to reveal an 18-karat-gold ring with a large diamond bordered by two emeralds.

"Holy fuck, Conor!"

"Jenna Christine Ballou, would ya do me the honor of becoming my wife?"

I struggled to suck in enough air to speak. "Conor, I…I… uh…"

"I know, it's last minute. But we've been dating a couple years. Your mother's been nagging ya about getting married for a while. If you're gonna run away with me, the least I can do is make an honest woman out of ya."

"Conor, I…this…fuck." My stomach knotted. "I want to say yes. You know I do. But it means giving up everything else."

"I know, but honestly, I can't live without ya." He put his hands on either side of my head and kissed me so deeply all I wanted to do was fuck his ever-loving brains out.

"I feel the same way."

My heart was hammering away like a piston. Could I give up my whole life for a man? I had reinvented myself once before when I became a girl at age eleven. But I had a lot of support then.

Here I was at thirty, looking at reinventing my world once more, assuming a new identity, and at the same time giving up all that support. It was insane. And yet one look into Conor's eyes and it felt as though it just might be worth it.

As my mind considered the possibilities, I imagined a completely new life and what that would do to my family. Before I could reply, my phone rang. It was Caden.

"Juanita's awake!" His voice rattled with a combination of exhaustion and joy.

"Seriously? What are the doctors saying?"

"She's really confused, but she can move her hands and feet. They have the infection under control. She's having trouble speaking and walking, but the neurologist said she might recover with therapy. Jinx, she's alive!"

Before I could stop myself, I was bawling from a combination of gratitude, guilt, fear, and who knew what else. Conor put a hand on my shoulder.

When I was finally able to speak, I said, "Caden, that's great. I…I can't believe it."

"You think you can come by this afternoon?"

"Yeah, give me about an hour or so, but I'll be there."

I hung up and shared the good news with Conor.

"I'm happy for her. I know how much she means to ya."

"I have to go see her, Conor."

He nodded. "I understand."

"Ask me again."

"Ask what—oh! That!" He knelt down again. Jenna Christine—"

"Yes! Yes! I will fucking marry you!" Maybe it was gratitude that Juanita was on the mend. Or maybe it was a reaction to the trauma of the past few days. Or maybe I'd gone completely insane. But all at once, I had no doubt about who I wanted to spend the rest of my life with.

He slipped the ring on my finger. It fit perfectly. Seeing it glitter in the light made me feel so girly, a feeling I could only describe as gender euphoria. Like the time my mother took me shopping for my first bra. I was going to get married. How weird was that? Me married. It didn't seem real.

"You think it's okay for me to wear? What if the feds and that inspector from Northern Ireland want to question me?"

"If they ask about the ring, tell them I proposed a few days ago. But if you think it will cause too much trouble, you can take it off until we're ready to leave."

I looked at it. "I'll leave it on."

"That's my girl. I'll reach out to Picardo and my other contacts to make the arrangements. And darlin', you're gonna love Spain."

40

Conor slipped out the back door, and I found Reggie sitting in the corner of the living room, watching the news coverage of the bombing. Much of it was speculation and updates of body counts. So far, eight were confirmed dead.

"Hey, sorry about the confusion earlier," I said. "Conor's a bit protective with all the craziness going on."

"Man nearly kilt me. Pointed a gun at me."

"I'm sorry. It won't happen again. Last year, I had someone stalking me. People died. So when he found a stranger in my house, he went a little overboard."

"I'll say." He stared at the TV as a reporter interviewed someone. "You down there when that explosion went off?"

"I was." The euphoria I'd been riding evaporated as memories of the chaos returned. "White Nation set off the bomb after driving the crowd toward it with tear gas."

"You still in one piece, though, right?"

"I am." I sat down next to him. "My friend who's in the hospital just came out of the coma. I need to go spend some time with her."

"What about your man?" Reggie looked a little concerned.

"He has to run some errands, but he understands you're staying here for the time being. Shouldn't be a problem anymore."

"Well, let's hope not. I don't mind fixing your roof to help pay for my lodging and food, but ain't nothing worth getting shot at."

I caught myself looking at the ring. The emeralds reminded me of the green of Conor's eyes. I took off my ballistic vest and my utility belt, then secured the Glock in the small gun locker in my closet. I kept the revolver in my ankle holster just in case.

An hour later, I walked into Juanita's hospital room. The ventilator was out. White bandages peeked out from under the scarf on her head. Her face was blank as she stared at the television mounted across the room.

"Hey, look who it is!" Caden smelled of BO and looked as though he hadn't slept since the last time I was there.

Juanita turned to me. Her eyes narrowed for a moment, as if she were trying to remember who I was, then she gave me a faint smile. "*¡Mi'ja!*"

I blubbered up right away and gently hugged her.

"I'm so glad to see you, *tía*." I wiped my eyes and sat on my haunches, my head level with hers. "You had us all worried."

She nodded. "I worry."

The tears kept coming. It broke my heart to see her like this. I missed my sassy, sarcastic fairy drag mother. I hoped I would get to see her again before I left for Spain.

"They treating you all right here?"

She made a face. "Nurse *puta*. Kept waking me up."

"I'm sorry. They tend to do that in places like this."

"Doctor good, though. Knows her shit. Kept me alive." She turned to Caden and pinched her nose. "*Apesta.* Caden stinky."

Just like that, I burst out laughing. Caden covered his face in embarrassment, but I caught a hint of a smile.

"Yeah, he's a bit ripe. But considering he's been by your bedside nonstop for days, maybe we'll cut him a little slack."

One side of her mouth curled up in a grin. "Maybe slack."

I spent the next few hours with her while Caden ran home to grab a shower and a change of clothes. Someone brought in dinner, which consisted of chicken broth, Jell-O, and weak tea. Juanita drank half of the broth, turned her nose up at the Jell-O, and took a few sips of the tea. Not bad for a first meal.

When Caden returned, he noticed the ring on my finger. "Hey! Is that what I think it is?"

I blushed, a mix of embarrassment and guilt. "Conor asked me to marry him."

"Congrats, girl!" Caden hugged me. "Isn't that something, Juanita?"

"'Bout damn time," she whispered. Maybe she was in there after all.

"Speaking of time, I better be heading home. But I'll stop by tomorrow, okay?" I hugged her again, then Caden.

"You better, *mi'ja.*"

I stepped out of the room and found myself getting choked up again. At this point, I didn't know what the hell I was feeling. The only word that came to mind was *overwhelmed.* I needed to put some cream on my burned hand and could use a few beers for the pain.

As I walked outside into the chilly early evening, my phone rang. No name came up on the caller ID, but it was a local number. "Hello?"

"Jinx?" asked a familiar voice.

"Who is this?"

"Peyton. Peyton Dietz." He was speaking in hushed tones.

"Well, well, Peyton Dietz. How's life as a Nazi terrorist?"

"I didn't know it was going to happen like that. I didn't think...I didn't realize people would be hurt."

"Then you're dumber than you look, Peyton. Bombs tend to have that effect."

"I tried to warn you. You should thank me for saving your life."

"Oh yeah, and what about the people you killed? Doesn't exactly make you a hero in my book."

"Jinx, we need to talk."

"You want someone to talk to? Try the cops or maybe the feds. I know an Agent Lovelace who'd love to chat with you."

"I need to talk with you, Jinx. Those things I said earlier, I didn't mean them. I was just trying to piss you off enough to get you to leave. Remember in high school, you and me watched that *Lassie* marathon on TV. That one episode where the ranger's coming to take Lassie away, so the kid tells Lassie he hates her."

"So in this scenario, I'm the dumb dog. Yeah, that makes things *so* much better."

There were voices in the background on his end of the line. He started whispering. "I still care about you, Jinx. I know my father's done some awful things. That's why I wanted to talk with you."

"Fine, so talk."

"Not on the phone. In person."

"In person? How stupid do you think I am? First you have no idea your father's in town. Next thing I know, you're planting a bomb that killed ten people. And now you want me to meet you? I know a setup when I see one."

"It's not a setup. And I wasn't the one that set the bomb."

The voices in the background got louder. Peyton spoke to whoever it was. The phone got bumped around until finally he came back on the line. "They're planning something big. I need your help to stop it. Please. I'll even help you bring my father in."

"Fine, where do you want to meet?"

"Take Carefree Highway and turn south on Fifty-First Avenue. It's basically a dirt road, but there's a sign. Go about a mile and it dead-ends at an old abandoned ranch."

A ranch, huh? The ranch. "When?"

"Tomorrow around eleven o'clock."

"I'll be there. But if this is an ambush, you *will* regret it, I promise you."

"It's not, I swear." The line went dead.

"Shit." I had every reason not to believe him, but in my gut,

I felt Peyton was on the level. Still, who was I to stop White Nation's next act of terrorism? This was something better suited to the cops.

I dialed Hardin's number in Homicide. It rang twice before a male voice answered. "Detective Hardin's desk."

"I need to speak with Hardin."

"He's not available at the moment. Could I take a message?"

"Who is this?"

"Detective Loughlin. Who is this?"

I hung up. Last person I wanted to leave a message with was Loughlin after he'd arrested me for shooting Overcash. Chances were he was clean, if a bit too eager to arrest people for defending themselves. On the off chance that he, too, was in with White Nation, I didn't want to tip them off that Peyton had turned on them.

I called Hardin's cell number. After three rings, it went to voicemail.

"This is Ballou. Call me when you can. It's important."

It might still be a trap, but this proposed meeting with Peyton was now my best chance at catching his dad and possibly Rudy Pratt. But I didn't want to risk it alone. Safety in numbers and all that shit.

I called Rodeo first, though I knew it was a long shot. "What's up, Jinx?"

"How's the arm?"

"Not bad. Only hurts when I move it. Or when I think about it. Or when I'm sleeping. Basically all the damn time. How's your friend, Juanita?"

"She's awake. Docs are optimistic." I wanted his help meeting with Peyton, but if things got rough, he'd be more of a liability than an asset.

"Good to hear. Incidentally, Jake called, begging me to take him back and promising to work on his internal homophobia."

"Is that so? Who knew my brother had it in him."

"Seems someone gave him a good talking-to."

"Huh. I wonder who that could've been."

"I told him I'd give him another chance. So I guess we're un-broken up."

"I'm happy for you two."

"Thanks, Jinx. Jake's lucky to have you as a sister. I owe you one."

"You take care of that arm, Rodeo."

"Roger that."

I hung up and called Caden.

"Everything all right?" he asked.

"I got a call from Barclay Dietz's kid. He's offering to help bag his father. Wants to meet at an abandoned ranch off Carefree Highway and Fifty-First Avenue."

"Sounds like a trap."

"I thought so too. But my gut's telling me he's legit. You think you can step away from Juanita for a little bit tomorrow?"

"I think I can manage that. What time?"

"Meet me in the parking lot of the Ben Avery Shooting Range at twelve thirty. The meet's not until one, but I want to get there early. Just in case."

"Smart. I'll see you there."

A calm came over me as I drove home. I even caught myself humming Christmas tunes, which never fucking happened. I had no idea what I might face in my meeting tomorrow with Peyton. But with Juanita on the mend and this crazy ring on my finger, I couldn't help feeling hopeful, even cheerful.

When I walked in the door of my house, I found Reggie watching *A Christmas Carol*, the one with the guy who played Patton as Scrooge.

"I hope you don't mind, but I made a meatloaf for dinner. There's plenty left over if you hungry."

"Wow! You can fix roofs and you can cook? How come you're not already married?"

He laughed. "Yeah, who wouldn't want a homeless junkie for a husband?"

"Ex-junkie. You seem all right to me. Lot of people ended up homeless during the recession. Shit happens. Hell, if I wasn't already"—I almost said "engaged"—"dating someone."

"Girl, I'm old enough to be your grandfather."

"Father. Maybe. Look, we all got a past. Doesn't have to define us."

"Maybe you right."

"Conor around?"

"He snuck in the back door while back."

"Didn't give you any more trouble, did he?"

"Naw, not so far."

"Good. I'm going to freshen up a bit, and then I'll grab some dinner."

I walked into my bedroom and found Conor on the floor in the dark, typing away on a laptop.

"Peyton wants to meet tomorrow. Possibly a trap, but it may be my last chance to grab his dad. You in or are you still laying low?"

"You know I've always got your back. I'm in."

"Thanks. What are you working on?" I sat on the floor next to him and leaned my head on his shoulder.

"Plane tickets from Puerto Peñasco, Mexico, to Valencia, Spain. We should get our new passports in two days. What do you think of the name Eileen Anne Crawford?"

"Hmmm, I'm not sure it suits you."

He shoved me playfully. "Not for me, ya daft girl. For you."

"Sounds very British. Eileen Anne Crawford," I repeated in a posh British accent.

"Well, technically, you're Canadian."

"Am I?"

"At least according to your new passport."

The reality hit me like a clue-by-four. "Shit, this is really happening? Tomorrow may be the last time I see my folks." The excitement mixed with a deep sadness and guilt.

"It is. Having second thoughts?"

"A few. But I want to be with you. I just hope they'll understand."

"When I was a wee lad, my da told me about the American wakes."

"American wakes?"

"When someone in Ireland decided to venture to the New World, his family knew they'd not likely see them again. So they'd throw a wake, as if they were dying."

"Sounds very sad."

"Aye, a bit. But also happy for the lad or lass going on to new adventures in America."

"Did your family throw an American wake for you?"

"Not sure. They didn't know I was leaving."

"Are we going to have to keep doing this? Building lives, then running away?"

He kissed my forehead. "I bloody well hope not. From now on, I'll try to keep a lower profile than I have."

"Where will we live?"

"My mate Tuckey's working on securing us a villa in Valencia. You like the ocean?"

"I've been to the beaches in San Diego a bunch of times. It's okay. Water's too cold to swim in."

"Valencia is nothing like San Diego. Mediterranean is warm and beautiful. Not cold and clogged with kelp like the Pacific. Great music. Great food. Hot wom…well, that last part's not important anymore."

"Damn straight! You're gonna be a married man, Mister, uh, what is your name going to be?"

"Damien Ellsworth Crawford. Also Canadian."

"Yeah, well, you're going to need to do something about that Dubliner accent of yours."

"Hey, I can talk with a Canadian accent, eh?" The result sounded like a Southerner faking a bad Minnesota accent.

I burst out laughing. "That is the worst Canadian accent."

"Where's my tuk? Did I leave it in the washroom? How about some poutine?"

I laughed so hard I could barely breathe. "Oh...oh, shit, that's fucking horrible." Another spasm of giggles took hold of me until I was snorting. "I suppose I can't go wrong with a man who makes me laugh like that."

41

The next morning, I showed up at my parents' place for Sunday brunch. Conor wanted to come, knowing this would be hard for me. But we decided that with him on PSNI's Most Wanted List, he should stay put.

Jake and Rodeo were already there when I arrived, looking like two teenage lovebirds who couldn't keep their eyes off each other. My mother doted on Rodeo because of his injured arm. My dad was busy cooking strawberry crepes, which were being eaten as fast as he could make them. When they asked about Conor, I told them he was on a stakeout that ran long.

Christmas music was playing on a radio on the kitchen counter, and the whole place was decked out for the holidays. The twelve-year-old artificial Christmas tree gleamed in the corner, covered in lights and decorations that dated back to my childhood and before. Some of the glass ornaments were at least a century old.

And while I tried to join in with the holiday spirit, an emptiness gnawed at me. Never again would I groan at my father's corny jokes or roll my eyes at my mother's nudges to have a family of my own. Jake would no longer ask me to help him renovate a run-down house he was planning to flip. I wouldn't even be spending Christmas with them, which was only ten days away.

After breakfast, I helped my father with the dishes. Despite having a dishwasher, he preferred the "zen of washing them by hand," whatever that meant.

"Dad, you know I love you, right?"

"Course I do, *cher*. Why would you ask?"

"Just wanted to make sure. Mom and Jake too."

He set down a glass and held my gaze. "Something wrong, sweetie?"

"After what happened to Juanita, it got me thinking about how quickly things can happen. I just wanted to make sure you all know."

"You know we all love you, too, don't you?"

Tears pricked behind my eyes. "Yeah, I do."

"How's Miss Juanita doing, by the way?"

"She's out of the coma. Got a long recovery ahead of her, but it looks hopeful. I think the worst is over."

"That's so good to hear. When you came out, we weren't sure how best to help you. That girl, she really stepped up and became a mentor for you. Your mom's been lighting a whole lotta candles for her."

"Huh. I didn't think Mom liked her."

"I'll admit, your mother wasn't sure what to make of her. That whole intense drag queen act and all. I think Juanita scared her a bit."

"She can be a bit scary at times."

"But your mother saw how much Juanita helped, especially with matters your mother and I didn't know much about—the dysphoria, the misgendering, things that only a trans person understands."

"Yeah." It made me sad all over again, thinking how much I would miss Juanita. "She's something special."

The silence between us grew until my father said, "We received a visit from the FBI the other day. A gentleman from the Northern Irish police was with them, looking for Conor."

Shit. "Really?"

"Conor in some kind of trouble?"

"They have him confused with someone else," I said as convincingly as I could. "Kirsten, my attorney, is helping to straighten it out."

"Are you in some kind of trouble?"

He cupped my head in his hands. Worry troubled his eyes.

"I'm okay, Dad." He didn't look convinced. I hugged him. "I love you so much."

At eleven o'clock, I hugged them all again. I tried to act normal, as though I would be seeing them all again within the next week, if not sooner. But my heart felt like lead.

I cried all the way back to my place. I wiped my face before I walked in the house. Conor pulled on one of my spare Kevlar vests, with his Walther tucked in his waistband. I grabbed the Colt 1911 I'd taken off Daniel Warren. If things went sideways, I'd rather not have any spent rounds traced back to me.

Before we left, I checked outside to make sure there weren't any suspicious cars on the street. It was clear. No sign of the feds. Still, Conor kept low as I drove the Gray Ghost north to meet Caden at Ben Avery.

42

Conor and I pulled into the Ben Avery Shooting Range parking lot a few minutes before Caden, who arrived decked out in his body armor and gear.

"How's Juanita this morning?" I asked as he approached the Gray Ghost.

"Pissed that she's on a clear liquid diet. Pissed that I had to leave. Pissed that you're not there."

"So pretty much her usual self."

He shrugged. "For the most part. Still having problems with speaking, walking, and some fine motor skills, but the doctors are optimistic that will come back with therapy."

"Good to hear." The fact that she was improving eased the guilt of my impending departure but only a little.

I pulled out a printed map of the area. "On to the business at hand. Peyton's only expecting me. He's supposed to come alone himself. However, I don't trust him. So Caden, I need you to be our lookout. I want you here, concealed if possible." I pointed at a spot on the dirt road for the ranch, just off Carefree Highway. "Give us a heads-up on the walkie-talkies when you see vehicles headed our direction."

"Roger that."

I turned to Conor. "You'll be with me down by the abandoned ranch. I suggest we leave Caden's car here in the shooting range parking lot so Peyton doesn't get spooked when he sees it. Any questions?"

We climbed into the Gray Ghost and drove the half mile down the road until we came to the turnoff. A short ways down the road, I stopped. Caden turned on his walkie-talkie, stepped out of the Gray Ghost, and took cover behind a cluster of palo verde trees.

Closer to the ranch, the gravel road deteriorated into a seldom-used Jeep trail riddled with ruts and creosote bushes. Other trails intersected it here and there, but we continued south until the trail dead-ended at the remains of an adobe building. Nearby, cracked wooden posts dangled from rusted barbed wire clinging to ocotillo plants in the corners of the corrals.

I backed up the Gray Ghost next to the ranch house. If things went south, I didn't want to waste time making a three-point turn.

Conor and I got out and inspected our surroundings. The roof of the ranch house was gone. The adobe walls were worn and crumbling from the brutal heat of countless summers and the intense storms of the monsoon seasons. A cracked wooden door hung from one hinge, squeaking in the slight breeze. Only fragments of glass remained in the windows.

"Why does this feel like high noon in some spaghetti western?" Conor asked.

"You've watched too many Clint Eastwood movies." But I felt it too. A sense of impending doom.

The radio squawked. "One bogie headed your way," called Caden. "Dark-red Honda sedan. Driver is a white male, no passengers visible."

"Thanks, Caden. That'd be our guy. Keep an eye out in case we have any unexpected company."

"Roger that. Over and out."

A dust cloud rose, and I spotted Peyton's Accord. I had my hand on the Colt. Conor drew his Walther and held it at his side.

Peyton pulled alongside the Gray Ghost and got out. He shuffled up to us, his eyes wary. "I wanted this to be just the two of us," he said to me. "Who the hell's this?"

I was tempted to say he was my fiancé. "Fellow bounty hunter. I needed to be sure you were on the level. And I wanted help bringing in your father. Where is he?"

"At a ranch near Cave Creek."

"He alone?"

Peyton stared at the dirt, kicking around a stone. "No. There are others there."

"So what's the plan, boyo?" Conor took a step toward Peyton. "Ya setting Jinxie up like ya did the other day with the bombing?"

"No!" Peyton backed away. "I never meant for anyone to get hurt! You have to believe me."

"Oh?" I approached him, my fists clenching. "And what did you expect would happen when you set off that bomb?"

"It wasn't me!"

"Then who the bloody hell was it, ya fucking wanker?"

I stepped into his personal space, forcing him to look up at me. "It was Evans, wasn't it?"

"Yeah, he's the one that left it by the anchor." His face colored. "They're planning another one. Bigger."

"Where?" I pressed.

"I don't know yet. They always speak in code. Site A. Site B. But wherever it is, I get the impression they plan to kill a lot of people. They said it'd be bigger than Oklahoma City. Maybe bigger than 9/11."

"When, ya little shit?" growled Conor.

"I don't know. But soon."

I shook my head. "You need to be telling this to the cops, Peyton."

He chuckled darkly. "The cops? Who do I tell? Evans *is* a cop. If they find out I talked, I'm a dead man."

"And yet you're talking to us," replied Conor.

"Because I thought I could trust you, Jinx. And you were always smart. I hoped you could stop them somehow."

"We're just bounty hunters, Pey. We're not the bomb squad or SWAT."

"Fine." He turned on his heel and shuffled back to his car.

I hustled after him. "Peyton, wait!"

He stopped and stood with his car door open.

"You help us arrest your dad, we'll see what we can do to stop this other bomb." I glanced at Conor. He had a disapproving look on his face.

"Can you bring him in alive? I know he's done a lot of bad things, but he's still my dad. I'm afraid if I went to the feds, they'd kill him." He looked as though he were about to cry.

I put a hand on his shoulder. "I don't think he'll come along quietly no matter who tries to bring him in. After what he did to me, I'd fantasized about killing him a gazillion times."

"I can't blame you. But I'm asking as a favor to me. If you promise not to kill him, I'll set it up so you can bring him in."

My radio crackled. "Jinx, we got two bogies inbound. A red pickup truck and a black sedan. Both coming in fast."

"You expecting anyone else?" I asked Peyton.

"No!"

"You're a fucking liar." Conor rushed him, putting his Walther to Peyton's temple.

"I swear I didn't tell anyone I was coming."

The staccato beats of automatic gunfire caught my attention.

"I'm taking fire," Caden shouted.

The gunfire ceased, replaced by the roar of engines.

"Caden!" I shouted into my walkie. "Caden, do you read me?"

No response.

Conor grabbed my arm and pulled me toward the ranch house. "Jinxie, we got to get to cover."

I followed him into the ruined adobe building and crouched at a broken window, my Colt pointed at the rising column of dust. Conor took a position standing inside the door.

Movement caught my eye. Peyton was still out there.

"Peyton, get in here!"

He ignored me and instead walked past his car toward the approaching vehicles, waving his arms in the air. What the hell? Had he set us up? Or had he been followed?

A red pickup truck crested a small hill. In the bed of the truck stood a man armed with a large assault rifle.

"Peyton, get your ass in here!"

The guy in the back of the truck opened fire. Peyton's body exploded in a blast of red.

Conor and I returned fire. The gunman turned to us. The ground shook as bullets peppered the adobe wall. I fired until the gunman's chest blossomed red and he collapsed in the truck bed. The pickup veered off and turned back the way it had come, then passed the black sedan roaring down the trail.

The sedan skidded to a stop. It looked like the Caprice that had opened fire on me the day before. The dust became a wall, engulfing the cars and the old ranch house. Everything outside the building became an eerie tan shadowland. Gunshots pinged off the side of the building. I raised my pistol to return fire only to realize the slide was locked back. I was empty.

As I ducked behind the wall to reload, Conor yelped and fell. I rushed to his side. He lay in the doorway, gripping his chest. I pulled him out of the line of fire as the bullets hit all around me.

"You okay?" I gasped, not finding any blood.

"Aye. Bloody bastard got me in the vest." He pulled himself to his feet.

Voices outside caught my attention. "Shit." I peeked out the doorway. Two figures emerged from the car as the dust thinned. I fired at the taller of the two. The other figure fired and dove back into the driver's seat. His shots went wide. I continued firing, but the Caprice whipped around and sent a shower of dirt and rocks in my direction as it charged back down the trail.

43

I approached the figure I had shot and immediately recognized him as Officer Evans. Blood pooled around his body.
My first two shots had hit dead center, the third in his throat.
My ears rang from the sudden silence and from the realization
that I had killed a cop. A dirty, murdering, racist cop but a cop
nevertheless. I was in a shitload of trouble unless I could prove
he was dirty and that I had acted in self-defense.

Conor came up from behind me. "Looks like ya got the
fucker. Good shooting, love."

"He's the cop who set off the bomb at Wesley Bolin Plaza."

"Shite! Bloody wanker. Glad ya got him." He kicked the body.

"We need to check on Caden and…and Peyton."

Conor gave me a look. "I'll see to Caden. You check on
your boyfriend."

"Ex-boyfriend!" I shouted as he hustled off the Jeep trail.

I found what was left of Peyton lying on his back, his blood
soaking into the sand. I checked for a pulse but knew there
wouldn't be one. He was already cool to the touch.

"Fuck, Peyton. What'd you get yourself mixed up in?"

I didn't want to cry. I shouldn't be crying. He hadn't been
my boyfriend in over a decade. I tried to tell myself I was just
wiping sweat and dust from my eyes. My heart ached as I
squeezed his pale, cold hand.

After a while, the rational part of my brain kicked in. I

needed to find his dad and Rudy Pratt. I rummaged through his pockets and found a phone, a set of keys, and his wallet. I kept the phone, hoping it might help me track down my fugitives. The rest I stuffed back into his pockets.

"Jinx? Ya there?" Conor called on the radio.

I wiped my face again. "I'm here. How's Caden?"

"He has a through-and-through on his right thigh. It's bad. Using a belt to stop the bleeding, but he needs medical attention now. How's the ex-boyfriend?"

"Dead. I'm coming to you." I took a final glance at Peyton. I hated leaving him for the vultures and the ravens, but there was nothing else to do.

A couple of bullets had torn through the Gray Ghost's rear seat but hadn't hit anything mechanical. I raced up the dirt road, passing another body I assumed was the shooter from the truck.

I skidded to a stop by the palo verde trees, where Conor was tending to Caden, and hopped out to assist. Caden was groaning and gritting his teeth. His skin was pale. Conor had pulled off his vest and was using his shirt and belt as a makeshift tourniquet to stop the bleeding from Caden's leg.

I tossed Conor's vest into the Gray Ghost. "How's he doing?"

Conor looked worried. "Lost a lot of blood from the exit wound. We gotta get him to hospital fast."

"Nearest one's Deer Valley. Let's get him in the truck."

"How you holding up, Caden?" I asked as we set him into the back seat of the SUV.

"Fucking goddamn hurts," he whimpered, draping his arm over his face. Conor knelt on the floor and snapped the seat belts to hold Caden in place.

I jumped behind the wheel. "We'll get you to the hospital soon, okay?"

"No." He gulped air, trying to get a grip on the pain. "Last time, they kept calling me ma'am. Treated me like a freak."

"Look, mate," said Conor. "You'll die if ya don't get proper medical attention."

"Mika from the support group," Caden grunted. "She's a doc."

"She's a fucking psychiatrist, Cade. You need a trauma surgeon." I jammed my foot hard on the accelerator, fishtailing onto Carefree Highway and hoping I didn't get pulled over by a cop. My mind raced for ideas. "Reggie served as a corpsman in the Marines back in the day."

"Are ya daft? You're gonna trust Caden's life to that free-loading bum?"

"You got any better ideas?" I shot him a look.

"All due respect, love, I spent enough time in Afghanistan and Iraq to know corpsmen just bandage people up long enough to get 'em to a proper surgeon. That's what we're doing. Your mate Reggie can't fix this."

"Fine. Deer Valley it is."

"No! Please," Caden yelled, his voice hoarse and ragged. "I'd rather die than get treated like that again."

I understood how he felt. Most medical personnel were cool, but some were so judgmental and shaming they made you want to slit your own wrists.

"Don't worry, Caden," I said. "We won't let them treat you like that again."

"Just hope he doesn't bleed out before we get there," snapped Conor.

At the on-ramp for the Black Canyon Highway, we passed two county sheriff's cars with lights and sirens, racing back the way we came. Neither turned and came after us, thank the stars, because I wasn't stopping and didn't want to turn this into a wild police chase.

I screeched to a halt in the ER pass-through, and Conor and I carried Caden through the sliding glass doors. As soon as medical personnel had Caden on a gurney, a woman in business attire approached asking questions about Caden and what had happened. Before long, police officers would be there asking the same questions and more. I wasn't prepared to answer questions that would connect us to their dead racist colleague a few miles away.

I told her I needed to park the truck in the lot and we'd be right in to provide her with answers.

We hustled to the Gray Ghost, tears running down my face. Once behind the wheel, I got back on the southbound Black Canyon Highway.

Guilt felt like a millstone on my chest. I hated myself for abandoning Caden to the care of strangers. First thing, they'd cut off his pants and shorts, only to discover he was trans. I could only hope they'd treat him with more dignity than they had the last time. I needed to focus on finding my fugitives and getting the hell out of town.

"Where we headed, Jinxie?"

"Home."

"Not a good idea, love. There were security cameras at the entrance to the ER. Won't take the cops long to connect Caden getting shot with what went down at that old ranch. And then to me and you."

"Suppose you're right."

"I'm sorry, love."

"Not your fault."

"Ya all right?"

"No." Tears made it hard to see the road.

"I'm sure he'll make it. He's a tough lad."

"Hope so."

"You want me to see if Picardo's got our new docs ready a day early?"

"I gotta find these fuckers and take them down." Sorrow squeezed my heart.

Conor put a hand on my leg. "You've done all ya can. Meeting with Peyton didn't accomplish anything. Maybe it's time to throw in the towel on this one."

"After what they did to Juanita, Rodeo, and now Caden and Peyton, I'm not gonna stop until I bring the whole lot of them down."

"Jinxie, I understand you're pissed, but we're not equipped to take on all of White Nation. It's not our bloody fight anymore. It's bigger than just the two of us."

"Then call Deez and the rest of your crew."

"I can't put anyone else in danger."

"People are already in danger. Didn't you hear…" My voice choked. "Peyton. Bigger than Oklahoma City."

"I understand, but that's for the FBI to handle. And ATF and all those other three-letter organizations. You and me just need to get outta town."

"That's always your answer, huh? When the heat gets too much, just cut bait and run."

"Maybe it is. But I'm only thinking of you."

I pulled off at the Camelback Road exit, sat at a red light, and stared down at the blood on my hands and clothes. Peyton's phone felt like a lump in my pocket. I pulled it out. It was a flip phone, the kind often sold as a burner.

I grabbed my own phone and called Becca, hoping she could somehow use Peyton's burner to lead us to this Lodestar Ranch. The call went to voicemail, and I left a message for her to call me. The light turned green, and I turned left onto Camelback.

"What's the plan, love?" asked Conor.

"No idea."

"Where are we headed?"

"No idea."

He put his hand on mine. I resisted the urge to push it away. My phone dinged. I glanced at it, hoping it was Becca. Instead, Reggie had texted, "Cops looking for you. Didn't tell them nothing."

"Shit. Cops are at my house."

"That's it. Turn south on Central when you come to it. There's a tattoo parlor on McDowell, across the street from Grumpy's Bar and Grill."

"Tattoo parlor?"

"You'll see."

44

It was about five thirty when we pulled the Gray Ghost into the parking lot of the Prowling Tiger tattoo studio on McDowell, one street south of Conor's place.

"I wasn't aware getting new ink was part of the escape plan."

"We're not getting any new ink," he said with a grin.

"Then what?"

I followed him into the tattoo studio. In one of the chairs, a man with long hair, multiple piercings, and a full tableau of ink across his body was working on a female client.

"Weevil!" said Conor in greeting.

"Danny boy! How's it going?" The two of them went through a series of handshakes, grips, and a fist bump.

"Good."

"Who's the pretty lady?" Weevil cast a smile in my direction, and I felt undressed.

"Weevil, this is my old lady, Jinx!"

"Nice to meet you, uh, Weevil." I reached to shake his hand.

"Pleasure's all mine, Miss Jinx." He kissed my knuckles.

"Need to use the back door, mate." Conor pointed at the back of the shop.

Weevil raised an eyebrow. "Expecting company?"

"Yeah, but it bloody hell ain't Father Christmas."

"You need backup?"

"Naw, we got it covered, but thanks."

"Keep it real, man." Weevil went back to work.

I followed Conor through a curtain and past a storage room full of ink and other supplies. "Danny Boy?" I asked with a chuckle.

Conor shrugged. "It's what he calls me." He moved aside a mop bucket to reveal a metal plate in the floor with a keyhole. He pulled out a set of keys, inserted one in the lock, and lifted the plate to reveal a three-foot-wide hole in the floor. A ladder disappeared into the pitch-black hole.

"Are you shitting me?"

Conor climbed down into the darkness and switched on a light. "Come on. It's safe."

I followed him down. Ten feet below the tattoo studio, a tunnel led off to the north, lit by bare bulbs set in the solid concrete wall. "This tunnel leads to your place?"

"Clever girl. When I was a teen working with the IRA, a bloke named Gerry McFadden told me that rabbits always have multiple entrances to their burrows. In case one gets blocked, there's always a way out. Or *in,* as the case may be."

I gazed in amazement down the length of the tunnel. "Doesn't it flood during monsoon season?" I asked.

"It's fairly watertight." He beamed. "Brilliant, eh?"

"How the hell'd you build this without anyone finding out?"

"One of my mates from Dark Horse Security knows a lad who builds these things. I did him some favors."

"Do I want to know what kind of favors?" I asked hesitantly.

"Just some security work. Nothing black ops or anything."

"And why am I just learning about all of this? I thought you'd told me all of your secrets."

Conor stared at his feet for a moment then up at me. "I hate keeping secrets from ya, love. But a few things like this are on a need to know. And you didn't. Least not at first."

"We've been dating for two years!" My voice echoed along the corridor.

"Aye, we have. It just never came up."

"Anything else you haven't told me?"

He shook his head. "That's the last of my secrets, love."

We reached the end of the tunnel. A series of rungs built into the wall rose to another trapdoor. Conor inserted a key into the lock and pushed it open. He vanished for a moment and flicked on a light.

I followed him up and found myself in his coat closet. "Okay, I admit this is kinda cool."

"Thought you'd like it, seeing as how you're into superheroes."

We stepped out into the hallway to his bedroom. The windows were covered with his security shutters, leaving the place dark. He turned on a bedside lamp. Without thinking about it, I pulled off my vest and utility belt and curled into a fetal position on the bed. Conor snuggled in behind me, cradling me in his arms.

"I wish I could make it all better for ya, love."

"I know. But you can't. Maybe no one can."

I opened myself up to a storm of emotions I'd been struggling to contain for the past few days and sobbed uncontrollably for ten minutes. My whole world felt as if it was coming apart and me with it. But for the first time in days, I felt safe.

When I was cried out, I turned around and faced Conor. He wiped my face and kissed me. He became the light at the end of a very dark tunnel, the fragile strand connecting me to what was left of my sanity. He reached under my shirt as his kisses drifted to my throat. I pulled off my shirt and bra. Conor slipped out of his clothes, then teased my hardened nipples with his tongue, sending me into the stratosphere of ecstasy. My mind swirled as I shimmied out of my pants.

The firmness of his body coupled with the soft ginger curls covering his chest washed away the last of my worries. I ached to feel him inside me. But Conor took his time, leaving a trail of kisses down my stomach to the inside of my thigh. I gripped the hair on his head tightly, knowing if I didn't, I might go spinning off the earth into space.

He parted my labia with his tongue, teasing my clit, while squeezing my ass with his strong hands. My breath grew ragged. I pressed my pelvis into his face. I wanted to beg him to fuck me, but I couldn't form words.

As if he read my mind, he squeezed on some lubricant and pressed himself inside me. His face was next to mine again, and I kissed him hard as we thrust toward one another. He tasted like me.

I squeezed him hard and pressed his ass to drive him deeper into me. I was so close. His face contorted in pleasure, and I knew he was too.

"Oh, baby, yes," I whispered. A couple more hard thrusts and my brain short-circuited, as if it had been Tasered. My entire body contracted in orgasm so hard it almost hurt. I felt him release inside me. My heart raced like a hummingbird's. I felt at once as light as a feather and at one with the earth below me. "Thank you."

He peppered my face with gentle kisses. "You will always be my love."

The next thing, I knew my eyes fluttered open. We had fallen asleep. A small clock told me it was after five in the afternoon.

The sorrow, guilt, and anger raged like a storm that was miles away. For the moment, I floated on a cloud of bliss and gratitude. And for the first time in a week, I felt hopeful. I would find a way to stop White Nation from detonating another bomb. And I would bring both Rudy Pratt and Barclay Dietz to justice.

A while later, we got up and fixed a light dinner. I sent a text to Becca with a list of numbers on Peyton's burner phone, asking if she could narrow down a location, ideally in the Cave Creek area. She replied that she would get back with me as soon as she had something.

I wanted to do more research, but my printouts were back at my place. Only a few streets north of me, and they might as well have been across the country for all the good they did. I tried to study a few of the documents Becca had sent me over the past week on my phone, but they proved useless.

When I was at my wit's end trying to locate this mysterious Lodestar Ranch, I dared a phone call to Deer Valley Medical Center. I told the person on the other end of the line that I was Caden's mother and that I'd just heard he'd been injured. I was transferred.

"Hello?" asked a weak voice.

"Caden, it's Jinx."

"Where are you guys?"

"Sorry, man. But we couldn't stay. Too much heat on both of us. How's the leg?"

"Hurts like a fucker. Broken femur. Damage to several major blood vessels, which I can't remember the names of. Femoral artery was okay, though. Got so much metal holding my leg together I could open a Hardware SuperCenter."

"Glad you're alive, at least. How's the staff been?"

He actually giggled. "I think a couple of the nurses have the hots for me."

"Ever the ladies' man." I managed to smile. Damn, I was gonna miss him. "What'd you tell the cops?"

"Told them I don't remember much. Last thing I remember, I was out hiking near the Ben Avery Shooting Range, since that's where my car was. They asked me about the shooting by the abandoned ranch. I told them I didn't know anything about that. I think they bought it, but don't know for sure."

"Okay, man. You get better. We'll see you soon."

"Thanks, Jinx, for saving my life."

A lump formed in my throat. "Any time."

It was only eight o'clock, but Conor and I crashed not long after my call to Caden. A few hours later, my phone rang. Caller ID revealed it was my friend Amber.

"Sorry to call so late, Jinx, but I have some information on those two guys you're looking for. My friend Chloë says they and a couple other guys came in earlier this evening. That ex-boxer invited her to come up to some ranch near Cave Creek. Lodestone or something like that."

"Lodestar?"

"Yeah, that's it. Lodestar. She went up there with them and partied for a bit. But then she got real creeped out when she recognized them from the photos I'd shown her. She made an excuse to use the bathroom and got the hell out of there."

"She get an address?"

"Yeah." She gave it to me and sighed. "Jinx, from the way she talked, these are some freaky guys. And not the fun kinda freaky. More like crazy, dangerous freaky."

"Don't worry. This is what I do. Thanks for the tip. Tell your friend Chloë to keep a low profile for the time being. Especially since they know where she works."

"Thanks, Jinx. Be careful, sweetie. I want you in one piece when I give you your lap dance."

I hung up and woke Conor. "We got an address."

45

I used Conor's laptop to locate the ranch on Google Maps. The ranch was a few miles northwest of the town of Cave Creek.

The satellite photo revealed a large main house, roughly three thousand square feet, if I had to guess. A second building that looked like a garage stood about fifty feet away. A dirt parking lot separated the two. Both buildings sat at the base of a small hill.

I printed out a copy of the map and stuffed it in a pocket in my ballistic vest. "Let's do this," I told Conor.

Conor opened his walk-in closet to reveal his personal arsenal of pistols, rifles, knives, and box after box of ammunition. My own arsenal wasn't nearly as impressive, but then, I didn't usually take some of the bigger jobs he did.

"For the record, I'm still pissed off you didn't tell me about your secret tunnel until now," I said as I loaded two spare magazines for my Glock. "We've been dating for two years, for fuck's sake."

"Aye, we have, love. But if the feds or the Brits ever interrogated you about my past, the less ya knew, the better." He pulled out a green duffel and loaded it with weapons, ammo, and related gear.

"Conor, they did interrogate me. I told them nothing. I can't believe you couldn't trust me."

He stopped what he was doing and turned to me, clearly

crestfallen. "I hate ya had to go through that for me. If I had to do it over again, I never woulda gotten involved with the bloody IRA." He shook his head. "I've been working my whole life to make up for it. To make the world a better place than I found it."

I took him in my arms. "You're a good man, Conor Doyle. I wouldn't have agreed to marry you otherwise."

A loud rumble outside caught my attention. At first I thought it was one of those new jets from Luke Air Force Base, but the rumble intensified.

"What the hell's going on outside?"

Conor opened the laptop on his desk and pulled up his security feed. Several black trucks with "FBI" on the sides had pulled up in front of the house, choking the street. Blue lights were blazing.

"Holy shit! How'd they know we were here?" I asked.

"My guess is your phone."

My stomach sank. "Shit. Can they do that?"

"They're here, aren't they?" Conor replied, grim-faced.

A woman in a ball cap and body armor stepped between the vehicles, holding a bullhorn. It took me a moment to recognize her. Lovelace.

"Liam O'Callaghan and Jenna Ballou, we know you're in there. Come out with your hands behind your head. No one needs to get hurt."

"Not gonna fucking happen." Conor went back to loading his duffel bag.

The reality of our situation sank in as it never had before. I was in love with a wanted man. And if I ran away with him, I too would be a wanted fugitive. We were Butch Cassidy and the Sundance Kid. Or Thelma and Louise. It hadn't worked out well for any of them.

"What's the plan?" I asked, feeling my pulse quicken.

He zipped the duffel closed. "Go out the way we came. Then you and me are going to grab your fugitives. You're going to take them down to lockup. If you get stopped by the feds, tell them you haven't seen me. That you only stopped by to feed my fish."

"You don't have any fish."

"They don't know that."

Just as he said that, my phone rang. There was no caller ID.

"Don't answer that," he warned, but it was too late. I'd already pressed Accept.

"Yeah," I said.

"Ms. Ballou, this is Special Agent Lovelace. You and your boyfriend need to surrender right now. Or we will come in there and get you."

"What are you talking about, Lovelace?" When in doubt, play dumb. "I just stopped by Conor's place to feed his fish."

"Don't fuck around with me, Ballou."

"You've got the wrong man, Lovelace. Conor's from Dublin. He didn't set off that bomb in Northern Ireland."

"He's welcome to tell that to DCI Collier. I'm giving the two of you one minute to come out. After that, we're coming in."

I met Conor's gaze. He had slung the duffel over his shoulder. "Hang up," he mouthed silently.

"Fine, Lovelace. Just give us a few minutes. This may be the last time I get to see my boyfriend." I hung up and pulled the battery out of my phone.

"Let's go," I said.

"I'm not surrendering." His face was firm.

"No," I replied. "*We're* not."

46

We returned to the coat closet. The top of the trapdoor was covered with a square of carpeting that matched its surroundings. No wonder I'd never noticed it before.

He reached into his pocket, then patted himself all over. "Shite! Where's my bloody keys?"

"They must be in the bedroom. Hang on, I'll get them." I hurried to the bedroom and scanned everywhere for the keys. Outside, a SWAT team was moving into place, armed with assault rifles, a very heavy-looking battering ram, and what appeared to be some sort of launcher, most likely for teargas. Lovelace was making more demands over the bullhorn, but I ignored her.

"I can't find them, Conor." I searched the bed, the closet, the bathroom.

The pounding of the battering ram on the front door rattled my teeth. These guys were serious.

Conor rushed into the room. "They've got to be here somewhere."

"We got no time."

"The door's reinforced with steel rods that go into the floor and ceiling. It'll hold for a little while."

I checked behind the nightstand. How could he lose his keys in a room with so few furnishings? I bent down and looked under the bed. "Bingo!" I handed him the keys just as something smacked hard against the window. Concentric fractures appeared in the Plexi, but the window didn't shatter. Outside, clouds of smoke billowed from a teargas canister that had failed to penetrate.

"That'll teach 'em," Conor said with a chuckle.

He unlocked the trapdoor and sent me down first. I descended into the tunnel, then helped him lower the duffel bag. It weighed a ton. He shimmied down the ladder in a flash.

"Do you need to lock it?" I asked.

"It relocks automatically. Now let's move before they breach the front door."

Moments later, we emerged from the tattoo studio, giving Weevil a wave. The acrid scent of teargas drifted across the parking lot from Conor's place. We hopped in the Gray Ghost and drove east to the I-17. It was after midnight, so traffic was light.

"I'm worried about my family," I said as I cut around a slow-moving Kia Sportage. "What are they going to think when I just disappear without saying goodbye?"

But I knew what they'd think. They'd assume I'd been killed or kidnapped or something worse. The image of my mother grieving my loss cut me deeply.

Even if the feds told them I'd run away with a wanted fugitive, would my folks believe them? The situation sounded like a rock ballad from the 1980s that my dad listened to sometimes. Styx or Queen or one of those groups.

"When we get to where we're going, you can write them a letter. I can make arrangements to have it delivered in a way that won't be traced back to us."

I felt a glimmer of hope. "I can write to them?"

"Once. Maybe twice. Any more than that, you risk exposing us, and we'd have to relocate all over again."

"I understand."

He took a deep breath. "If ya'd rather stay, I'd understand. I'd miss ya like hell, but I'd understand."

"You still want to get married?" I didn't know why I asked. The question just pushed its way out.

From his expression, my question clearly caught him by surprise. "Wha? Are ya daft? Of course I want to marry ya. Ya still want to marry me?"

"I do. I just never imagined it'd be like this. I don't even know what brides wear in Spain. Do you?"

A smile crept across his face. "Got no bloody idea, love. But whatever you wear, you'll look smashing."

It was almost one in the morning by the time we reached Cave Creek, where large homes gave way to the desert foothills with little but creosote bushes, cactuses, and large outcroppings of rocks stained black by the weather. Out here, coyotes, bobcat, and javelina roamed freely, largely unmolested by humans.

The landscape was dark in a way that Phoenix never was. Homes were spread out. Much of the glow of the city was blocked out by rolling terrain. What little light there was came from the moon rising in the east.

We parked on a side road a mile from Lodestar Ranch. Our first goal was to surveil the area from the top of the hill to get a feel for who was there.

Conor hefted the duffel onto his back like a pack and led us around the perimeter of the property, navigating by GPS to the top of the hill. The buildings lay quiet below us. Three vehicles sat in the parking lot, including the dark-blue Caprice and the pickup truck from our failed meeting with Peyton. A dirt driveway stretched into the darkness toward the main road.

Above us, Orion the Hunter hung from the heavens, searching for his quarry. I wasn't much of an astronomer, but Orion was one of the few constellations I could recognize. And being a hunter of sorts, I took its presence in the sky as a good omen. Not that I was superstitious or anything.

"Wish I'd packed a sweater," I said as the night's chill sent goose bumps on my arms.

"There's a windbreaker in the duffel," Conor said.

I pulled out a windbreaker with the logo of Conor's company, Viper Fugitive Recovery, printed on the left breast. It wasn't much, but it cut the chill to bearable levels.

Moonlight glinted off the stones of my engagement ring. *Am I ready to walk away from everything and everyone in order to live a life on the run with the man I love? A man with layers and layers of secrets?*

I felt so strongly pulled in opposite directions I thought I'd rip in two. "Ambivalence" was what my father called it. Not apathy but rather being torn apart by powerful yet opposing needs.

My father would no doubt accept whatever I did. My leaving would crush my mother. And Jake, I honestly didn't know how he'd react. Becca would be pissed off, as would Juanita. Could I survive without the safety net of people who'd supported me through so much? My transition, breakups, and career changes?

I studied Conor's moonlit figure as he watched the ranch through binoculars. He had rebuilt his life a time or two. If he could do it, perhaps I could too.

47

We watched the place in silence for about fifteen minutes. A few interior lights were on at the front of the house. The back of the building was dark. No one walked outside. No one drove up. The place was quiet.

At one point, a pack of coyotes starting yipping, no doubt over a kill. A rabbit or such. Their chorus would rise to a crescendo and suddenly drop off to a few random yips until the whole thing started over again.

There was something primal in their cries, something terrifying, though I knew we were in no danger. It haunted me and called to the darkness in my own soul. Something in my hunter brain awoke. A need to hunt, to subdue, to kill. A need for blood.

When the pack of canines finally ended their feral symphony, I stood up. My butt was cold and numb from sitting on a rock. I put away the binoculars and stuffed them in Conor's duffel.

"I'm going down there for a closer look," I announced. The moon was high overhead. It was bright enough that I could negotiate down the mountain without tumbling off a boulder or walking into a cholla cactus. At least I hoped so.

"I'll join you," he replied. "I wonder what's in that garage." He zipped up the duffel and heaved it onto his back.

"The garage? Why?"

"Your boyo said White Nation's planning to detonate another

bomb. Something bigger. If it were me, that garage would be the ideal place to put it together."

"Why?"

"It's away from the main house, for one. When my da and his mates were putting together bombs for the IRA, that's the kinda place they'd use."

"I'm not here for the bombs. I'm here for Pratt and Dietz."

"Jinx, if those bombs are in there and they go off, killing God knows how many, how are ya gonna feel if ya done nothing to stop 'em?"

I wanted to tell him he was wrong. But he wasn't. I might not have been a cop anymore, but protecting innocent people was a strong part of my moral compass. Making a buck by bringing in fugitives came second to that.

"Fine, we'll see what's in the garage. If there are bombs, then what?"

"I'll try to disarm the bloody things."

"Disarm them? Since when are you in the disarming-bombs business? You could get yourself killed and me along with you."

"I learned a lot watching my da. Also did a wee bit of bomb disposal when I worked with Dark Horse in Iraq and Afghanistan."

"I thought you worked as a bodyguard with Dark Horse."

"Aye, that was the official line. But our duties were often a bit more involved. They trained us to handle all kinds of situations we might face in our protection duties. And let me tell ya, it came in handy more than once. IEDs were as thick as scorpions over there."

"Fine. Let's go see what's down there. But once you've disarmed the bombs, if there are any, I'm going next door to find my fugitives."

The climb down toward the buildings was steeper than our approach around the outside of the property. At one point, I was a step away from a ten-foot drop. It wouldn't have killed me, but a broken ankle would have seriously wrecked our plans.

It was two thirty by the time we reached the garage. The large overhead doors were closed with no way to open them from the outside. Our only way in was a side door, which was also locked.

"Shite! Left my picklocks at home." Conor shook his head in disgust.

"No worries," I said with a smile. "I've got mine."

I retrieved the leather pouch from my tactical belt and unzipped it. Conor held out his hands expectantly.

I shook my head. "I can handle it, big boy."

He chuckled and turned toward the main house, drawing his Walther. "Aye, that ya can, love."

It took me a couple of minutes to defeat the seven-pin lock. As soon as I opened the door, Conor shuffled in behind me. I looked around for signs of an alarm system or a surveillance camera but didn't see one.

The place reeked of a deadly combination of fertilizer and diesel fuel. I flipped on a light switch. The place lit up, revealing two large stakebed trucks, similar to the kind landscapers sometimes used. Each held a dozen fifty-five-gallon drums. The cabs were painted with the words "Stewart's Non-Hazardous Transport" along with an address and phone number.

"Holy Mother of Christ," Conor said with a whistle. "These lads are fucking serious."

"No kidding. How big an explosion would this create?"

"Twice what brought down the Murrah Building in Oklahoma City," he said. "You could bring down a city block with just one of these trucks."

"So now what?"

Conor climbed into the bed of the nearest truck and atop the steel drums. "Eeny meeny miny moe. Catch a piggy by the toe."

"Enough with the nursery rhymes."

"Hold your horses, love." He removed the lid of a drum near the center of the truck bed and examined what was inside. What little humor remained in his face drained away.

"What is it?"

"An explosive package. Just a small one. But add the barrels of diesel and fertilizer and suddenly ya've got a weapon of massive fucking destruction."

"How'd you know where it was?"

"Lid had a white sticker on it. Others didn't. And it was in the middle of the stack for maximum effect."

My pulse quickened as he pulled out a jackknife and dug at the contents of the barrel.

"Looks like it's booby-trapped. Multiple redundancies. Charged capacitors will blow it if I try to remove the battery. Got a cell phone wired in to detonate it. Gotta give these lads credit, they know what they're doing."

My heart hammered like a piston. "Great, I'll be sure to nominate them for Terrorists of the Year. Now for the real question. Can you disarm it?"

Conor grunted, eyeing the explosive package from different angles. "Maybe. Good chance I could blow myself to kingdom come."

"Well, we wouldn't want you to do that."

"On the other hand, if I don't at least try, dozens of people could die. Possibly hundreds."

"Oh, that makes me feel a whole lot better."

"On the upside, if it blows now, we'll be dead before I can even say 'Oops.'"

"Conor!"

"Don't get your bloomers in a twist. Tell ya what, love. Go scope out the house. See if you can find a way in and who may be in there. I'll join you shortly once I disarm these buggers."

"Try not to blow yourself up, all right? I'd hate to miss my wedding night on account of you splattering yourself trying to play the hero."

"I'll do my best."

Conor was whistling to himself as I walked out. I was glad he was so confident. I sure as hell wasn't.

48

My walkie-talkie squawked from local radio traffic, so I turned it off. Didn't need it giving away my location.

I crept around to the back of the house and peered into the windows at a dark kitchen. I paused and listened for any sounds of activity. I had no idea how many people were inside. Didn't want to walk into an ambush if I could help it.

After several minutes of hearing nothing but the sounds of the desert, I figured I had the advantage of surprise. I pulled out my lockpicks and set to work on the back door. Both the door handle lock and the dead bolt were set. The main lock yielded in just a few minutes with little bother. Just a run-of-the-mill five-pin lock. The dead bolt, on the other hand, was a whole other story.

The security pins refused to cooperate. Just when I thought I had them all aligned, I'd put pressure on the tensioner only to learn one or more of them was still out of place. It didn't help that my hands were growing numb and achy from the cold. A snow bunny I was not. Give me the triple-digit heat over bitter cold any day.

Eventually, I was forced to pull my hands inside the windbreaker and stuff them under my armpits to warm up. My body was shivering. My knees aching. And it was all I could do to keep my teeth from chattering.

I looked at the kitchen window, hoping I could make entry

there. Unfortunately, it was a solid pane of glass that didn't open. I could break it, but that would instantly alert anyone inside. Not an option.

There were four other windows on the back side of the house. A small high window farther down had a frosted pane. A bathroom window, no doubt. The three remaining windows appeared to be located in the bedrooms. Super risky, especially if occupied.

I opted to try the bathroom window first. It would be awkward climbing in a small window set at chest height, but it seemed safer than climbing into an occupied bedroom. I studied the frame and looked for the telltale signs of an alarm but didn't see any. The window consisted of two panes, one of which slid horizontally on a track. I tried pulling on one of the two panes. It didn't move. I tried the other but with the same results.

I turned on my phone and activated the flashlight. If it drew the feds, so be it. But I needed to see, goddammit! I pressed my face against the icy pane, looking for a latch. As I did, I caught movement inside. I dropped to the ground as the bathroom light flickered on. *Shit, shit, shit! Did he see me?* My heart pounded so hard against my chest I thought it'd break a rib.

Someone hummed tunelessly inside as he did his business on the commode, accompanied by some award-winning farts. A moment later, the toilet flushed. After what felt like an eternity, the light from the bathroom window winked out. I took a deep breath to clear my head.

I waited another ten minutes before I once again peeked into the dark bathroom. I could just make out the outline of a hinged latch. If I had the right tool, a slim jim, perhaps, I might be able to squeeze it between the two panes and release the latch. I recalled seeing Conor slipping a survival knife onto his belt. Maybe that would work.

I shuffled through the shadows to the garage and slipped silently through the door. Conor wasn't atop the barrels any more. But the explosive package he had found remained in place.

"Conor?" I whispered.

"Over here, love."

I found him sitting at a workbench covered with bits of wiring and an assortment of screwdrivers, pliers, and wire cutters. A small electric kettle rested next to bricks of C-4. Conor sipped a steaming liquid from a tin cup.

"What the hell, Conor?"

"Sorry, love. Needed to warm up with a cuppa."

"Great time for a coffee break. I'm freezing my ass out there trying to find a way into the house."

"Tea."

"What?"

"Not a coffee break. It's tea. I woulda called ya on the radio, love, but didn't want to break radio silence. But since you're here, would ya like a cup? Ya look like a frozen fish finger."

I wanted to grab Pratt and Dietz and get the hell outa there. But as cold as I was, I would've drunk hot piss if it would warm me up. "Yeah, I suppose."

He pulled another tin cup from his duffel, poured some tea, and handed it to me. I wrapped my hands around it and let the warmth seep into my frozen fingers. "Any luck with the explosives?"

Conor shrugged. "Whoever wired up the fucker knew what they were doing. Multiple redundancies. Bloody nightmare to disarm without a schematic."

"So can you disarm it?" I took a sip of the tea. It was strong for tea but didn't have the level of kick I preferred from coffee.

Conor stared over at the trucks with their lethal cargo. "I'm sure I can. It'll just take time. What'd ya find at the house?"

"No luck at the back door. I think I can get through the bathroom window if I can borrow your knife."

He pulled it out of the sheath. The black blade was narrow with a saw blade on the back side. "Try not to damage it. It was a gift from a friend when I was in the sandbox," he said, referring to Iraq. "Saved my arse on more than one occasion."

"I'll be careful. You gonna join me, or am I supposed to apprehend two violent fugitives on my own?" My tone had a bit more grit in it than I anticipated. "I didn't invite you along to play Bomb Squad."

"I'll be along. See what ya can do with the window and wait for me before making entry. Don't want those blokes getting the jump on ya."

"Hurry it up, then." I set down the cup and rose to my feet.

To my surprise, he stood up and hugged me. His body heat felt delicious. "I love ya, Miss Jinxie Ballou." Something troubled me about the tone of his voice and the smile that didn't quite meet his eyes. I saw a sadness that sent chills down my spine.

I returned to the bathroom window and wedged the blade of Conor's knife through the rubber seal between the panes of frosted glass. With a little maneuvering, I used the teeth of the saw blade to catch onto the latch.

I twisted and pulled up on the blade to release the latch, but it slipped loose. I tried again, with more pressure, but it wouldn't budge. With my frustration rising, I put my body weight into it. The latch started to pull away from the track of the window. *Just a little more. Just a little more.*

The crack of the knife snapping sounded like a gunshot. The blade bit into my hand. I pulled out the handle and pressed my back against the wall. Conor was going to kill me if Pratt or Dietz didn't.

I waited another five minutes, listening for sounds of alarm from within, looking for any lights being turned on. But all remained quiet in the house.

Blood seeped from the cut on my hand. I was so cold I hardly felt it. What hurt more was the fact that these assholes were sleeping soundly while planning to kill who knew how many people.

I cast a glance toward the garage. Conor was no doubt still fucking around trying to defuse the damned bombs. Fuck him. I was going to bring these assholes down if it was the last thing I did.

I peeked through the bedroom windows, hoping to find one of the rooms unoccupied. The bedroom on the far side of the house had a bed that appeared empty. By luck, the window was open just a smidge. Guess one of the idiots forgot to close it all the way.

The crack between the window and the sill was enough for me to wedge the broken remains of Conor's knife into. I used it as a lever to nudge the window open a bit more. Then I inserted my fingertips and pulled, ignoring the throbbing in my injured hand. The window squeaked open.

"Why's it so fucking cold in this house?" asked a voice from inside. I suspected it belonged to Pratt.

I pivoted to the side, out of view of the window. *Fuck, fuck, fuck, fuck.*

"Thermostat's set at sixty-five," replied someone who sounded like Freytag. "If that's too cold for you, Mr. Pratt, you're welcome to find lodging elsewhere. But seeing as how we are only a couple hours from showtime, I suggest you take another comforter from the linen closet and shut the hell up."

"Whatever."

I stood there, trying to keep my teeth from chattering, and waited. After several minutes of silence, I peered through the open window. The bed was still unoccupied. Time to make something happen.

I put my left boot on the sill and pulled myself up to a crouch. As I stepped down on the floor, movement to my left caught my eye. Then everything went black.

49

Pain in my jaw and the taste of blood caught my attention as I came to. I squinted in the glare of a brightly lit room at the misshapen face of Barclay Dietz staring down at me with a cruel grin. Next to him stood Rudy Pratt, Eric Freytag, and a short guy with a mullet.

I was sitting on the floor in the front room with my back to the wall. My shoulder ached, and the steel of my own handcuffs bit into my wrists. My Rossi revolver lay next to a large green glass ashtray on a nearby rough-hewn wood table. No sign of my Glock. I was seriously up shit creek.

"Sleep well, ya little freak?" asked Dietz.

There were a lot of things I wanted to say to this asshole. Things I'd waited more than a decade to say. But I figured my chances of survival would be improved if I refrained from sharing them with the class just yet.

"Where's my son, faggot?"

I blinked, not expecting that question.

"They didn't tell you?" I glanced over at Freytag, then back at Dietz. My right hand fished into my back pocket, where I always kept a spare handcuff key. "One of your buddies shot him. He's dead."

"You're lying." Dietz kicked me in the knee, sending a shock of pain up my spine.

"Actually, she's telling the truth," said Freytag with a look of arrogance. "Your son betrayed us to our guest here. We were forced to deal with the situation."

Any hopes that this would create a conflict between them were quickly dashed. Dietz's anger was directed only at me. He leaned over and grabbed me by the collar, his eyes burning with murderous intent. "You seduced him with your filthy perversions. It's your fault my son is dead."

"He betrayed you because he saw you all for what you are—racist ammosexuals with nothing better to do than kill innocent people. Not to mention a sleazebag father who likes to beat up teenage girls."

He slammed me against the wall so hard I saw spots. *Note to self, don't piss off the assholes until you're ready to defend yourself.*

"I'm gonna enjoy killing you!" growled Dietz. He reached behind his back and pulled out a Glock. Mine, most likely.

Shit. Time for plan B. Or plan C. My brain was still fuzzy, so I wasn't sure where I was on the list. I locked my gaze on Freytag. "You realize Barclay here's working with the feds, too, right? Like father, like son. Or vice versa in this case."

All eyes turned to Barclay, who had a who-me look on his face that quickly morphed into anger. "She's lying. I ain't no rat."

"He's a CI for Special Agent Lovelace. Peyton told me before your goons showed up. They recognized the tattoo on his neck from security footage when he robbed banks on his way down from Canada. Busted him shortly before our little tête-à-tête at Dixie's. They made a deal, Freytag. He'd flip on you and your organization in exchange for a lighter sentence."

"You're a fucking liar!" He rushed at me, shoving the Glock in my face.

"Barclay!" said Freytag in a firm, cool tone. "Stand down."

"She's a fucking liar. I ain't no snitch."

"Regardless, put away the gun."

I inserted the key into the cuffs and released one hand then the other while the attention was on Barclay.

"You ain't gonna trust him for the deliveries, are you?" asked Mullet. "He could blow the whole operation."

Barclay turned the gun on Mullet. "Listen, you pipsqueak, I ain't never talked to no feds."

The two of them started shouting at each other, throwing shade and innuendos. Finally, something was working.

"Silence!" Freytag shouted as the two men were about to come to blows.

"Mr. Shepard," Freytag said, turning to Mullet. "You deliver the package to Site A. Go give those liberal snowflakes a convention they'll never forget. Pratt, you're still delivering the package to Site B."

"Now wait a minute here," Barclay started in, but Freytag cut him off.

"I'm in charge of this operation, Mr. Dietz. Not you. I'm not taking any chances. Mr. Shepard's making the drop. Since your son led this girl here, you're responsible for disposing of her."

"It," said Barclay with a sneer in my direction. "It ain't a she. It's an it."

"Whatever. Pratt, Shepard, you two get a move on. Rush hour traffic will be starting up soon." He locked eyes with Pratt. "I need that package delivered to that specific parking space in the City Hall garage to bring down the building."

"Will do," said Pratt.

"See ya later, traitor," Mullet said to Barclay, whose face turned dark red.

"This ain't right, Freytag. I drove all the way from Canada to help you guys out. Hell, I formulated the damned explosives for God's sake," bellowed Barclay.

"My decision is final. Now go outside and dispose of our guest. There's a trail out back that leads to a cave that pumas use as a food cache. Save you the trouble of burying the body. I have to retrieve Mr. Pratt and Mr. Shepard after they make their drops. See that this matter is taken care of before I get back."

Freytag turned to me. "Ms. Ballou, I must say I've been

impressed with your determination and resourcefulness. Sad we have to part. Better luck in your next life."

Fuck, fuck, fuck. Outside, engines roared to life. I wondered where Conor was and if he'd had any success disabling the bombs.

Barclay stood over me, holding the gun. My hands were free, but I needed to get to the Rossi revolver.

He pulled me to my feet. I reached for the revolver. Before I could get a solid grip on it, I caught a jab to the chest. I stumbled back, and the Rossi fell to the floor.

Dietz aimed the Glock at my head, and time slowed. I stared down the barrel, watching his finger tighten on the trigger.

In that instant, I was no longer that frail, frightened teenager facing off against a monstrous bull. I was Jinx Ballou, bounty hunter. I was a survivor, a scrapper trained in krav maga. For eleven years, I'd longed for this moment. Fire rose in my belly. Adrenaline blazed through my body. I was no longer human. I was a force of nature as powerful and unrelenting as the monsoons that tore through the valley every summer.

I pivoted right as the gunshot thundered in the room. A bullet buzzed past my left ear. Running on pure instinct, I twisted his gun arm. Dietz bellowed in pain, dropping the pistol.

A left hook barreled toward my temple. I turned my head in time so that it grazed only my forehead. The blow was enough that I tumbled against an end table and knocked it on its side. Blood dripped into my right eye, partially blinding me.

He came at me again. I pulled myself to my feet and drove him back with a barrage of punches and kicks. He stepped back in a pugilist's pose, mallet-like fists at the ready. I fell into the fighting stance I'd learned from years of krav maga training.

He advanced with a couple of jabs, which I blocked and followed up with an elbow to his chin and a heel to his instep. He stumbled but quickly regained his balance and charged at me like an enraged bull.

I tried to sidestep, but he managed a couple of blows to my abdomen. I doubled over in pain, gasping for air. An uppercut knocked me on my ass. Before I knew what was happening, the Beast was on top of me with his hands around my throat. I tried using the techniques I'd learned to break free, but his grip was like steel.

Out of the corner of my eye, I noticed a green glass object. The ashtray. My fingers clutched it, and I slammed it against Dietz's head with all of my remaining strength. The air filled with fluttering bits of ash. Dietz tumbled over, losing his grip on my neck. I swung again, but he grabbed my arm, forcing me to drop it.

With both of us struggling to stand, I rotated my arm inward, breaking his grip, and caught his left arm in a lock. He reared back for another punch, but I twisted till I heard the satisfying crackle of his radius and ulna snapping. He dropped to one knee, cradling his broken arm. I pressed my advantage with a couple of elbow strikes to his face. He fell back against the hardwood floor, coughing and spitting blood, his chest heaving.

I snatched up the Glock and stood over him with the gun aimed at his god-ugly face. My finger slipped into the trigger guard.

He glared at me. "Do it," he growled. "Or don't you got the balls?" He coughed as he tried to laugh at his own joke.

"I dreamed of this day for thirteen years. The day I got my revenge on Barclay 'The Beast' Dietz. The day I got to blow his fucking brains out. And you know what I realized? You aren't worth it. I'd rather you live a very long life knowing you got your ass handed to you by a trans woman."

"Fucking bitch," grumbled Dietz.

"Now get on your belly so I can cuff you."

"Kiss my ass, you goddamned freak. You broke my fucking arm."

I aimed the Glock at his crotch. "I might not kill you, but I have no problem blowing your goddamned dick off. Now roll over like a good dog."

He glared at me but slowly turned over, cursing at the pain. I snapped the cuffs on him. As I contemplated my next move, my phone rang. It was Conor.

50

"Where are you?" I asked Conor.

"In the Caprice that was parked by the garage. I'm pursuing one of the lorries south on the 51. The other was headed west on the Loop 101 along with a chase car when they split up."

"Did you disable the bombs?"

I heard him sigh. "Afraid not, love. That's why I at least gotta stop this one lorry. Shot at the wheels, but the bastard's got dual tires in back. Trying for the front, but traffic's bloody thick. Hard to get a clear shot. Oh shite!"

I heard tires squealing and Conor grunting and cursing.

"Conor, are you there?"

"The wanker tried to push me off the road. Just passed the Glendale exit. If I can—"

I heard an exchange of gunfire. An engine roared followed by crunching metal. More shots, then the clunk of a car door being slammed.

"Conor? Are you there?"

Conor was yelling at someone to get out of the truck. I couldn't hear the response.

Outside the house, the wail of police sirens approached, accompanied by the chut-chut-chut of helicopters. The cavalry had arrived. Late as usual.

"Conor, can you hear me?"

I heard more urgent shouting over the phone followed by

a deep thump and dead silence. "Conor?" My phone beeped. The call had dropped. "Shit."

The front door burst open in a shower of splintered wood. Men in assault gear and automatic weapons flooded into the room.

"Down on the ground. Get down on the ground now!"

I put my hands behind my head and got down on my knees. It was all I could do to keep my shit together while wondering what was happening to Conor. "There are two trucks delivering explosives—"

"Get on the ground now! Or we will shoot you!" One of the SWAT team members bore down on me, holding the barrel of his rifle a foot from my head.

"I'm on the ground. Now, listen to me!" I pleaded. "I'm a bail enforcement agent. This man is my fugitive. His cohorts are driving two trucks full of explosives."

He cuffed my hands, hoisted me up, and escorted me outside. The eastern sky was a pale yellow with the coming dawn.

"That truck already exploded, lady," he said.

Tears pricked my eyes, and I gasped for breath. "Conor." I struggled to control my emotions. More lives were on the line. "There's another one. My fugitive knows where it's headed."

They hauled me inside a large black FBI mobile command vehicle and stuffed me in a small room with a table mounted to the floor. The cuffs chafed, but I barely noticed. My body shivered from adrenaline withdrawal, cold, and despair.

"Please be okay, please be okay," I muttered repeatedly.

After what felt like hours, Special Agent Lovelace and another agent walked in with a couple of case folders. "You can uncuff her."

The agent did so and left. It was just Lovelace and me.

"What's happening out there?" I asked.

"I'm asking the questions here." Her tone was assertive but not mean. "You're shivering. You need a blanket?"

"I need to know what's happening with Con—with the trucks."

Her eyes narrowed. "Was Conor Doyle driving one of the trucks?"

"No! He tried to stop them. And now…" Tears ran down my face. I'd hit my limit.

"Miss Ballou." She put a gentle hand on my arm. "Jenna, I'm sorry. We have reports from Phoenix PD of a large explosion on the 51 just south of the Glendale exit. The blast zone is the size of a city block. I don't know how many casualties there are, but last count there are at least thirty-three dead and countless injuries. I expect those numbers to rise dramatically. If Mr. Doyle was anywhere near that truck…well, you have my sincere condolences."

Even though I was expecting it, the news hit me like a ton of bricks. I sobbed uncontrollably. At some point, a blanket was put around me, and I felt Lovelace's arm on my shoulder.

"I…I need to see him," I choked out.

"Who?" asked Lovelace.

"Conor."

"Jenna, you won't be able to get anywhere near the site. It's a massive crime scene. It's going to take some time to identify remains."

I wanted to believe that somehow he had survived. But he'd been right there. There would be little left to identify.

"Now I hate to do this, but I need some answers from you. What are you doing here?"

I reminded her of my attempts to locate Pratt and Dietz. She asked about the shooting off Carefree Highway, and I filled her in on how our meeting with Peyton had gone off the rails. Apparently, she and her team had been on to Officer Evans for some time.

Pratt, as it turned out, was driving the truck that blew up. So no bounty for me. The other truck was intercepted before it could be detonated at the Gila River Arena. The driver, Bennie the Mullet, apparently got pulled over for speeding and was promptly arrested.

Lovelace had me write out a statement. When I was done, I slid it over to her.

"Now what happens?"

"DCI Collier wanted to charge you with harboring a fugitive. And you're on my shit list for interfering with a federal investigation. Again."

I said nothing. I no longer cared what she did.

"However, in light of recent events, Collier has agreed to return to the UK empty-handed, and the FBI will not be filing charges against you."

"Thank you."

"I know you have a job to do, Ms. Ballou. But in the future, stay out of our way. Do I make myself clear?"

"Crystal."

I walked out into a bright-blue morning that left me dead inside. The ride home was a blur. I remembered turning off the radio and driving in silence. I slogged through traffic on I-17, which was no doubt a result of the closure of Highway 51 following the explosion.

The next thing I knew, I was walking into my front door. In the pantry, I found the bottle of Jameson I had bought for Conor. I drank a few glasses. At some point, Reggie walked in and put me to bed.

51

I spent the next week staying at Becca's, being waited on by her and her new cuddle-buddy. Easton was cute with long blue bangs, freckles, and a fondness for bow ties and suspenders. Both Becca and Easton seemed to tiptoe around me as though I was apt to fall apart any second. And maybe I did that a few times.

My parents and Jake stopped by several times bearing food, including a ton of holiday sweets. My folks begged me to stay with them for the holidays, but I declined. I wasn't in the mood to be psychoanalyzed by my father. Neither did I feel like being in a house filled with nativity scenes and heralding angels and all that Christmas shit.

Caden called, and we talked for a while. He was expected to be released from the hospital soon but would be out of commission for a while. His sister had come in from Santa Fe to help him while his leg healed. He was thinking about applying to law school at ASU. I told him I'd miss him but supported whatever he decided.

I referred the few bail-jumper jobs Sadie Levinson had over to Deez, who was now in charge of Conor's bounty-hunting team. He and the boys dropped by to bring me flowers along with their condolences.

"Whenever you're ready to get back to work, you're welcome back with the old team," Deez said in his deep bass voice. I told him I'd think about it.

Despite everyone's hospitality, nothing could fill the gnawing emptiness inside me. I caught myself sniping at anyone who got near me.

"You know what you need?" said Becca one morning over coffee.

"A frontal lobotomy?" I joked darkly.

"A dog."

"Yeah, right."

"No, I'm serious," she insisted. "You need someone to take care of. Someone who will love you and shower you with kisses no matter what."

"Becks, I know you mean well, but a dog won't replace Conor."

"Not replace. But a dog might help you through the grief. Sometimes having someone to take care of can get your mind off your own troubles."

"You sound like my dad. He keeps pushing me to join a grief support group."

"Might not be a bad idea."

I scoffed. "Yeah, right. Don't see me sitting around a circle singing 'Kumbaya.' 'Hi, my name's Jinx, and I used to date an Irish terrorist who got himself blown up by a white nationalist.' Not gonna happen."

"We're all just trying to help, Jinx. We love you and hate to see you suffering."

"I know. Nothing anyone can do. I just feel dead inside."

"But you're not dead. I know Conor is, and it fucking sucks. But dammit, Jinx. Life goes on."

I pushed away my untouched cup. "I think it's time I move back home." I stood up and walked to the guest bedroom where I'd been staying.

Becca followed me. "Don't leave mad."

"I'm not mad. I'm just...I just have to figure this shit out for myself." I turned and hugged her. "You're the best bestie a girl could have. But I've been crashing here long enough. I know Easton's tired of me hanging around."

"Easton adores you. They just think you're a little..."

"Scary?" I asked.

"Intense. I mean, it's Christmas in a few days. Easton's used to everything being all cheerful and merry. They don't know what to say after what you've been through."

I made the bed, threw my clothes in my bag, gathered my toiletries, and tossed them in, too. "All the more reason to give you two some space. I don't want to be harshing anyone's holiday spirit."

She held my gaze as I shouldered my bag. "You gonna be okay?" She had the look of a worried puppy.

I nodded. "I'll be okay. I think I need some time to think. Sort through some feelings. Maybe I'll even show up to one of those grief support meetings."

"I'm always just a phone call or a text away. You're welcome back as long as you need."

"I know." I gave her another hug, and she walked me to the door. "Thanks, Becks. Thanks for being there for me all these years."

At home, I gathered up my pile of mail and spent the better part of an hour sorting it, tossing out the junk, and creating a pile for bills to be paid and another for Christmas cards. One serious-looking letter was from the Federal Bureau of Investigation. "Shit."

I opened it, expecting some sort of summons or threats of legal action. Instead, I found a check for two hundred grand for apprehending Barclay Dietz. Considering I lost out on the bounty for Pratt and had missed a week's worth of work, I could use the dinero. In fact, I could probably take the next few months off if I wanted.

As I pondered what else I could do with the money, my phone rang. I didn't recognize the number.

"Ms. Ballou, this is Harvey Mashburn with the law firm of Mashburn, Steele, and Wallace. Is now a good time to talk?"

Ugh, lawyers. "Not really. What's this about, Mr. Mashburn?"

"I understand. I represent the estate of Conor Doyle. He has named you as the sole beneficiary of his trust."

"His trust?"

"His property and other belongings. It's like a will but avoids all of the problems of probate. At any rate, I'd like to schedule a time to meet with you so that I can go through all of this with you."

"Can we do this after the holidays? I'm…I'm not ready to deal with all this right now."

"I certainly understand. You take your time." He gave me his phone number, even though it was on the caller ID. "You get in touch whenever you're ready. And I am truly sorry for your loss. Merry Christmas."

I hung up. "Merry fucking Christmas."

For two days, I stayed at home, not going out for anything. Reggie, who had started working for Jake remodeling houses, wasn't around as much. I did manage to move aside my workout equipment and set up the spare bedroom for Reggie so he wouldn't have to crash on my couch anymore.

For the most part, I just ate kids' cereal, binge-watched British crime serials on Netflix, finished off the bottle of Jameson, and let my body steep in its own juices.

Try as I might, I couldn't keep from thinking about Conor. The feel of his arms around me, the exhilaration of making love to him, even his proclivity for getting under my skin. I missed it all.

At eleven o'clock one night, I climbed in the Gray Ghost and started driving. Traffic was all but nonexistent. I had no destination in mind. I just needed to be in motion, to get out of the stinking, stifling house.

To my surprise, the holiday lights and other decorations through town started to cheer me up despite the fact that I hadn't much cared for Christmas since I was a kid. Sure, I bought a few token gifts for immediate family and the closest of friends, but I avoided parties and serious shopping expeditions in search of the perfect gift.

I found myself sitting in a parking lot at the corner of Glendale Avenue and Sixteenth Street, a block away from the highway that was still cordoned off due to the bomb blast. I wrapped my coat around me and wandered off with a flashlight in hand.

A makeshift memorial of flowers, candles, and stuffed animals lay at the barricades to the highway's on-ramp. I stepped past them, paying them no mind, and shuffled down the ramp until I reached another set of barricades that marked the edge of a crater. To my right, the water in the Arizona Canal glimmered in the moonlight.

I stood there. This was where he'd died. The man I loved. A man who'd been caught up in violence of one sort or another his whole life. And this was how it ended. Dozens of people had died here on the 51, but Conor had saved thousands at City Hall. And now I didn't have anyone.

A patrol officer startled me as I walked back up the ramp. "Ma'am, this area is off-limits."

"Sorry. I just needed to see it."

"I'm sure you can find better things to do on Christmas Eve than wandering out here in the dark."

"Is tonight Christmas Eve?" I'd lost track.

"Yes, ma'am. You lose someone in the blast?"

I fingered the ring that now hung from a chain around my neck. "My fiancé."

"I'm sorry for your loss, ma'am, but you need to be on your way."

"Yes, Officer."

I wandered back to the Gray Ghost and started driving again. Thirty minutes later, I found myself at Juanita's hospital room.

"*Ay, ay, ay!* It's Wonder Woman," she said as I stepped into the room. I'd forgotten I was wearing a Wonder Woman T-shirt.

Juanita was propped on her bed with a scarf wrapped around her head. *It's a Wonderful Life* was playing on the TV. She muted it.

"No superheroes tonight, I'm afraid, *tía*. Just little old me."

Juanita patted her bedside. "Don't stand there like an IV pole. Come here, *mi'ja*, and snuggle next to me."

She winced as she scooted over and made room for me. I carefully slid in next to her, afraid of hurting her. But it felt good to be near her.

"You sound more like your old self." I asked, "How you feeling?"

"I feel like fuck on stale toast," she said with a chuckle. "Staff can't wait to get rid of me. Moving me to rehab in a few days to help me walk again."

I nodded quietly. Even though she was improving, it hurt to see her like this.

"How you holding up, Miss Thang?" she asked.

"Everything feels wrong with Conor gone. I feel like I'm ruining everyone's Christmas."

"Fuck them, *mi'ja*. You been through hell and back."

"I don't know how to get on with my life. It's hard to explain."

"Ain't nothing to explain, *chica*. Back in the eighties, all my friends were dying. That *pendejo* Reagan called it the gay plague. Like it was God's judgment on us queers."

"I've heard the stories."

"My boyfriend, Esteban, got this spot on his face." She shook her head. "After the clinic confirmed he had AIDS, he admitted he fooled around on me. Got infected by some *pinche* white boy."

I shook my head, not knowing what to say.

"For weeks I refused to get tested. Couldn't face it. Then he got real sick. I go down to the clinic. Sure as shit, Esteban had infected me too."

"What happened to him?"

"Sorry motherfucker died on me. I was devastated. Wanted to die myself."

"Oh, Juanita, I'm so sorry." I leaned my head on her shoulder.

"But then I realized, no! I was not gonna die. And you know why?"

"Why?"

"Because fuck them. Fuck them all. Fuck Reagan. Fuck them haters. Fuck them cheating *maricones* getting everyone sick. I was gonna live just to spite them."

She took a few breaths as she started to get winded. "Don't get me wrong. It was touch and go for a while. I earned some frequent flier miles in the hospital. But thanks to my friends and medical science, I pulled through."

"I'm glad you did, *tía.*"

"I ain't telling you this for some bedtime story, *mi'ja*. Your man is gone. And it fucking sucks. Unlike my Esteban, Conor died doing right. Going after them White Nation *hijos de puta*. He gave his life trying to save people. Best thing you can do is say 'fuck you' to them racist assholes by living your life."

"I suppose you're right."

"Tía Juana is always right."

Fatigue was seeping into my bones as the movie dragged on. Juanita needed her rest too.

I pulled myself to my feet as she started to drift off to sleep. I kissed her cheek, wished her a *Feliz Navidad*, and drove home.

52

I woke the next morning to my doorbell ringing. I ignored it, hoping whoever it was would go away. It rang again. I continued to ignore it. A moment later, someone was knocking on my bedroom door. Instinctively, I rolled out of bed and drew a pistol I kept next to my nightstand.

"Don't shoot! It's me." Jake stood in the doorway, holding a golden retriever puppy on a leash. Rodeo stood next to him.

I put away the gun and ran a hand through my hair. "What are you two doing in my house? With a dog?"

Rodeo beckoned me with his hand. "Come on. You'll see."

I followed them into my living room. My parents were arranging stacks of wrapped presents around a hastily set up Christmas tree. Rodeo's seven-year-old daughter, Gwyneth, and Reggie were helping decorating the tree with lights and ornaments.

"Merry Christmas," my parents said in unison.

"What's all this?"

"You didn't show up for Christmas breakfast, so we brought Christmas to you," said my mother. "We even brought panettones to make Italian French toast." She held up the odd-shaped yellow boxes. It was a weird family tradition, but Italian French toast had always been my favorite part of Christmas morning.

"You guys, you shouldn't have." I caught myself feeling emotional.

My father reached out and hugged me. "I've been worried about you, kiddo."

"I'm actually feeling a little better." And I meant it. Juanita's talk was starting to sink in.

"So what's the dog's name?" I asked Gwyneth.

"I don't know," she replied with a coy smile. "Whatever you name it, I guess."

"Huh? Jake, whose dog is this?"

Jake grinned. "Yours."

"What?" I looked at my brother, then each of my parents. I bent down and petted the dog, who was all waggly tail and lapping tongue. "You're giving me a dog?"

"Becca suggested it," explained Jake. "Dad seconded the idea. Thought it'd do you good. They'll be over later, by the way."

"Who?"

"Becca and Easton." Jake rolled his eyes. I guess my brain wasn't fully functioning yet.

After a few rich pieces of my mother's Italian French toast and opening presents, we were sitting around my living room playing with the dog and semi-watching *A Christmas Story*.

I was feeling more alive than I had since the explosion. I even decided on the name Diana for the dog, which was Wonder Woman's cover name.

Just as Ralphie was getting his mouth washed out with soap on the television, my doorbell rang.

"About time." I figured it had to be Becca. "Great idea about the dog," I said as I opened the door. Except it wasn't Becca but a large white man with a buzzed head standing at my door. He was dressed in fatigues. "Sorry. Guess you're not Becca, huh?"

"No, ma'am," he said with a thick Southern accent. "The name's Tuckey. I was asked to deliver this to you." He handed me a small cardboard box.

As a bounty hunter, I'm suspicious of any hand-delivered packages. "Asked by whom?"

"Your fiancé, ma'am. He and I served in the sandbox a while back."

My legs felt like jelly. Gravity pulled at odd angles. I grabbed the doorframe to steady myself. *Is this a joke? Or a threat?*

"When'd he ask you to deliver this? And what the hell's in it?"

"Received it by mail just yesterday. Postmarked from Spain four days ago. As to the contents, I could not say."

"Spain?" I took a deep breath to clear out the gremlins. Suddenly things started to coalesce. "Thank you, Tuckey."

"Merry Christmas, ma'am." He turned and disappeared into a pickup truck on the street and drove off.

"Who's that at the door, honey?" asked my father.

"Just a delivery man," I said, closing the door before shuffling to the kitchen.

"On Christmas morning?"

I grabbed a knife and opened the package. Out slipped a flip phone with one number in its memory. My heart beat so fast in my chest that I wondered if I was having a heart attack. *It can't be. It can't be.*

I dialed the number.

"Feliz Navidad, love," said Conor. "You should see the view of the Pacific from this villa. Had no idea Ensenada, Mexico, was this gorgeous."

Conor and I sat on the sand at Playa Hermosa, drinking a local wine, while Diana the wonder pup chased after shorebirds. The cry of gulls and the pounding of the surf helped to untie the knots in my soul that had built up since early December.

I drove down just after New Year's, telling my family I needed time to think and heal. I made no mention that Conor was still alive. We had spent the past week exploring Ensenada, living on street tacos and fresh fish, and fucking like rabbits.

All the while, I wrestled with what to do about Conor. When

I arrived at his villa, he explained that he'd realized Pratt was about to set off the explosive. Conor jumped into the canal and dragged himself out a mile downstream. He hooked up with Picardo the document forger and headed south of the border.

Diana came running up to us and shook her fur, showering the two of us in salt spray and sand. I would have been upset if she weren't so cute.

"Never took ya for a dog person." Conor chuckled.

"Me neither. I guess people can change."

"Does that mean you're ready to become Mrs. Eileen Crawford?"

I took a deep breath, remembering what I went through when I thought he was dead. The soul-crushing grief would have consumed me if it hadn't been for Becca, Juanita, and my family.

"Don't suppose there's any way you could return to Phoenix now that the Northern Ireland police think you're dead."

"Afraid not, love. Too risky. Besides, the weather's better down here. And what's not to love about the beach? It's paradise." He sighed. "Or would be if you were with me."

I turned to him, gazing deep into his emerald eyes. "I love you, Conor. No one has made me feel the way you do. But my life is back in Phoenix." I slipped the engagement ring off my finger and put it in his palm. "I'm sorry."

He kissed away the tears. "Nothing to be sorry for, Jinxie. I should never have saddled you with my past. But do me a favor. Keep the ring. Remember me with love."

I took the ring back and hugged him. "Always."

A month later on a Saturday night, L Street was packed and rocking to the beats of the Pink Trinkets' latest album, *#MeThree*, a tribute to the #MeToo movement. It was only Groundhog's Day, but the bar was already decked out with rainbow-striped hearts in anticipation of Valentine's Day.

I'd had a couple of beers and was feeling relaxed, enjoying the Pink Trinkets' driving beats and searing vocals. Becca and Easton sat across the small table, chatting with me about some video game Easton was reviewing for a podcast they hosted. I was only half listening.

"I think it's a great improvement over the previous version of the game, but—" Easton waved to someone behind me.

I turned, and a shiver ran up my spine. This was such foreign territory for me. But if I could learn to be a dog person, perhaps I could learn other things.

CO Toni Bennett looked sexy in her uniform but a helluva lot sexier in her civvies. My heart went full hummingbird as she put her arms around me and kissed me. "Hey, gorgeous. Sorry I'm late."

Want to Read More?

Download a free ebook short story

by joining the Dharma Kelleher Readers Club

at https://dharmakelleher.com

Also by Dharma Kelleher

Jinx Ballou Bounty Hunter Series

Chaser

Shea Stevens Outlaw Biker Series

Iron Goddess

Snitch

Boosted (short story)

About the Author

Dharma Kelleher is the author of four novels. She is a pioneer in transgender crime fiction, writing gritty tales about outlaws, renegades, and misfits from a trans/queer perspective.

She is a former journalist and a member of Sisters in Crime, the International Thriller Writers, and the Alliance of Independent Authors.

She lives in Arizona with her wife and three feline overlords.

https://dharmakelleher.com

Acknowledgments

This book, and the entire Jinx Ballou series, would not exist were it not for my lovely wife, Eileen (not an alias). She is my first reader, head cheerleader, and holder of my heart. She came up with the idea of a bounty hunter and is always willing to let me bounce ideas off of her, no matter how ridiculous.

I would also like to thank the fantastic editing team at Red Adept Editing, most notably Angela McRae and Kristina Baker. They help debug my manuscripts and are always teaching me something new about grammar and style.

Thanks goes to the myriad podcasts who have invited me to blather on about my work and my life. Top of the list is the *Inciting Incident* podcast with Marissa Lennex-McCool and Bethany Futrell. Also Pam Stack of *Authors on the Air* and Janet Mason of *This Way Out*, both of whom have been amazing advocates of my work. And of course, Gabriel Pereira of *DIY MFA*, Marissa Lennex-McCool (again) and Ari Stillman of The *Cis Are Getting Out of Hand*, Caleb Arring of the *Beyond Gender* podcast, and S.W. Lauden and Eric Beetner of *Writer Types*.

To all of you, thank you for helping to make this book possible and for contributing to the visibility and representation of transgender people in crime fiction.